Margo's Reunion

Margo's Reunion

by

Jerry B. Jenkins

MOODY PRESS
CHICAGO

© 1984 by
JERRY B. JENKINS

All rights reserved

ISBN:0-8024-4328-1

ISBN:0-8024-4328-1

1 2 3 4 5 6 7 Printing DP Year 90 89 88 87 86 85 84

Printed in the United States of America

To each reader
of the Margo Mysteries
who has kindly taken the time
to write and let me know
of his or her enjoyment.
Your letters have meant more to me
than I can express.
Thank you.

Chapter One

It was my wife Margo's idea, and as usual it came in the middle of a discussion about something else. And it would become something totally unlike what she had in mind.

It was late on a Monday night, and we were sitting in the large outer office of the EH Detective Agency. Our boss, former Chicago Police Homicide Detective Sergeant Walvoord Festschrift, was debriefing us on a particularly bizarre case.

It had been so strange that Wally had taken both Margo and me off other cases, and the three of us had been working on it day and night for three weeks. We were tired.

Wally had turned one of the chairs backward and parked his bulk facing Margo, his meaty arms folded across the top of the back. He had just finished complimenting Margo on her intuition, which he credited for breaking the case.

An aging indigent, or at least a man who looked like one, had labored up our stairs one afternoon and flashed a lot of money to Bonnie, our receptionist. That earned him a brief audience with Wally, who was relieved to know that a man who looked and

1

smelled so bad had the necessary funds to engage a detective agency. Aging he was. Indigent he was not.

Simon Albert's problem, he said, was that an insurance company refused to take any action on the suspicious death of his friend, which had occurred behind a grocery store on the west side of Chicago. Wally had read of the case.

Found in a trash compactor were the mutilated remains of one Roosevelt Stevens. He had been a toothless man whose identity could not be confirmed by dental or medical records, and had it not been for an almost completely shredded wallet, police would not have been able to piece together a name and address.

That information led them to a tiny, seedy apartment in a converted hotel, where they found evidence that the dead man had been one of those rare misers who had apparently carefully invested most of the money he made as a young man and had seen the miracle of compound interest turn it into a fortune.

There was no known family, but a will and an insurance policy both named Simon Albert beneficiary of the estate, which was worth nearly eight hundred thousand dollars. The insurance policy alone was valued at a quarter of a million dollars.

The upshot was that the police decided the death was either a suicide or an accident, and because Simon Albert had no clout or connections, he could get neither the dead man's insurance company nor his bank to come through with any cash. They stalled and stalled, and he came to us.

Wally liked the old guy, but like I say, it was Margo who broke the case. The three of us ran down every lead we could think of and tried to put pressure on the financial institutions, but they rightfully demanded more positive proof of identity.

Margo found our client suspicious, but she couldn't convince Wally or me. So she married herself to Mr. Albert's schedule. He was an eccentric, she said, and he was forgetful and careless. He would trip himself up.

"What're you suspecting," Wally said, "that he murdered the guy?"

"No," she said. "I don't know." But she flashed Wally one of those close-mouthed grins of hers with the huge hazel eyes dancing and the delicious brown hair bouncing, and he just shook his head.

What Margo found was that when old man Albert went walking, he kept turning up on Roosevelt Stevens' street. Then he would curse himself under his breath and head for his cubbyhole room at a flophouse.

Neither Wally nor I liked the idea of her running the streets where the skid row types walked, but none of them seemed to have the energy to keep up with her, let alone accost her. She was careful, and of course she carried a weapon.

Anyway, the day came when Margo put it all together, wired herself for sound, and approached Simon Albert from behind. "Mr. Stevens?" she asked brightly.

"Yes, ma'am," he responded quickly, turning to face her.

"Mr. Roosevelt Stevens?" she persisted.

He nodded slowly, warily staring deep into her eyes. "I have something interesting here for you, if

3

you are indeed Roosevelt Stevens," she said, reaching into a large manila envelope and letting a wad of twenty-dollar bills spill out as she reached for a document.

He knelt as quickly as a weak old man can kneel and came up with the bills vice-gripped in both hands. "Name's Roosevelt Stevens, and I can prove it any way you want," he insisted, standing on tiptoe to peer into the envelope.

Margo reached for the bills in his fists, and he reluctantly let her tug them free. She showed him a copy of a section of insurance law, informing him of the penalty for attempting to defraud an insurance company and the state.

She, and he, were dead right. Simon Albert was Roosevelt Stevens. He was wealthy beyond most people's imaginations, yet he figured he could get his hands on another quarter of a million by turning up dead and leaving it to himself under another name.

When he discovered one of his old acquaintances dead of exposure—and who knows what else—behind the grocery store one night, he seized on his chance. He tossed his own wallet and the body into the trash compactor and hoped for the best.

He then disguised himself with different clothes, false teeth, a new location, and a full beard. But he kept forgetting that he had moved until the moment he found himself at his old building.

He had a neurotic need to amass an impotent fortune. He meant no harm to anyone, and he had no one to leave his money to even had he been successful. There were no plans to spend it. Only to save it and watch it grow.

The court chose to make an example of him, and in a strange decision he was sentenced to pay a fine of five hundred thousand dollars. The judge said he was not inclined to incarcerate the man, but to teach him a lesson and to make an example of him, he would get "some of that currency back into circulation where it belongs."

The public took a liking to old Simon Albert/Roosevelt Stevens, and a group of concerned citizens prevailed upon Amos Chakaris to take his case. They even talked the old man into parting with some of his remaining fortune in the hope of salvaging the huge fine.

Chakaris, a former secretary of the state of Illinois and a friend of the owner of our EH Detective Agency, Earl Haymeyer, was bemused by Stevens and the attendant publicity. And he agreed that the judgment had been too harsh. He put Hilary Brice, a star attorney from his former law firm, on the case. (Hilary and I had once traveled to California together on a case involving the suspicious death of Margo's mother.) Anyway, Roosevelt Stevens died before Hilary could even talk to him. The state inherited every dime.

And now Wally was capping the file with a final discussion. "I'm getting old," he said wearily. "How many times is that now, Philip, where one of you two has seen through someone I believed in?"

I shrugged.

"C'mon, Spence!" he scolded. "You know as well as I do it's been too many."

I shrugged and nodded. He pretended to be hurt.

"You *have* noticed it then?"

5

"Yeah, I guess," I said.

"Oh, yeah? Well, don't be invitin' anybody to the retirement banquet yet, pal."

"Wally!" I said. "You were the one putting words in my mouth."

"You could've spit 'em out," he said. Margo chuckled.

I shook my head and rolled my eyes.

"Anyway," he continued. "It was Margo who exposed Roosevelt Stevens. She's a better investigator than you'll ever be."

I couldn't argue with that.

"And a better judge of veteran talent," he said. "You never hear her sayin' stuff like you just said."

"What'd I just say?"

"You said, 'Yeah, I guess,' when I asked if you noticed I'd been slippin'."

I couldn't win. I didn't even try. "Guilty," I said.

"It wasn't what you said," Wally pushed. "It was what you didn't say."

"You wanted me to argue with you," I guessed.

" 'Course."

"You're the best," I said without emotion.

He laughed and smacked his knee, then stood and clapped me on the back. "And don't you forget it, Spence!"

The fact is, of course, that Wally Festschrift was and is one of the best detectives in Chicago and one of the best judges of character too. Sure, he's missed a few, but he stays on a case like a dog with its teeth deep in a postman's pantleg.

"So back to your suggestion, Mar," I said, hoping

to change the subject so we could start winding down and heading home.

"I was just saying that it was good to have a reason to see Amos and Hilary. It was great to see them again. We ought to keep in touch more with our old friends and acquaintances."

"Now *you're* sounding old," Wally said.

"Maybe I am," she said, though both of us were barely into our thirties. "I just don't like losing contact with people. Allyson Scheel's wedding is this weekend, and I wish Larry and Shannon could make it."

"Earl's comin' by this weekend, you know," Wally said almost absently.

Margo and I stared at each other. It had been so long. "No, we didn't know," I said. "Why didn't you tell us?"

"Thought I had," he said. "Some Illinois Department of Law Enforcement meeting in Schaumburg. And, 'course, Allyson's wedding." (Allyson is co-owner, with her mother, of the boutique on the first floor of our building.)

"How nice that he can make it," Margo said. "Now we just *have* to get Larry and Shannon to come over." She was referring to Larry Shipman, one of our former co-workers who married Shannon Perry—an old friend of his and a client of the agency.

"I thought he had just been promoted," Wally said. "From city editor to managing editor or something. Probably can't get away on short notice."

Margo nodded sullenly. "I miss them," she said. "Don't you?"

7

Wally shrugged. "I guess. I'm not big on sentiment, you know."

Margo winked at him. "Baloney. You're a softy. And you know I'll find a way to get everybody here. Even if I have to stage a phony case for everyone to work on with me."

Well, as it turned out that wouldn't be necessary, but of course none of us could know that at the time. Margo reached for the phone.

"What are you doing?" I said, rising.

"Calling Shannon."

"Have you looked at your watch lately?" I said.

"Oh, no! Twelve-thirty?"

I nodded.

"Then I'll call Larry at the paper."

"That's long distance to Indiana," Wally muttered.

"Dock my pay," she said.

"Mar," I said, "if Ship's really the new managing editor, he wouldn't be working nights like he used to."

"Then I'll leave a message."

"C'mon, call him tomorrow when we can talk to him personally."

I was dragging my coat on and carrying Margo's to her. She stood and stretched. "Gotta admit this has been a strange one," she said.

"You had the guy pegged from the beginning?" Wally said.

"Almost," she said, as if admitting it. "But I frankly thought he did in his friend."

"Then you were a little afraid when he was put back out on the street?"

"You bet. How did anyone know if Simon Albert

died before or after he was thrown in the trash compactor?"

"Either way, Stevens is dead now too," Wally said. "Get some sleep and take the morning off. Celebrate your good work."

"Me too?" I said.

"Why not?" Wally said, punching me on the arm—a little too hard. "You've been riding her coattails for a coupla years. Be in by noon tomorrow."

That sounded good, but not for long. When we arrived at our apartment, the phone was ringing. I left the keys in the lock and burst in to answer it. "Glad I caught you," Wally said. "Earl's in town already and wants to talk to us first thing in the morning."

"Tomorrow?" I said, pained. Margo shut the door and brought me my keys, looking puzzled. "I didn't know he was going to be here this early."

"Neither did I," Wally said. "He won't even tell me what he wants. Sounds kind of ominous, though. It's almost like he's got bad news for us."

"You mean he might want to shut down the agency?"

"I just don't know. I hope not. I can't afford to buy it, and I'm not ready to quit, either."

"Well, don't assume the worst," I said. "That's not like you."

"It is too," he said. "And you know it."

"We've been doing all right, haven't we?" I asked. "I mean we've been profitable for him and all that?"

"Oh, I don't think it's been as lucrative as he might have hoped, but we've done fair. Sleep well, Philip. I'll see you at eight."

Sleep well, indeed. Neither of us slept longer than a

half hour at a time. And we guessed Wally was up pacing a little himself.

We arrived at the office a half hour early the next morning, and Wally was already there. He was clean-shaven and had his thinning hair slicked back, and he was wearing his favorite green suit with the cuffs, white socks, and hush puppies. But he looked haggard. The only person I knew who could look good in the morning after a fitful night was hanging up her coat and heading for her desk.

"You guys look like death warmed over," she teased. "Let's assume he's announcing raises, not closings."

"Yeah," Wally said. "I guess we've got no reason to jump to conclusions. 'Cept that's how I make my living. At least up until now."

"Wally!" Margo said. "Stop with the pessimism already!"

Yet for twenty minutes we sat in silence in the outer office, Margo at her desk, I at mine, and Wally in Bonnie's—our receptionist's—chair. We each tried to read the paper, then gave up. We straightened our desks until they were disgustingly organized. Finally we just sat and stared at each other until gallows humor took hold.

"I never liked detective work," Wally deadpanned, after nearly forty years as one of the best in the business. "Would've rather owned a car wash."

We smiled. "Maybe you still can," I said. "I'm going back into art."

Margo shook her head. "I want babies, and lots of 'em."

We fell silent again. "Wonder if there'll be severance pay," Wally said.

"Not enough for a car wash," I said.

"All I need is the down payment," he said.

We stared at each other when we heard a car pull up outside. The downstairs door opened, but the steps on the stairs didn't sound like the old Earl—the lithe, bouncy, healthy head of the Illinois Department of Law Enforcement in Springfield. The steps sounded old, tired, heavy.

We craned our necks to peer out the double glass doors to see when his head would first appear from the stairwell. And we burst out laughing when the matronly head that arose was Bonnie's. "What's so funny?" she said as she entered. "I have a run in my nylons or what?"

Wally stood and hugged her, still laughing. "No," he said, "we just thought you were Earl."

"Hilarious," she said. "I'm often mistaken for a handsome bachelor."

Earl appeared on the stairs behind her. We got serious so fast, Bonnie thought we'd seen ghosts. We stood, formally, and shook hands with him.

"I haven't seen you for what, six months," he said, "and this is the reception I get?"

Chapter Two

Earl looked natty as usual, and as was his custom, he took a long time getting to his point. In response to his chiding about the reception, the four of us took turns embracing him and trading pleasantries. Bonnie dabbed at her eyes and asked what he was doing here.

"Well, IDLE has meetings in Schaumburg later this week, and then there's the wedding on Saturday."

"But why today and why so early? I mean, I'm glad to see you and everything—"

"It sounds like it," Earl said, feigning offense. "No, I just wanted to see you all and talk some business."

Bonnie, who had been with the agency since Earl had opened it several years before, knew that the business would not include her and quickly found busywork to occupy herself. "Would you like me to arrange your office for a meeting, Wally?" she asked.

Wally nodded with a vacant stare, and his eyes followed Earl as he moved to the coat rack and shed his trench coat to reveal a deep navy wool suit over a bright white shirt, with a pale burgundy tie and a stickpin at the collar. His shirt cuffs were linked and showed appropriately at the wrist from inside his suit jacket. He wore an expensive but tasteful watch, a wedding band on the left hand, and a college class ring on the right.

As usual, he was in shape, glowed with health, and moved as if unaware of his clothes. With his dark hair parted in the middle and softly layered back over the top of the ears, he looked several years younger than his forty-four.

Earl Haymeyer was the type of man who could have sauntered as cockily as he wanted, but he never did. He had always been tops at whatever he decided to pursue. Years before, he had worked for Wally Festschrift in the homicide division of the Chicago Police Department.

It hadn't taken him long to pass up Wally and become his boss, not because he wanted it that way, but because Wally had never aspired to be anything but an on-the-street man, a detective sergeant, a plainclothesman. He didn't even mind the younger Haymeyer becoming his boss, though he gave Earl a rough time for several years.

By the time Margo and I met Earl, which wasn't long after she and I had met in Atlanta, he had become a special investigator in the office of the U.S. Attorney for Northern Illinois. He was assigned the case when Margo's mother, a Cook County Circuit Court judge, was implicated in a murder.

Not long after that case was over, Earl turned down the chance to join his boss in Springfield when the former U.S. Attorney became the governor of Illinois. Earl wanted rather to start his own detective agency, and soon Margo and I joined him as trainees.

Wally and Earl ran into each other again a few years later when we were investigating a suburban murder that had ties to the Chicago mob. Though they squabbled some more, they reestablished the old relationship, and Wally became sort of a fixture around the office during his off duty hours.

When Earl finally succumbed to the governor's pressure and accepted the directorship of the Illinois Department of Law Enforcement, he installed Wally as head of the agency. We missed Earl a lot. He eventually came to Christ partly through Margo and me, but he had tried to convince Wally of the merits of the faith even before he had made his own decision.

When Wally too became a Christian, it created an unusually strong bond between the two veterans. Though Wally is much older, he treats Earl as his superior, and rightly so. But there's not a cop or former cop alive Earl admires more than Wally Festschrift.

Earl was a widower, despite the wedding band, which he used more as a defense than anything else. It revealed to me that he was at least aware that he was an attractive man, though I'm sure part of the reason he continued to wear it was also because of the deep love he had for his late wife. Their only son was a teenager confined to a state center for autistics.

Bonnie had pulled a couple of extra chairs into Wally's office, then shut the door behind us when we were inside. I know she hated being on the outside of such meetings, but she knew Wally would keep her posted on anything she had to know.

There was an awkward second when Wally didn't know if Earl wanted to sit in his old chair behind his old desk or if he wanted Wally to. Wally pointed to the chair. "May I?" Earl asked.

"You own it, boss," Wally said, pulling it out for him. Wally and Margo and I sat in front of the big wood desk, facing Earl. It would have been like old times, except that Larry Shipman wasn't there.

Earl looked briefly at each of us, but as he took a breath to speak, Wally interrupted. "I just want you to know, Earl, that everything is in order. The cases are up to date, the files are complete and properly documented. The bills are paid, the receivables are basically on track, and there are no law suits pending."

Earl looked a little surprised, but preoccupied. "Thank you, Wally," he said. "I never dreamed otherwise. You're doing a great job, and I appreciate the way you've kept me informed on Philip's and Margo's progress." He smiled at us, but Wally looked uncomfortable, as if he thought Earl assumed he had said that because he wanted a compliment.

Then Earl did something that shocked all of us. He opened the meeting by praying. It moved me to think that he felt free to do that now that we were all Christians. When he finished we all just smiled at each other.

"Good job on that indigent murder, Margo," Earl said finally.

She nodded and smiled. "You thought it was murder too, then?"

"Oh, of course. No question. Didn't you all?" He looked to Wally and me. I cocked my head noncommittally; Wally shrugged.

"Probably," he muttered.

Earl winked at Margo. He unbuttoned his suit jacket and leaned forward in his chair, resting his

15

elbows on the desk and entwining his fingers. "There's something very important I want to talk to all of you about. It's more than important, really. It's complex, it's widespread, it has many ramifications. I need your help."

I still thought he was talking about closing down the agency, and both Wally and Margo would tell me later that they thought the same thing. But what he said next made us realize how wrong we were.

He reached inside his breast pocket and produced a triple-folded sheaf of six yellow legal sheets with his neat, block printing covering one side of each. "I can't copy these for you," he said. "I can't even keep them in my briefcase."

Almost involuntarily, we all edged forward.

"I don't know where else to turn," he said. "I need a private investigation by people I trust, but I don't want to use a state agency. And, of course, I cannot take any percentage of the fee the state will pay for this job, so there will be no hint of a conflict of interest. The only other person who has any knowledge of this is the governor himself, and he had authorized the funds. Will you have the time, if the money is made available?"

"Sure, Earl," Wally said. "Will we get to decide on whether we take the case, or is this an assignment from the owner?"

"It's an assignment."

"Of course we won't turn it down."

"Of course. The problem is, we need more people, but we'll have to do with what we have here. Another big problem, Wally, is that this concerns the Chicago PD, so you're no good to the case either—as an inside person, I mean. You'll be invaluable as coordinator, adviser, and consultant."

Wally was curious, I could tell. But speechless. He knew Earl would get to his point without prodding.

"There's something the Chicago Police Department has not publicized at all. In fact, when the questions have arisen, they have denied it." Earl was speaking in just above a whisper, obviously emotional. "You see, there's a leak in the Internal Affairs Division."

"Oh, no," Wally said.

Earl nodded. "And it's having the worst result imaginable."

"Covers are being blown?" Wally asked.

"Worse than that."

"Threatened?"

"Worse."

"Hurt?"

"Worse."

Wally shook his head. "How many?"

"Three."

Wally shook his head again.

"I'm not following you," Margo said.

Earl stood and came around to the front of the desk and sat on the top. "The Chicago PD Internal Affairs Division has a tough time talking cops into ratting on each other, but if they don't, no one ever will. And as you know, there have been scandals among the police that have rocked the city."

Margo nodded.

"When a cop comes forward, he often wants to give information without getting personally involved in the operation. Because once he does, he becomes a target, and so does his family. When things get bad

17

and a cop *has* to get involved, it's almost impossible to keep his identity hidden from his colleagues. If he's involved in the bust of a bunch of cops, he has to be moved away and given a new identity."

"I've read about that," Margo said. "It sounds horrible. Wondering if anyone in the new town knows who you really are. Having your kids try to remember their new, phony name. Leaving all your friends and relatives and familiar spots. Terrible!"

"It *is* terrible," Earl said. "And now it's worse than terrible. Two of the informants who had been set up with new identities have been murdered, and one is missing. The city and the state will be the targets of heavy lawsuits from the families, but that's not what concerns me. The families don't want to say anything publicly for fear of their own lives, now that they have lost husbands and fathers. The problem is, the leak has to be coming from inside IAD, because the identities and new locations are so top secret."

"What can *we* do?" I asked.

"That hasn't been totally determined yet, Philip," Earl said. "But my hope—and my dread—is that you and Margo might be able to infiltrate either IAD or the regular police force and find out who the major contact is. Wally's too well known, of course."

"Sounds like dangerous duty."

"You bet. And you have the right to refuse it, of course."

"You mean we would become bogus cops?" Margo asked.

"No," Earl said. "That would take too long. You'd have to start as cadets and you wouldn't get into the action quickly enough."

18

"But they can't pose as transfers either," Wally said. "The IAD guys and everyone else check that out pretty carefully."

"I know," Earl said. "I was thinking they might pose as fences."

"I don't get it," I said. "I thought this business was all centered around dope. What would we be fencing?"

"I'll get to that," Earl said.

"More important," Margo said, "do we look the part?"

"Neither of 'em look the part!" Wally said. "You can take them out of Sunday school, but you can't take the Sunday school out of them!"

Earl stood and paced the room. "I know it's a long shot," he said. "That's why I think it might work. You don't look like undercover cops or private investigators either, but that hasn't hurt your effectiveness here."

Wally agreed. "It's come in handy more than once."

Margo and I looked at each other. "What happens if we're successful?" she asked. "When it's all over, will you have every last one of 'em behind bars where they can't hurt us either?"

"There are never any guarantees, Mar," Earl said. "You know that."

"Then we'll be moving away from home and friends and family and church to some remote place where we know no one and no one knows us?"

"We hope not."

"You hope not," she repeated.

Chapter Three

"You said our roles had not been totally determined yet," I said. "Who will determine them, and
when will that happen?"

"We will," Earl said. "All of us. And right now."

"I'm still curious about this fencing question," I
said. "What is there to fence?"

"What *isn't* there to fence?" Earl said, returning to
Wally's chair. He pulled out the top left drawer and
propped his feet on it, tilting way back in the chair.
"These guys who've taken so much heat for the
cocaine and heroin pushing—I mean the ones who've
been under suspicion but haven't been caught—are
trying to hedge their bets now by branching out.
They're buying and selling stolen property."

Wally looked as if he wanted to spit. "There oughta
be capital punishment for crooked cops," he said.

Earl nodded and fell silent, staring at the ceiling.
He looked weary. I was getting nervous. I didn't want
to get Earl and Wally talking about cops on the take,
betraying the public trust, violating their call of duty
and their oath of office. It wasn't that they weren't
both eloquent and articulate, Wally in his own way. It
was just that I was selfishly worried about what Earl

had in mind for my wife and me, and if they got on a favorite hated subject, we'd never get to it.

"I'm going to draw you a picture," Earl said, "and before I leave here, I'm going to tear it into little pieces and throw it away. So watch carefully."

He scribbled on the back of another yellow legal sheet, drawing a rudimentary building in an alleyway. "This is in Oak Park," he said, "and notice the address." He wrote *9679* on the brick wall above double garage doors with a standard door between them. "Memorize it," he said. "It's on Cornell Street North, or—I should say—behind the small businesses and apartments and dingy homes on that street."

"What happens there?" I asked, but Earl was carefully holding the sheet before Wally's and Margo's eyes, then mine. He waited until he had the attention of each and nodded at us. When all three had nodded back, he did as he said he would and tore the paper into tiny scraps, which he put in the wastebasket under the desk.

"That's their combination warehouse and outlet," Earl said. "Anything that might sell is shipped there, sometimes in broad daylight. Buyers are friends and acquaintances or referred by the same. If you showed up uninvited, they would play dumb, not understanding why in the world you thought you could purchase anything in their garage."

"A garage is their front?" Margo asked. "Is that their phony business so they can make deliveries in the daytime without arousing the suspicion of the neighbors?"

Earl nodded, retrieving a scrap from the basket and

21

writing: "AUTOMOTIVE REPAIR BY APPOINT-MENT ONLY."

"But no phone number," Wally said.

"Or even name or address," Earl added. "They have at least one panel truck and one van, both with that same sign painted on the side. They come and go day and night, along with a variety of cars of several vintages. A man in a blue service shirt and cap, carrying a legal-sized clipboard, emerges from a standard-sized door between the garage doors and greets them as they pull onto the concrete apron in front of the garage. He chats with the driver, scribbles on the clipboard, then opens the garage door with a remote control device."

"They're delivering goods?"

"Or buying," Earl said.

"How do you know about this place?"

Earl's eyes seemed to glaze over. He looked above our heads and took a deep breath, as if preparing to speak, but he said nothing. He pressed his lips together and shook his head slowly. "It, ah, was shown to me," he said deliberately, fighting emotion. "By the inside informant who is now missing."

Earl covered his mouth with his hand, and we sat in awkward silence for several minutes. Finally, he pulled his wallet from a back pocket. There, along with a photograph of his late wife, one of his son when he was seven years old, and Earl's various iden-tification cards, was a mug shot of a youngish black police officer in his dress blues. "Johnny Ray Robin-son," he said.

We stared at the picture, and Earl explained. "He was one of the best inside men Internal Affairs ever had, and he wasn't even officially part of their operation. Came to them three years ago upset about the drug thing. Said he was offended that just because he was black and outspoken, he was presumed to be part of the crowd that was on the take, had access to dope, was a dirty cop. Interesting guy, though. He would never take part in a sting operation."

"Where you actually bust some cops," Margo said.

"Right. He never, ever used names."

"What was the point?" Wally asked.

"He just felt he could be more valuable and stay with the program longer if he wasn't directly involved with fingering anybody on the inside."

"He wasn't protecting someone, was he?"

"We never thought so, Wally. He was amazingly effective."

"How?" Margo said. "What did he give you if he didn't give you names?"

"Places. Times. Details. And we'd read down a list of names, and he'd either shake his head or stare directly to his left. We learned to know what he meant. Sometimes we'd read a name of a cop we knew was straight, in fact maybe another informant. He never looked surprised. He would just stop with his mysterious glances and gaze directly in our eyes and smile slightly, letting us know that he knew we were just testing him."

"By his telling you when and what and where, you and IAD were successful?"

"You read the papers. You know the last two sting operations were winners. Problem was, we had some casualties."

"Robinson?"

"Nope. He survived both unscathed. But then he told me about the automotive repair shop. Where is it?"

"Ninety-six seventy-nine Cornell Street North, Oak Park," Margo rattled off, as if she'd been waiting for him to ask. "Double garage doors with a regular door between them." She had a way of reciting just what the teacher wanted without being smug.

Earl nodded. "He and I drove by there one time. Three days later his life was threatened. He wouldn't say by whom. He said he'd give us every other name and detail he could think of if we'd move him and his wife and his three daughters—all under six—a thousand miles from Chicago and set them up with a new home, new identity, the whole bit. We were sorry to have to do it, but eager to help in any way. What he gave us put a lot of men away."

"I still don't get it," Wally said. "Why were you involved, Earl?"

"At the request of the head of IAD."

"Oh, that's right. You and Bubba go back a long way, don't you?"

"Bubba?" Margo said. "I thought the IAD chief was Jasper Buchanan."

"That's Bubba," Wally said, smiling. "What would you go by if your name was Jasper? I could never stand the man."

"I've never been able to figure that out," Earl said. "He thinks the world of you. I've never heard him say a negative thing about you. In fact, he told me he wanted you in IAD from the beginning."

"Yeah, sure. By then I was twenty-five years into homicide, and I never felt about a mass murderer the way I feel about dirty cops. Bust a guy for dealin' dope and see him get reprimanded, suspended, maybe fired? Ah, nah! Not for me. All very quiet and dignified like. I'd have joined his IAD boys if he woulda let me have at some of those creeps in a back alley for ten minutes apiece. Don't get me started."

"But that's no reason to take it out on Bubba," Earl said.

"Maybe," Wally conceded. "But he was always a little smooth, a little elegant, a little soft for me."

"He's seen a lot of guys go to prison for what they did while wearing the Chicago PD uniform."

"But a lot of 'em were quietly dismissed, too," Wally said. "They shoulda been stoned at Daley Plaza."

"Give Buchanan a break," Earl said. "You're probably going to have to work with him on this case. He's one of your long time admirers."

Wally waved off the suggestion. "So what happened to Robinson?" he said. "Though I'm not sure I want to hear this."

"Me either," Margo said.

"All we know," Earl said, "is what he said to his wife the day before he disappeared. This is all more confidential than anything I've told you up until now, OK?"

We nodded.

"It's been leaked in the paper that we relocate our informants to the northeast and the southwest. That's as specific as we get. The truth is, Robinson was relocated to Tallahassee so he and his family would be within a half day's drive of his boyhood home in Biloxi, Mississippi. He could never go there, of course, but his mother could prearrange a visit to somewhere between the two cities and be able to see her granddaughters and her son and his wife."

"He couldn't go to Biloxi because—?"

"Because someone might be watching his mother's place to see if he'd head that way."

"So what happened? He went there anyway?"

"No, his mother went to Tallahassee. All the way there. And not six months after he'd been relocated. It was too soon. We think someone followed her to him."

"But that could have happened even if she met him halfway."

"Maybe. But he would have known how to play it safe and coach her on how to tell if she was being followed. Her visit surprised him. He was quite upset about it, according to his wife. He put his mother's car in his garage and kept her inside the house for a long weekend. Apparently it was too late. She left before dawn last Tuesday morning. He went to work, teaching civics and coaching in a junior high school under the name of Willie Banks. Just before noon, as far as we can piece together the story, Johnny must have spotted someone watching him. He asked the secretary in the physical education department to call his wife and tell her 'IAD.' She said he said it almost as if it was a practical joke, an inside thing that his wife would understand. The secretary said she called his wife and said, 'Mrs. Banks, this is Judy Prewitt at school. Your husband said I should tell you he said IAD and that you would understand.' Mrs. Robinson said, 'That's all he said?' Miss Prewitt said yes. Mrs. Robinson said, 'Let me talk to him,' and—according to Miss Prewitt—sounded alarmed. Miss Prewitt couldn't find him but promised his wife she would have him call as soon as he could. No one has seen or heard from him since. His car and all his belongings were left at the school."

"*No* one saw him?"

"Several students said they saw him with two men, but the descriptions vary. They range from tall and black to short and white, one black and one white, both black, both white, glasses and not, hats and not, a big new car, a small old car, you name it."

"What do you make of that?" Margo asked.

"Only that he must have been making a great effort to look nonchalant with the men and go with them without making a scene. His walking across the parking lot from the gym to a car with a couple of friends or acquaintances made little impression on anyone until they realized he was gone and probably not coming back."

Wally swore, then apologized. "Excuse me," he said. "I'm still getting used to the idea of not talking like that."

"Me too," Earl said. "This case has caused me to slip more than once myself."

"Do you think Robinson's dead?" Margo asked.

"I hope not. The other two that have been killed and the one who was beat up pretty bad were used as examples, I think. If they were going to use Johnny Ray as an example, they'd have done it already—left him somewhere or something."

"So what are they doing with him?" I said.

"Maybe trying to get information out of him?"

"How?"

"Who knows? Scaring him. Threatening him. Warning him of danger to his mother and wife and children."

"Where are they?" Margo asked.

"Safe."

"All of them?"

"Yup."

"Where?"

"There's no need to say, not that I don't trust you."

"In Tallahassee?"

"Nope."

"Biloxi?"

"Nope."

"Do you *know* where they are, Earl?"

"Yes."

"And you're convinced they're safe?"

"I know they're safe."

"That's all I wanted to know."

"I know, Margo."

"What kind of information do they want from Robinson?" I asked.

"Names. Just like we did. Only they want to know who all the stool pigeons are. He may be forced to tell them. The only hope we have is that he was in the service, fought in Viet Nam. He's been trained not to betray official secrets. But then, he was never a prisoner in Nam, and even if he had been, the Viet Cong didn't have access to his family. If he's alive, and if they're using the psychological and physical torture they're capable of, he's under the greatest pressure a person can endure."

Wally stood and stomped to the window, then

28

turned to face Earl. "And he tipped his wife off that these were IAD guys."

"Is that how you interpret it, Wally?" Earl said.

"Is that how I interpret it? How else is there to interpret it? How do you interpret it?"

Earl shrugged. "He may have simply been trying to tell her that he was in trouble because of his own involvement with IAD. We don't know that he was fingering IAD for what was about to happen to him. How could he tell his wife without having the secretary get suspicious? Anyway, no one from IAD was out of Illinois that day."

"I'd still start looking in IAD's backyard."

"That's why I'm here, Wally. That's why I'm here. Are you in or out?"

"I'm in," Wally said without hesitation. "For whatever you think I can contribute."

"And you two?" Earl said, looking first at me, then at Margo, then back at me. Margo and I looked at each other. Neither of us spoke.

Chapter Four

"I don't think we're in—yet," Margo said after a long silence, during which she had held her face in her hands and stared at the floor. Earl looked genuinely surprised, Wally disappointed. "For myself," she said, "I think I'd risk my life for Wally's ideals alone. Knowing how deeply he feels about this, and seeing how deeply you feel about your friend and brave colleague, Earl, no sacrifice would be too great. There's no one in the world I admire more than you and Wally, and there's nothing I wouldn't do for you. But my life, my body, my self isn't mine anymore. I belong to Philip, and he belongs to me."

No one knew what to say or how to respond, especially me. At first I wasn't sure what she was driving at. Was she saying she would willingly risk her life if she didn't have me to think about, or was she saying that she didn't want *me* to risk *my* life when I had *her* to think about?

"Are you saying it's up to me whether you involve yourself in this thing?" I asked.

"To a point," she said. "I wouldn't think you'd have a right to force me to if I didn't want to."

"But I could keep you from it if you wanted to, which you apparently do."

She nodded. Wally and Earl looked as if they had found themselves in a wholly befuddling conversation of which they wanted no part. "The only problem is," she said, "what if you are willing to let me involve myself, yet you don't want to yourself?"

"I'd be a coward."

"Or you'd be thinking of me."

"What if I wanted in and you didn't want me to be?" I asked.

"That's a very real possibility. What are our odds, Earl? For living through this, I mean. Without having to relocate under phony names, which is obviously not that successful anyway."

"No guarantees. No promises. No odds."

"That's what I was afraid of. But Philip, I'd have no right to ask to be involved if I wasn't willing to let you be involved as well."

My brain was hurting. There was some convoluted logic in there somewhere, but she'd long before flown past my limited capacities. "The question," I said, "was whether we were in or out."

"My sentiments exactly," Earl said.

Without hesitation, Margo said, "I'm in, but I want to have to talk you into letting me be. And I want you to want to be in, but against my wishes and better judgment."

I looked to Wally and Earl for help. Neither would return my gaze. "Let's just say we're in and forget the logic or lack of it," I said. I realized when I said it that it had come out wrong. Margo was hurt.

"I thought I was being very logical," she said.

"I'm sure you were. If you were trying to say that we both want in but are each worried about the other, I think we all caught that, didn't we?" This time Wally and Earl nodded, and though I think Margo thought what she had said was a little more sophisticated than that, she was through trying to explain it. "If you want in, Margo," I said, "we're in."

"I'm not in," she said.

I hadn't realized I had offended her that deeply, but I couldn't think of any other explanation for this change of direction. It came soon enough. "I want conditions put on it," she said.

Earl looked blank, as if he didn't know whether to laugh or cry, shout or whisper. Wally was intrigued— as usual—with Margo. I could tell he was tired of the word games, but she had aroused his curiosity, and if you can do that with Wally, you've got him. He even quit fidgeting and fixed his eyes on her.

"I'll bite," Earl said. "Let's hear the conditions."

"Just one," she said. "You said yourself you need more people on the case. There aren't enough of us on the front line. Philip and I will not be enough if neither of you can be visible."

"Will you let me worry about that?" he suggested.

"No," Margo responded quickly. "Remember, if we're in, we're thinking about each other just in case no one else does. I'm not saying you wouldn't, but if you think an operation this big and this complex— and especially this dangerous—can be handled by two people, you're not thinking of everyone involved. You need at least one more person."

Now Earl was exasperated. "Margo," he said slowly, "there isn't anyone else available that I trust.

It's not easy work. It's going to be difficult and demanding. The pressure will be unbearable. You'll be passing yourself off as someone else, as a personality and character that are the opposite of the real you. Not a lot of people can do that. And the ones who can are too close to this situation to do us any good. The people I would go to first are recognizable by the people we'd be trying to sting."

"I can think of someone," Margo said, just short of smugly.

"Who," Earl said, "Bonnie?"

"Don't be sarcastic. I'm thinking of Larry Shipman."

Earl hesitated long enough to reveal that he had been caught off guard, that indeed he had not thought of Larry. But he tried to recover. "I couldn't do that to him," he said. "His life is settled. He's enjoying his work and his marriage and his new location."

Margo smiled thinly at Earl. "He's the best con man in the business," she said. "Even better than the ones you said you'd go to first if they weren't already cops or IAD or IDLE. Admit it."

He didn't. But he didn't deny it, either. He appeared preoccupied, cocking his head and staring at the wall. "I couldn't do that to him," he said without emotion, but it was clear the idea was working on him.

"Remember that time he got himself on the bank staff as a teller and exposed the embezzler?" I said. "That was a classic." Earl nodded and smiled, still staring at the wall. He was remembering something else, another incident, a slice of life the way it was with the agency when the original staff was around. But he wasn't sharing it.

"I always liked the kid," Wally said. "He was a natural. I could tell from the minute I laid eyes on him."

"Don't give me that," Earl said, smiling, finally turning to look at Wally. "Ship drove you crazy from the evening we found that body behind the wheel of a Corvette in the parking lot at Proviso West High School."

Wally waved at him as if to disagree, but he said, "Not sure as he'd be comfortable around here now. I may have put him off by writing to him a few times too many."

"What're you talking about?" Earl said, his attention suddenly riveted to Wally. "What'd you write to him about?"

"Oh, you know, what's been happenin' around here."

"You didn't tell me that," Margo said.

"Didn't know I was s'posed to check in with you on everything," Wally said.

"That explains it!" Earl said, slapping the desk.

"Explains what?"

"Why he told me to back off."

"You've been in touch with Larry too?" Margo said.

Earl nodded. "I wrote to him about Wally and me becoming Christians. He ignored those parts of my letters when he answered, so I quit writing about that. Then he finally wrote and told me that he and Shannon were happy, and that he'd like me to meet her sometime, but he'd appreciate it if I didn't try to foist my religion off on them. I thought about going into

34

your spiel, Mar, about how it's not a religion, it's a Person, but I figured you'd already been through that with him."

"More than once," I said.

"That's *exactly* what I told him in my letters," Wally said. He turned to Margo. "Now were we doing what we were supposed to be doing, or did we blow it and turn him off completely?"

"I don't see how you can be blamed for telling someone about your faith," she said. "Unless you beat him over the head with it."

"I don't think I did," Earl said. "That's why I was so surprised when he ignored it when I was writing about it, and he reacted to it when I didn't. It must have been the combination of Wally writing from this end and me from that end, both hitting him with the same thing at once."

"Yeah," Wally said. "He musta thought we were in cahoots or something."

"So that's the real reason you don't want him in on this case," Margo said.

"That's not it at all," Earl said. "I just don't think he'd want to. It's not going to be a short-term thing."

"How long?"

"Well, longer than whatever his vacation is. What does a hotshot editor get for vacation these days—three, four weeks tops?"

Margo shrugged and nodded.

"No way this'll be that short," Earl said. "I want you and Philip to set up a stolen goods operation that asks no questions and answers few. It has to be good and solid and made to work in the best interests of the cops' fencing business. It could be a few months; it could be longer."

"Give Larry a choice," Margo said. "Give him a reason to leave the paper and get back into the business he loves the most. Shannon has been away long enough that people have forgotten her story, and she could handle the memories. I can't believe Larry likes a desk job, even if the pay and the security and the future are good. That just isn't him. Supervising people? I can't imagine."

Earl stood and opened the door. "Let's move out here where we can get some air," he said. We followed him and sat on desks in the outer office. Bonnie pretended not to listen.

"You're saying you're not in unless I put someone else on the case with you?" Earl asked Margo.

"Not just someone else," she said. "Larry Shipman."

"Or someone just as good."

"You said that anyone as good would never be able to pull this one off. Can't you just at least try? I don't want to be a pest on this, Earl, I really don't. You know me better than that." Wally turned his head away and covered his mouth. Earl fought a smile. "C'mon, you guys know I know who's boss!" Margo continued.

"Yeah," Earl said wryly. "I'm the boss and you're the one with the conditions."

"*You* asked us if we were in or out!" Margo said. "Well?"

"We're in. If Larry's in."

Earl rolled his eyes. "I can't afford him."

36

"If you can afford a big phony fencing operation, you can afford the guy who'll make it work for you."

Earl's eyes glazed over as if he were tired of talking about it. "You guys have your breakfast before you came in this morning?" he said.

We nodded. Wally said, "Not much. You hungry?"

"Ravenous. You want to go out and grab something?"

"Need you ask? Always." Wally turned to me. "Can you and Miss Prima Donna hold down the fort?"

"You guys!" Margo whined.

When Earl and Wally returned nearly two hours later, they had a deal for Margo. "You get him here," Earl said, "without telling him what we have in mind, and we'll hit him with it." Margo nearly squealed. "*But*!" Earl cautioned, "I'm not going to twist his arm. There may be plenty of good reasons why Larry simply would not want to uproot his wife and leave his job, even with a temporary leave of absence. No undue pressure. No badgering. No talking him into it. If he does it as a favor to you or me or anyone else, it'll grow old mighty quick."

"Larry loves this kind of stuff."

"Don't kid yourself, Mar. This is the big leagues. These aren't two-bit hoodlums or bank tellers. These guys would kill you if they knew what you were up to. Anyway, do we have a deal? You get him here under another pretense and we'll talk with him about it?"

Margo nodded. "I just don't know if he's been invited to Allyson's wedding. Shall we call him and find out and invite him for a party even if he hasn't?

It would be on the premise that so many of us are back that we wanted to include him in a reunion."

"Why don't we just call Allyson downstairs and see if she's invited Larry and Shannon," I suggested. "She knew him fairly well."

Margo grew stony. "You forget, dear, that *I* wasn't even personally invited. I'm the 'and Mrs.' on *your* invitation."

Earl and Wally were embarrassed. They knew well that Allyson was the only girl who had ever come between Margo and me, but—of course—that was long before we were married. "She's not snubbing you," I said. "She thinks you're special, and she's thrilled with this new guy. You could call her."

She shook her head. "I'm not being bratty," she said. "I'd just rather not."

"I'll call her," I said.

"I'd rather you didn't either," Margo said, not unkindly. "If you don't mind."

I shook my head but didn't say anything. "I'll call her," Bonnie sang out. "Erin, my granddaughter, is going to be standing up for her, you know."

We knew. Bonnie had only told us maybe twenty times. We also knew Erin Gibbons had made the Olympic gymnastics team and that her parents had reconciled and were living together as husband and wife again. I was relieved that she had taken the burden of calling from Margo and me.

Within minutes we had the news. "Allyson was out shopping," Bonnie reported, "but her mother checked the list for me. They're coming."

"Call 'em, Margo," Wally said. "Tell 'em you

wanted to know if they could come in a day early.
When's your party, Margo?"

"You tell me."

"Make it Friday afternoon. A picnic. And it'll continue into the evening if necessary."

"A picnic this early in the year?"

"Hey! It's May. Could be in the nineties."

"Could be in the forties too, Wally."

Chapter Five

Late that Tuesday afternoon while Margo and Bonnie worked on arrangements and invitations for Margo's big reunion and Wally tried to clear the decks so we could work on the Chicago PD IAD case, Earl asked me to take a ride with him. He headed south on Route 53.

"So Wally thought I was shutting down the agency, did he?"

"Yeah," I said. "Had me convinced too. Though I couldn't imagine why you'd want to."

"You got that right, Philip. That agency, and knowing it's in good hands, is what keeps me going. Getting back into the agency someday is like the light at the end of the tunnel."

"Really? I thought maybe you'd stick with Jim Hanlon until he was president and become head of the FBI or the Secret Service or his chief of staff or something."

Earl laughed. "No. I had no idea what I was getting into with a political job. I took it as a favor to Jim, and I thought I'd be able to stand it for four years. Now I'm not so sure."

"What's the problem?"

"Too administrative. Too political. Too tentative. When I was working for Jim in the U.S. Attorney's office, we could get our teeth into a case. With IDLE, it's admirable work and we provide a service, but, ah, I don't know. I'm still young enough to want some action."

I sensed he wanted to tell me more. "Does Hanlon know how you feel?"

"Oh, I think so. He should. Knows me well enough. I haven't actually come out and said it, but, yeah, I think he knows. That's one thing I have to admit, I have access to him. I was afraid I might not. Most department heads complain that they don't. Some were jealous of the time I got with him, but if I didn't get it, along with a few special assignments like this one, I'd go crazy."

"You said the time you *got* with him, as if it was all in the past. You gonna stick with it through his term?"

Earl shrugged.

"And what if he's reelected next year?"

Earl was strangely silent. I realized I'd hit on a sore spot when I asked if he was sticking out the first term, because it wasn't like him to not respond. I knew if I waited long enough, he'd feel obliged to answer.

"I may not have a choice," he said finally.

"You mean he might replace you if he's reelected?"

"He might replace me before the end of *this* term."

"Why?"

Earl studied the rearview mirror, then stole a glance over his shoulder and past my head so he could move to the far right lane and slow down. He set his cruise control at about fifty, and I knew he was eliminating distractions so he could tell me a story.

41

"I made the mistake of publicly criticizing the governor," he said.

"I didn't read of that."

"It just happened recently, and if it hits the Chicago papers, I'm as good as gone."

"What did you criticize him about?"

"Well, my predecessor eliminated several sub-departments within certain divisions of IDLE and in the process caused several casualties to our personnel force."

"People you would have kept in some capacity even if their departments had to be eliminated."

"Exactly. One of those was the Department of Local Assistance in the Support Services Division."

"You wouldn't have dropped that department even with the need for cutbacks?"

"Oh, yes, I probably would have. But I would have reassigned its chief. He was a man with thirty-some years experience, almost half of that as a chief on the local level. He had a lot to offer in the way of counsel to local departments. He was a feather in IDLE's cap. That department may have been a luxury, and I didn't even attempt to bring it back under the new administration when I took over. But I did speak frankly to Jim about finding a place for the former chief, even if it wasn't in Support Services. There were many areas he could have contributed to. Kill programs, yes, but don't expend talent."

"But the governor didn't let you?"

"Well, not exactly. It's just that there was some red tape that would have had to have been cut through, and he's the only one who could've done it. He didn't see it as a priority, and we lost the guy. He's chiefing on the local level again, and he feels a sense of commitment to the department that hired him, so we'll never see him in Springfield again."

"Did Hanlon know how badly you wanted him?"

"Sure, and don't misunderstand; I can appreciate Jim's view that some things are priorities and some are not. To me, this man was a priority; to the governor, there were other things he had to consider. Cutting through the red tape to rehire a man who had been lost in a cutback shuffle would have cost Jim some very expensive chips in the political poker game, if you'll excuse that old nature metaphor. He just wasn't willing to spend the chips when something more important might come along. Totally his prerogative."

"Then how'd you get in trouble?"

"I shot off my mouth before I had a chance to cool down and become levelheaded about it. And I didn't say anything that I hadn't said to Jim's face. I told him, 'Jim, I want you to know that I disagree with you on this and that I wish you would see that human resources should be a top priority for you. But I will abide by your decision.' He said something about that being why he respected me so much and that his decision was that he wasn't in a position to help me rehire the guy I wanted. Somehow the story leaked that I had lost one with my old buddy, and some press people showed up at my office to ask about it before I had put it all in perspective."

"So you told them what went on behind closed doors."

"Right."

"And that made the governor look bad."

"A little. But it made me look worse."

"How did *he* react?"

"Well, I called him as soon as the press left and told him I didn't know what was going to appear in the media, but that I had blown it. He was a little cool but very appreciative of my telling him. Before the stories hit, though, the press ran to him with my complaints and demanded to know what he was going to do about one of his trusted people showing such disloyalty."

"And he said?"

"He gave them some double-talk about not wanting 'yes men,' and that he respected and admired me and all that, and that he was happy to give me a verbal vote of confidence. Something about our not having to agree on every detail to work well together."

"That was nice."

"Yeah, and I think he was sincere, but it was a grave error on his part. He should have told them that he was upset about my breaking his confidence and violating a cardinal rule of high-level management, implying that I was on the ropes. Then he would have appeared strong; showing no favoritism, and he could have let me dangle for six weeks and then kindly pardoned me out of the goodness of his heart."

"You mean the press didn't like his generosity?"

"That would be an understatement. They murdered him. They made me out a teacher's pet, someone he was defending because of his own insecurity. They said he was spineless, wouldn't clean his own house, wasn't tough-minded, the whole bit. They wrung their hands over what this incident would mean to the future of state government, how if one of Hanlon's

44

own men could get away with showing such disfavor in public, what would the Chicago democrats do to the poor governor. Where is the mettle that put him in such revered stead as U.S. Attorney. All that."

"Wow."

"That's what I said. Then I proceeded to blow it again. See, I'm not a media animal, and I'm not a political one either. I should have just let the thing drop and forgotten it. That's what Jim was going to do, and it's what he told me later he would have advised me to do if he'd known I had no more sense than to run back to the press and try to defend him. It was dumb, but I didn't know what to do. I had been burned, so I stuck my hand back in the fire to try to put it out."

"And you got burned again."

"I sure did. I tried to resign through the papers. When the calls started coming, asking me how I responded to the governor's reaction to my spilling the beans, I should have done what I've always done. I should have said no comment and ignored them as I've been doing for years in criminal cases."

"That *has* been your technique, I know. Even when there was glory at stake."

"You know my philosophy on that, Philip. Wally's the same way. If a guy's in this business for the spotlight, he ought to move up to where the air is thinner, the lights are brighter, and the risks are smaller. Grandstanders get promoted or killed, that's the rule. I've never been one and never want to be."

"But you tried to fix things this time."

"Like a dummy. I drafted my resignation and read

45

it to the first three or four reporters who called to get the follow-up story."

"Without informing Hanlon first."

"Right."

"Ouch."

"You're telling me. And I didn't even think to tell him before the news hit. Can you imagine?"

I shook my head, yet who knows what I, or anyone else, would have done in that situation? "You knew he would see it."

"Of course I did! That's what was so foolish about it. I really thought I was going to fix everything by offering to resign, making it appear as sincere as it was, and doing it publicly through the same media in which I'd unintentionally hurt my boss."

"What'd he say this time?"

"He hit the roof. He was livid. It was one of those phone conversations that begins, 'We've been friends a long time, Earl, but I've got to tell you. . .' Know what I mean?"

I nodded. "Not too thrilled, huh?"

"Hardly. Told me he was of a mind to call my bluff and accept my resignation now that I had insisted on putting the ball in his court. What was he supposed to do now, he wanted to know, with the press and the public saying he was a weak leader who let his under-lings get away with things. 'It was salvaged when I passed it off as a minor infraction I could live with,' he told me, 'and let the media have their fun with it. Now they're really going to have a field day. Earl, I thought you had more sense.' "

"What'd you tell him?"

"What could I tell him? I was sorry. I blew it. I

didn't know better. Maybe he *should* accept the resignation. I'd survive. I told him it certainly wasn't a bluff, that I meant it sincerely. I said that even though I saw how it was a further embarrassment that I alone was responsible for, he should do whatever he felt was necessary. I really felt like a clod. He had done so much for me and made me feel good about what I had to offer, which was expertise in law enforcement and crime detection and prevention. But I should have just kept my nose out of politics and the media, where he has always shined."

"Did he tell you what he was going to tell the press?"

"No, and I was on pins and needles until the next morning."

"So, tell me, tell me."

"The papers quoted him as saying that he had not asked for my resignation, nor would he accept it. He said that he hadn't asked for an apology either, but that I had offered one, and he was accepting it. 'End of controversy,' he concluded."

"What a classic," I said. "The guy's really got it, hasn't he?"

"I was impressed," Earl said wryly. "He let a day pass, and then called me into his office. Told me maybe the time was right for me to get to Chicago for the secret mission he had approved funds for a few weeks before."

"This one, you mean? The IAD business?"

Earl nodded. "The press wasn't letting up on him or me, though a few editorial writers finally put it in perspective and begrudgingly complimented him on how he had handled it. If the press has let me go in

47

peace, which of course I don't know yet, we may survive it. If the press and the public, and most of all
Jim, get tired of it and it refuses to die—like I say, I
may be out."

"Would you be disappointed?"

"Not terribly. Embarrassed, yes. Ashamed of having made my boss look bad, yes. But I'm also realistic. I would survive. I'd come back to my own agency
as a consultant, let Wally keep running it, have some
fun. Nobody knows or cares much about who is or
isn't, or was and isn't, the head of the Illinois Department of Law Enforcement. I'd quickly be forgotten,
and most people wouldn't have been aware of me or
the situation in the first place."

Earl had exited Route 53 and headed west a mile or
so to Roselle Road at Illinois Street, just south of
Schaumburg Road in Schaumburg. At the east end of
a small two-story building, the other end of which
housed an animal clinic, was the field office for the
Division of Support Services of IDLE.

"About a half-dozen people work here, including
clerical help," Earl said as he pulled into the lot. "We
used to have an office upstairs for the chief of the
Department of Local Assistance when he was not in
Springfield, but that's empty now, as are the conference rooms up there. At least, they're supposed to be
empty."

"But they're not?"

"That's why we're here, Philip. Only I have access
to those offices. No one who works here does, and
they know better than to ask. They have a vague idea
that it's computer equipment. They just think it's

48

something that doesn't concern them. Which is only partially correct."

Earl was warmly welcomed into the office by the receptionist and three men. He chose not to introduce me, and they all but ignored me except for the cursory glance—common to all cops—toward my right hip to see if I was carrying a piece. I was, of course, so they probably assumed I was from IDLE in Springfield.

One of them asked Earl if he could speak with him for a moment. Earl looked as if he really didn't have the time, but the agent's tone was so conspiratorial and urgent that Earl allowed himself to be dragged into the corner. He was shown a document and then became engaged in an earnest discussion, where he appeared to be pleading with his subordinate. They shook hands as they parted, and Earl was visibly moved.

He motioned for me to follow him out the door and down the hall to a back stairway, which was locked. He produced the keys and let us into the stairwell, then turned and locked the door behind us.

"You wouldn't believe what the people in that office wanted to do," he said as he trotted up the stairs, his voice thick. "Everyone in the Schaumburg office had signed a letter to the editor of the *Springfield Capitol Record*, critical of the governor and supportive of me. It was all I could do to convince the writer that he would do me more harm than good."

"But you assured him you appreciated it?"

"Oh, yeah," he said, unlocking the door to a huge room and ushering me in. "I think he understands."

"Unbelievable!" I said as Earl flipped on the light. "What *is* all this stuff?"

Chapter Six

"That means the *Capitol Record* didn't let me leave in peace," Earl said, ignoring my awe of the approximately twenty-square-foot room filled with what appeared to be the latest in space-age technology.

"Huh?" I said.

"The guys here received the Springfield paper, and apparently Hanlon and I are taking heat because I've supposedly 'fled' to Chicago on 'non-business.' That's probably for the best, considering why I'm really here."

"Yeah," I said absently, still ogling all the equipment. "So what's all this stuff for?"

Earl pointed to a chair and pulled one up for himself. "Did you notice the command post downstairs?"

"Uh, no, not really," I said, hating to admit it. He was so observant and always encouraged Margo and me to be too. But I wasn't on a case—at least not that I knew of—and we were in a law enforcement facility that Earl was ultimately in charge of, so I hadn't thought to check the place out as thoroughly as his colleagues had checked me out.

"Well, a smaller version of what you see here is located downstairs. It was probably ten feet from your eyes as we passed through the receiving area. The receptionist was sitting before a console and two video screens. It's new. There used to be no computer hookup here. This office was mainly for support personnel who helped local departments with record keeping and reporting to the state.

"But now the LEADS system has been installed downstairs, and while it was being installed, we had this room equipped too."

"Surely there's more equipment up here than down there," I said, trying to cover for the fact that I had missed the console downstairs.

"Oh, yes. This is something much more complex."

"Did you say LEADS? What's LEADS?"

"Law Enforcement Automated Data System. Local departments, besides inputting the records they are required by law to report to the state, can use the system to record all kinds of administrative reports, time charts, fuel usage, man-hours, whatever. But we're also connected to the NCIC, the National Crime Information Center in Washington, D.C., where we have access to listings of missing persons, stolen cars, wanted subjects—you name it."

"So if the people here don't have access to it, what's it for?"

"For me. For us."

"Us?"

"You and me. Margo and Wally. Bubba Buchanan. It'll be our command post, and we'll have access to all the data anyone has on the whereabouts of Johnny Ray Robinson, a.k.a. Willie Banks."

"What about Larry Shipman?" I asked. "Is he part of *us*?"

"I hope so."

"You do?"

"I sure do. Margo hit it right on the head when she said he was better than anyone else I could think of, available or not."

"Can I tell her you said that?"

"If I wanted her to know that, I would have told her myself."

"You would not have, Earl. Even you have a little pride."

"More than a little! But I'll tell you this: I'll bet, knowing Margo, that she wouldn't be a bit surprised to know that I really want Ship on this case very badly. In fact, that I want him back with the agency."

"If he takes a leave of absence long enough to do justice to this case," I said, "he'll probably be looking for work. How does Wally feel about Larry?"

"I think he knows Larry's good. I kind of had to talk him into the current plan though, because he was under the impression that Larry liked the undercover angles a bit too much and that it made him careless."

"When was he careless? I remember when we were on the case where the girl kept finding clues in her apartment that someone had been there while she was out. Larry and I were checking the place out from the patio balcony when she came in the front door, and he tried to help me down onto a grassy knoll. I wound up falling on top of him, and we laughed so hard we cried."

"Not too professional," Earl acknowledged, smiling. "But it wasn't really an undercover assignment, either. Remember the time he walked in on Bonnie's daughter, Linda Gibbons, and her boyfriend, dressed as a maintenance man? That could have been one that Wally didn't appreciate."

"Maybe. But I bet they'll hit it off famously."

"You're assuming Larry will want to be in on this case, Philip. I hope you're right. Wally and Ship may hit it off, but I have this fear that having Buchanan and Festschrift on the same case will be like putting two cats in a bag."

"Margo and I will enjoy it. We'll learn a lot, even if Ship can't be in on it with us."

On the way back north on Route 53, Earl admitted there was something he had hoped to be able to talk to Margo and me about. "Something we're doing wrong?" I asked.

"Not at all. It's about my new life. You know, it's never been easy for me to talk about God, and for some reason, now that I'm a believer it's no easier. I mean, I love my church down there, and the young pastor has kind of taken me under his wing. But it seems I have as many problems now, if not more, as I had before I became a Christian."

"You mean this thing with Governor Hanlon?"

"That's only part of it. I haven't told you and Margo yet, but I was dating a woman in Springfield for about six months."

"You were? Why didn't you tell us?"

"Wanted to surprise you. I really thought I was going to marry this woman, Philip. I wanted to just drop a surprise wedding invitation bomb on you."

"But it didn't work out?"

He shook his head.

"Who was she? What was she like?"

He cocked his head. "Well, fact is, she was older.

53

Forty-five. Could have passed for ten years younger."
He chuckled to himself. "Took her a couple of
months to admit her age to me, as if it would have
mattered. I was surprised, but not bothered by it in
the least."

"You meet her at church?"

He nodded. "She sang in the choir, and I couldn't
take my eyes off her. I don't know why. She's a good-
looking lady in a prim and proper sort of way, but
not the classic beauty that turns everyone's head. But
she sure turned mine. She has medium-length black
hair that falls in curls to her shoulders, and she has
sort of a studied gaze, a look of character. I can't
describe it. All I know is that I couldn't concentrate
on sermons or anything. I just kept looking at her,
and when she looked back, we both looked away."

"Good grief, Earl, you sound like a high school kid
with his first crush."

"That's what I felt like! But of course, that's not
uncommon for me, remember?"

I nodded, remembering a seemingly warm and lov-
ing woman who turned out to be a phony and broke
his heart. "You weren't going to even think of dating
again," I said.

"And I didn't, until I saw Gail."

"Gail?"

"Gail Durning, the woman in the choir. For weeks
I fought the urge to introduce myself to her. I told the
pastor I was intrigued by her. He said, 'Who isn't?',
which I thought was a rather insightful and human
response from a pastor. He told me a little about her.
That didn't help. When I found out she was single,
which I had hoped after not seeing a ring, it was

harder and harder to keep from approaching her. I still stared at her during the services, and I quit looking away when she glanced at me. Within a couple of weeks she quit looking away too. You won't believe it, but after we got used to smiling at each other occasionally on Sunday mornings when we were both supposed to be concentrating on the service, I actually winked at her a few times. Even made faces and tried to make her lose her composure. Almost did a couple of times. I knew I had to meet her when I found her looking my way even before I looked hers once in awhile."

"How did she remain unclaimed all these years?"

"Oh, she had been married, but it was when she was just out of high school and not a Christian. Her husband had mental problems apparently, and they were divorced before she turned twenty. No children. She became a Christian a couple of years later and spent about twenty years in Europe as a missionary."

"A divorcee as a missionary? I didn't know a board would accept her as a candidate."

"She was under a board that was lenient about the divorce because it happened before she was a Christian, and because she was the innocent party and had tried to keep the marriage together until the end. Their rule was that if she remarried, they would not sponsor her any longer."

"That must have been difficult for her."

"It was. It confused and hurt her, but she accepted it and even turned down a couple of marriage proposals because she didn't want to give up her work. She had gone first as a short termer and proved valuable. Within a few years, she was one of the more respected veterans. Her former husband died during her sixth year in Europe, so she was free to remarry without threatening her status with the mission board, but she just never did."

"So how did you meet her?"

"It was just by chance. The choir members go to the basement to put their robes away after the service, so they are often the last ones out of the church on Sunday. I try to get out quickly, because you know I don't like lines and crowds and all that. Well, for some reason I got held up; I don't even remember why or by whom, but I wound up slowly filing out past the pastor as he shook everyone's hand. Suddenly he looked over my shoulder and said, 'Oh, Gail, have you met Earl?' "

"That was it? Love at first sight?"

"I could have died. I knew when I turned I'd be seeing her close up and would have to shake her hand and speak to her, and my knees were about to buckle. I felt like a fool. I was blushing by the time I turned around, and all the lines I had prepared for our first big meeting—whenever it might be—went right out the window. I'll tell you though, it was a thrill to see her blushing too. We staggered through the formalities, and I said something about my usually being gone by the time the choir left, and then she said the line neither of us will ever forget." Earl laughed at the memory of it. I waited.

"She said, 'Well, we have to disrobe after the service, you know.' I just nodded and smiled, and the pastor cracked up. She walked past us, shaking her head and looking as if she hoped a hole would appear in the ground and swallow her."

"I'm surprised she'd show her face in front of you again."

"That same night I made a point of greeting her by name as she went by, and I got the impression from the look on her face that she had gotten over her embarrassment. She stopped to chat, and I reminded her of my name. 'I know,' she said, which made me think that either she had known who I was before we were introduced or was interested enough that she listened well. I said, 'I was wondering if you were free for lunch next Sunday after church. I'll give you time to, uh, put your robe away.' "

"And that was the start of it?"

Earl nodded. "She said she'd be delighted, and I said something about how we had to quit meeting only with our eyes. She blushed again. We saw each other only on Sundays for about three weeks, then we went out Fridays and Sundays, and then on Fridays, Saturdays, and Sundays."

"It got serious, huh?"

"Very. I was in love. I thought she was."

"But she wasn't?"

"She never said so."

"That doesn't mean she wasn't."

"That was my hope. But she said it had been so long since she even felt as if she were in love, she had nothing to compare it to. She just didn't know."

"That's rough."

"Nah, not really. Not at that time, anyway. We were still seeing each other every weekend, still making eyes at each other during the morning service. I was patient. I had time. I figured I had at least until the end of Hanlon's first term."

"And now you're afraid you'll be sent packing before you can win her."

"Worse than that. Even if I stay there, I'm not sure she wants to see me anymore."

"Why not?"

"That's just it. I don't know. She wanted some time to think. It wasn't that our relationship had progressed so quickly. There was nothing inappropriate going on or anything. It was just apparent that we cared a great deal for each other. I was in love and had said so. She wasn't, or didn't think she was, or didn't know if she was, but still we were having great times together."

"And then out of the blue she wanted a cooling-off period?"

"Exactly."

Earl looked depressed. "There were no promises that your life would be easy after you received Christ, Earl. I hope no one misled you that way."

"No. No one did," he said. "It's just that of all the problems I had before, these seem worse. I've blown it and embarrassed my boss and may lose my job—which wouldn't be all bad—but now it looks like I may lose a fantastic Christian woman who could have made my life complete again."

I didn't know what to say, so I said nothing.

"And that's not the worst of it," he said. "My son is worse."

I flinched. "He's worse?"

"You know the prognosis is generally poor for autistic children who don't improve by the time they're five?"

I didn't know that, but I nodded so as not to interrupt him.

"Well, he's going to be thirteen soon. He's still never spoken. And the state would like me to put him in an institution for older autistics where he'll be of no danger to himself or anyone else. And I don't want to do it."

When we arrived back at the office, Bonnie told Earl he had a message to call Springfield.

Chapter Seven

Bonnie handed Earl the message slip, and I saw his expression cloud over. She began gathering up her things to leave and informed Earl that he could, of course, "use the phone in Wally's office. He and Margo are out shopping for the reunion. They'll be back around six looking for dinner partners."

I wished Earl had called from the outer office, because I was dying to know who had called him and what it was about. It had been unlike Earl to open up to me so much, but then he was a much different man than I had met in Atlanta several years before.

Since he had told me so much, I went through the same thought process he must have gone through before he read the message and saw whose call he was to return. Was it the governor? Was his tenure over? Was it a subordinate? Was there trouble? Was it his pastor? Could it be Gail Durning? Did she even know where he was?

I tried to busy myself at my desk while he spoke on the phone in the other room, but except for some junk mail—including a flyer informing me that I could save big dollars on brand name weapons if I bought before the summer—there was little to occupy me.

When Bonnie left, all I could do was pace the room and stare out the window. I was tempted to stroll past the closed door behind which Earl was talking—more and more loudly now—but it would be just my luck that he would slam the phone down and come out just as I happened by.

There was no way I could punch in from my phone and listen in without his knowledge, but don't think I wasn't tempted. The curiosity of the Earl Haymeyers and Wally Festschrifts had rubbed off on me.

Earl was shouting now. I couldn't remember ever having heard him shout. I still couldn't hear what he was saying though. It was ironic, I thought, that I had never seen or heard him lose his cool during the years before he was a Christian, and now he was coming apart for some reason.

Could it be something with Johnny Ray Robinson? The governor? He couldn't be losing his job. That wouldn't upset him this much, unless someone was impugning his character. Yet even he had criticized his own judgment. One thing was certain: he wasn't talking to his pastor.

He slammed the phone down and burst through the door, banging it shut behind him and tearing off his trench coat. The usually impeccable Earl Haymeyer tossed the coat in the vicinity of the coat-rack and wheeled Bonnie's chair out from its place behind the switchboard. He dropped into it and buried his face in his hands.

My mind was reeling. This was so unlike Earl. I'd seen him upset before. Down. Depressed. Angry—though not out of control. Usually he tried to hide it. I couldn't understand why he wanted to display his emotions before me. Why hadn't he stayed in Wally's office with the door shut? Maybe he didn't know either.

I decided that he must have wanted me to share his grief or anger or whatever it was that was controlling him. Maybe with no wife, no girlfriend, and a disappointed—and maybe former—boss and old friend, all he had left were his employees and associates. In a strange way, I felt honored that he felt he could share this with me, although he had said nothing yet. I knew he would, though. As out of character as this was, he had established the scenario by not leaving and driving off. He was here to stay, his coat in a heap by the rack, his trim self planted in the chair, his face still in his hands.

Something told me that when he did speak, it would be more a monologue than a conversation. He looked up, his face red and his eyes teary. "I never would have let 'em do it," he said. "How could they do it without consulting me, then tell me later?"

I didn't answer. He stared at the floor, then leaned back and gazed at the ceiling. "We noticed the symptoms when little Earl was about one and a half," he said. "Took him to the doctor. He told us little Earl—we always called him that—was one in twenty-five hundred. Real comforting. Happens mostly to boys, he said. That didn't help us much. All we knew was that he had started repeating a few baby words and imitating sounds, and then he suddenly quit. He quit talking altogether. All he would do was moan and cry. We thought it was a stage. Then he looked, um, gone or something. I don't know. A vacant expression. He would just sit for hours, not touching anything, reaching for anything, playing with anything, making any sounds at all.

"He was a beautiful boy, blond and fair-skinned, with blue eyes. Soft and sweet. After the doctor diagnosed autism, which didn't tell us much except that he was supposed to be unable to use language or process input from his environment—whatever that was supposed to mean—we kept him at home for another six months. We were sure we could get through to him. Were we ever wrong."

Earl shook his head slowly, probably remembering those days a dozen years ago when he was a Chicago cop, his wife was alive, and his son was at home. Finally he looked directly at me, as if forcing me to share the pain of the many things in his life that had changed so drastically.

"We were ignorant," he continued, nearly in tears again. "The doctor tried to tell us to institutionalize him, but we were both convinced he was better off with us. We were going to love him back to health, whatever was wrong with him.

"Naive? We actually got angry with him, because he seemed to lose interest in everything on purpose. We learned, of course, that it wasn't his fault at all, but how were we supposed to know back then? Here was this precious little guy who could walk and almost talk, who looked in your eyes and laughed and giggled and played peekaboo, and now he wouldn't look at anyone or anything.

"I would bound into his room singing and laughing and clapping, and he wouldn't even respond. At first we thought he was deaf, but apparently that wasn't the case either. It wasn't that he couldn't hear; it was that he couldn't make sense of what he was hearing. Or something."

Earl pressed his lips together tightly. "He looked as if he didn't care about anything, and as if he didn't want to care. He ignored all his favorite toys except one, and that one took on an altogether different sort of fascination for him. He found a little mechanism inside a teddy bear that made the thing play a song, and he would wind that key time and time again for hour upon hour. We had to almost force-feed him because he wouldn't complain even when it was obvious he was hungry."

Earl looked as if he was sorry he had got into it and was maybe worried that he was boring me with his personal recollections. I didn't know how to tell him that nothing right then interested me more right then. I felt for him, I was curious about his background, I cared for him, I wanted to help or at least encourage him, and especially, I wanted to know what had caused this outpouring. What was happening to Earl Haymeyer, Jr.?

"What finally made you and your wife decide to institutionalize him?" I asked, trying to assure him I was interested.

"We couldn't get through to him," he said, still showing the frustration. "We tried everything. If either of us even attempted to take away that teddy bear, even for meal time, he'd have a fit. He wouldn't look at us or try to communicate with us. That pretty little face and those vacant eyes would just erupt into wailing. All he wanted to do was sit in the middle of the floor and wind the crazy key on that teddy bear. You know, to this day, when I hear that dumb song, it gets to me. I couldn't tell you the name of it, but it's got to be one of the more common songs they put in toys, because I've heard it a dozen times over the years.

"Little Earl wouldn't even walk anymore. We'd try to stand him up, and he would crumple to the floor, staring at nothing, moaning and whining and crying until we brought him that teddy bear. Then he would sit up and either stay where he was or crawl to his room and sit in the middle of the floor, winding and winding, always letting the song play through to the end before winding it again.

"One day I tried getting rid of the thing, but when he woke up that morning he was so miserable I finally had to dig it out of the trash to pacify him. He never learned to walk. Was never toilet trained. To this day, he crawls if he has to get anywhere. He's getting big now. Apparently that's part of the problem."

I wanted to ask what problem, but I didn't. Earl continued.

"We finally realized we were getting nowhere with him. And as much as we loved him and were devoted to trying to reach him, we came to the decision that his living at home was not the best thing for him or for us. The doctor was convinced that autism was the result of a chemical imbalance, and for years he treated little Earl with heavy vitamin doses, especially B complex. But we never saw any progress.

"The only time anyone ever even claimed to get a reaction from him was when Paige—remember Paige?—said he smiled at her. But she claimed to have made progress with many of the autistics and was a proven pathological liar. So, it probably wasn't true, though I wanted to believe it, even after I learned the truth about her."

Earl appeared exhausted. But he was getting to his point. "The doctor kept telling me that if they could get little Earl to speak a little, preferably before age six or so, they might have a long-shot chance at recovery. I had to hand it to them; they had him almost walking for awhile. They tried taking advantage of his interest in mechanical things by trying a special education program, teaching him little by little every day for a couple of years. But he never really progressed.

"It's strange to see him now. Big and bony and lanky—like a lot of thirteen-year-olds—the start of peach fuzz on his chin. Yet his legs are atrophied from lack of use. He still stares into space. I've never felt that he's seen me, even when I can get him to look into my eyes. I talk to him when I see him every month, but the doctor tells me he's sure little Earl doesn't know me. I wish he'd lied to me about that. What harm would it have done for me to pretend that my son at least knows who I am, even if he can't respond?"

"It seems like there wouldn't be anything wrong with that, Earl," I said gently. "But maybe the doctor doesn't want to give you false hopes."

"False hopes are better than nothing," he said quietly. "I have to admit, it has taken me years to realize that the doctor is probably right. You see, I have built this scenario in my mind that is altogether different from the current thinking about autism. I know it's because my own son is a victim, and his mother and I were victims. But I didn't care. I convinced myself that since no one knew, no one *really* knew what was going on behind those pretty, vacant, faraway eyes, my son, and others like him, were actually just trapped in noncommunicative bodies."

"You thought he could hear and see and understand, and that he knew who you were?"

Earl nodded. "It was a form of cerebral palsy to me, Philip. I have known cases of cerebral palsy where the person can communicate laboriously, either by writing on a chalkboard or in dirt in large, awkward letters, or they can type slowly on a special keyboard. And what you discover is an incredibly gifted and well-read and well-rounded individual who is smart and sensitive and aware and who is limited merely by a body and tongue that will not cooperate. I remember asking a CP victim how he felt about the way people viewed him, assuming he knew they thought he was retarded or deaf or whatever.

"'Embarrassed,' he typed out for me. 'Embarrassed for them.' A lot of insight, wouldn't you say?"

I nodded.

"That's what I told myself about little Earl. That though he couldn't even type or communicate in any way, if he could—by blinking or waving or nodding or whatever—he would tell me he wished he could read. He would tell me he could hear and understand and that he knew words but just couldn't make them come out. He would tell me he loved me and missed me and needed me and missed his mother and where was she and what happened to her?" With that, Earl broke down and wept.

And I made a mistake. I wanted to be of help and encouragement, and I don't know what made me say it, but I said it, and I regret it. "Of course you know,"

I said, "that your theory is likely not valid." I don't know why I thought that would be of any help, but it sure wasn't, and even my tone of voice had not softened its awfulness.

A disgusted look grew on Earl's face, and he stared at me. "Yes," he said coldly. "I'm fully aware of that, Philip. When I visit my child who is growing up, yet wears diapers and only makes sounds he has heard but that don't make sense, I realize that maybe I've been living in a fantasy world. When I realize he doesn't see me or hear me or think about me or care about me, when I think about the fact that he doesn't know how much I love him and want the best for him, yes, I know that my theory is wrong."

"Earl, I'm sorry. You know I didn't mean any harm by that. Forgive me."

He lowered his head. "Now they want to take him out of the facility he's been in for more than ten years, the one place where he's at least familiar with the surroundings, if he even has that capacity. They say he's too old, too big for the attendants, too big for the other kids. And they have seen some success with other patients there. I guess that hurts the most. They have seen autistics come in before the age of five, begin speaking after awhile, wind up making real progress, and returning home—even being integrated into normal schooling. That makes me want to not give up on the possibility that he will progress, but I know it's long past the encouraging point now."

"And they want to move him?"

"They've moved him already. Without even consulting me. I knew they wanted to. We've talked about it. I argued with them. I thought they'd wait until we came to some conclusion. I guess I thought maybe with some state government pull, I could get some consideration. I don't mind losing the argument, but I mind their doing it without my knowledge. The only consolation is they're moving him to a facility in Springfield. It's for severely retarded adolescents, though, and that was what I was trying to avoid."

"At least you'll get to see him more often and more conveniently."

"Don't be too sure. If I'm out of my job, I'll be moving back up here and will be farther from him than I was before."

Then we heard Wally and Margo on the stairs.

Chapter Eight

"I know you don't think I can pull this off," Earl whispered just before Wally and Margo entered, "but please don't say anything at dinner about what we talked about, and I won't either. Do I look terrible?"

I shook my head, doubting he could hide his depression from his friends, but when they came in he turned on a neon smile and started kidding Wally about having probably already decided on a place to eat.

"Don't s'pose you know any good prime rib and steak places?" he said. "I could eat a side of beef."

"You kiddin'?" Wally bellowed, in his glory now after being dragged out to shop for picnic supplies. "There's a lot of those Cattle Company type places down by Woodfield. Wanna go that far?"

"Why not?" Earl said, clapping him on the back and leading us down to the car. "You guys have to tell me all about these reunion plans anyway."

"I thought we'd get dibs on a corner of that playground near Hubbard Woods," Margo said in the car. "We can carry everything over there on foot and come back here when it gets dark. We'll just have a cookout."

"Who all's coming?" Earl asked.

"Who isn't?" Wally muttered. "Bonnie was on the horn all afternoon. Ol' Amos'll be there, and I guess he'll bring Hilary. By the way, Earl, she's still single. Always thought she had a crush on you, ya know." Earl ignored him.

"She's in court that day," Margo said, "but the judge is Pincham—which I think is a great name for a judge—but anyway, she said you would know what that meant, Earl. So what does it mean?"

Earl laughed. "That means she'll probably not be too late for the picnic. Pincham enjoys his long weekends and likes to recess Friday sessions in the middle of the afternoon at the latest."

"Bonnie wants to bring her daughter Linda and her husband, and Erin, of course," Margo said. "If that's all right."

"Why not?" Earl said.

"Linda's husband might be a little embarrassed," Margo said.

"Why should *he* be embarrassed?" Earl said. "She was the one who ran off, right? Anyway, theirs is an all-American success story, if it lasts. So who else?"

"Allyson's going to bring her fiancé, who will have just gotten in from Pennsylvania the night before. Has anyone met him?"

We all shook our heads.

"Me either," she said. "Should be interesting. Their rehearsal is later that evening, so they and Erin will have to leave early. Pity."

I looked sharply at her and was relieved to see mischief in her smile. "And guess what?" she asked.

"Larry and Shannon can come early," I guessed.

"Oh! How'd you know? Did Bonnie tell you?"

"No! She's innocent. I just guessed. Am I right?"

"Yes. Isn't that exciting? Earl and Wally can talk to Larry whenever they want."

"So that's how many?" Earl asked. "Including all of us."

As Margo counted on her fingers, I wondered if the others detected the fatigue in Earl's voice. "Fourteen," she announced.

"Mrs. Scheel's not coming?" Earl said.

"No, and that's a story in itself," Wally said. "She told Bonnie she thought it was ridiculous to have it the night before her daughter's wedding, and if Allyson and her husband-to-be had an ounce of sense, they wouldn't attend at all."

"Is she offended that we're having it?" Earl said.

"Oh, I don't think so, but she thinks either we shouldn't have invited Allyson and her man, or they shouldn't have accepted. She wants to know what happens if he—or worse, she—gets sick on a hot dog or something! Can you imagine our throwin' a bash and cookin' hot dogs?"

"What *are* we serving, Wally?" Earl asked.

"Same thing you're eatin' tonight, chief."

"Out of whose budget?"

I had to fight to keep from studying Earl's face in the dim light of the restaurant during dinner. His shoulders sagged, and it was all he could do to force himself to stay in the conversation. A couple times I got the impression that Wally and Margo suspected something, but both times Earl must have sensed it too, because he rallied to get the spotlight on someone else.

72

When Earl showed up at the office the next morning, Wednesday, Wally quickly folded up the *Tribune,* and Wally and Margo and I tried unsuccessfully to nonchalantly work our way back to our desks. Earl stopped ten feet from us. "Oh, no," he said simply. "I made the morning paper?"

Wally nodded.

"Did you read it all?" Earl asked, resignation in his voice. Wally shook his head. "Well, then haul it out and let's have a look."

"There have already been calls for you this morning, Earl," Bonnie said as Wally spread the paper out on her desk again. "Both papers and a TV station." As she said it, the phone rang.

He waved and shook his head. "Not available," he said. "I at least have to see how the *Trib* is treating it first."

"EH Detective Agency," Bonnie said. "No, ma'am, I'm sorry, he's not available right now. . . .Whether he's here or in outer space is really none of your business, is it? Either way, he's unavailable right now. . . .No, you might as well not leave me your number. . . .I wouldn't suggest trying again this morning, anyway. . . .You're welcome."

Earl gave her a thumbs up but winced as he read the headline: *IDLE Chief On the Ropes.* The article told the story virtually the way Earl had told me the day before and promised a lengthier and more indepth story in a later edition, adding that "Earl Haymeyer has been, up to now, unavailable for comment."

"I'm going to stay that way, too," Earl said. "I've made enough trouble for Jim as it is."

"They're going to find you here," Wally said. "Where're you gonna go?"

"I don't know. Maybe Schaumburg. Nah, they'll be staking that place out. Maybe I ought to just head back to Springfield and quit once and for all. Make it easy on Jim."

If he was waiting for an argument, he was disappointed. It wasn't that quitting was necessarily what any of us really wanted him to do, but it sure didn't sound like a bad plan. By the time the Chicago media got finished with one of its local-boys-made-good-and-gone-bad, Earl would wish he had done just what he was suggesting.

"If you really go down there, can I come along?" I asked.

"Right now it sounds like a fun trip," Earl said. "A relief. You could even help me move back."

"Let's not jump to conclusions," Wally said. "Anyway, Spence here still works for me, right?"

"Of course," Earl said.

"Yes, sir," I said.

"Good," Wally said. "Until further notice, you report directly to Earl."

"Philip," Margo said, "I can't go with all I have to do here. You guys *will* be back in time for the reunion, won't you?"

"Sure," Earl said. "I'm going to need it more than ever now, especially if I'm going to be a new resident. Wonder when the welcome wagon will make the rounds."

"Earl," Margo said quietly, "this is so sad. I don't know what to think. It certainly doesn't sound like you did anything so terrible, and even if it *was* bad, it wasn't on purpose. Doesn't Governor Hanlon understand?"

"He understands, Mar," Earl said. "He just has to do the right thing politically, and there's little doubt but that it will be to dump his political liability. And you're looking at him."

"Well, if it has to be, it has to be," Margo said. "It'll be great to have you back, but I don't want to see you suffer."

"Thanks. I'll survive."

"Uh, Earl," Margo said. "What will happen to this case?"

"I've been wondering that myself," he said. "Maybe I'll get a chance to talk to Jim about it. I'm sure he would still trust me with it, but with state funds, and no contact between him and me? I just don't know."

"Excuse me, Earl," Bonnie said, "but the answering service just called. They took a couple calls for you from Springfield last night."

Earl read the two slips, stared straight at me, and shoved them in his pocket. "If we leave now, we can make Springfield by early afternoon," he said. "Wally, you and Margo sure you can let Philip go for a couple of days? I promise we'll be back by Friday."

Margo drove me home, and I packed while Earl was checking out of his hotel. "Did you know about this?" she asked. I nodded. "Why didn't you tell me?"

"He asked me not to."

"We don't keep secrets."

"I know, but I knew it would come out and that he would want to tell you. There's a lot more to the story that'll have to wait until I get back."

"Tell me now."

"It isn't something that can be told quickly."

"Oh, Philip! You have to tell me."

"I will! When I get back." A horn sounded outside. "That's him."

"Careful," she said, holding my hand as I moved out the door. "Call me."

Earl handed me the call slips after I slung my bag into the backseat and slid into the front. One was from an aide to the governor, requesting his presence in Springfield as soon as possible. The other was from Gail Durning, no message.

"Shouldn't you call her?" I said.

"I tried," he said. "That message is the brightest spot I've had in weeks. She wanted two weeks of no contact. It hasn't been that long. Wonder what she wants."

"You said you called her?"

"No answer. And she doesn't work except for lots of volunteer stuff. Who knows where she could be? Hope she doesn't just want to offer moral support or sympathy or something."

"She might. She know about all this?"

"Sure. She reads the papers. And now that it's made the Chicago media, it'll be even bigger downstate."

"What do you make of the governor's request?"

"What do you make of it, Philip? What can I say? It's over. I don't know whether to visit him first and pack later or vice versa."

"Better visit him first," I said, stating the obvious. He nodded and smiled.

A few miles south on Route 55, Earl exited and

76

tried Gail's number again. No luck. He did, however, reach the governor's office, where he was not put through to Hanlon but was able to leave a message of his estimated arrival time.

"Even told his aide you were with me," he said. "I asked him if it was all right if you came with." Earl laughed. "He said, 'You mean for the meeting with Hanlon?' I said, 'Yeah!' He said, 'I don't know. I doubt it.' I said, 'Check it out. Tell Jim it's all right with me.' "

"Is it really all right with you?"

" 'Course."

"But aren't you fairly certain you're going to get the axe, pardon the expression?"

"I'd bet my life on it."

"And you want me there?"

"You don't seem to understand, Philip. Unless I get hold of Gail and find out otherwise, you represent one of the few people in the world I have left. If I can talk my way into your joining me for this meeting, I'll do it. If I can't, I can't."

He tried Gail four more times before we arrived in Springfield but got no answer. Not even his pastor had a clue where she might be. He was, however, concerned for Earl and asked how he was holding up. "Not bad," Earl assured him. "And even better if Gail is as tired of the cooling-off period as I am."

We stopped to eat lunch but were both so nervous that we each rushed through a fastfood sandwich and kept moving. We reached the state capitol building at one o'clock, and I followed Earl straight to the aide's office.

A short, thin, Ivy-Leaguer, he told Earl that his

boss had assumed he was kidding with his request that a friend be in on the meeting. "You told him the name, Philip Spence, right?" Earl said.

"Well, no, but I got the impression that it wouldn't make any difference."

"Can you still try?"

"I really don't think—"

"I know you don't think," Earl said, exasperated. "I want you to try again."

"Well, I'm not going to do it by phone. Let's go."

He bustled off down the hall with us on his heels and held up three fingers as he passed the guard at the end of the hall leading to the governor's office. The guard counted us as we went by, the aide included. *Tough job,* I decided.

"Let me speak with him for a moment before the meeting, Loretta, may I?" the aide asked the secretary in the huge reception area.

"Sir," she said over the intercom. The response was nonverbal, just a tone.

"Mr. Wissy would like to see you a moment." I almost cracked up at the name and realized why she hadn't tried the "Wissy wishes to see you" tongue twister.

"Haymeyer here?" came the governor's voice.

"Yes, sir," Loretta said.

"Send him in."

"Which, sir?"

"Haymeyer."

Wissy appeared at a loss for words.

"May Mr. Wissy join you briefly?" she asked.

The response was the tone again, which was apparently affirmative. They both went in, and with the door open, I heard the formalities, then Ivy League explaining that Earl still preferred that I join them.

"You're kidding, right, Earl?" Jim Hanlon said. Earl said something I missed, then the governor said something to Wissy. He exited quickly and told me, "The governor *and your boss* request that you wait out here."

I'll bet, I thought. I sat down, smiled awkwardly at Loretta as if to tell her I wasn't disappointed and that it hadn't been my idea in the first place, and waited. Wissy hurried back down the hall.

Less than a minute after the door had shut behind Wissy, the governor's voice came over the intercom. "Wissy still out there?"

"No, sir. Shall I ring him?"

"No, just bring me a Coke, will you?"

Loretta looked terribly puzzled. "A Coke, sir?"

"It's a soft drink, Loretta. Maybe you've heard of it."

"Yes, sir." She glared at me as she opened a drawer and pulled out some change. She locked her desk, punched several buttons on her phone, and trotted off down the hall. A few seconds later the door to the governor's office opened, and Jim Hanlon's six-foot four-inches filled the frame. I stood.

"How ya doin', Spence?" he said. "Haven't seen you since the Salerno murder case that put us both on the map."

I was speechless.

"Get in here," he said. "You think I sent my secretary for a Coke for the first time ever just for her health?"

Chapter Nine

Earl was sitting in a formally relaxed pose, with his legs crossed, his hands folded, and his suit jacket unbuttoned. It was as if he had been invited to join the governor for tea. He didn't look the least bit nervous.

Governor Hanlon, with his shirt-sleeves rolled up and his suit jacket folded carelessly on a credenza near one wall, had one shirttail threatening to break free from his trousers. His hair was a couple days overdue for a trim, and the shock in front hung down over his forehead—the way he was never photographed.

He was a big, lunky sort of guy in private but was able to pull a string that tied the whole package together just before he stepped into public view. Then he was a giant, strapping, pin-neat, youthful-looking politician in the John F. Kennedy mold, though he was a Republican.

"Sorry about that charade," Hanlon said, dragging a heavy, wing-backed chair close to his desk so I could sit next to Earl. The governor flopped into his big chair and let it tilt way back. "It's just that I couldn't let my secretary or my aide think I'd let Earl call the shots right up to the end, could I? By the time they get back, they'll think I invited you in when I was good and ready. And I did, didn't I?"

I nodded, still reeling at the thought of the governor of Illinois casually ordering me into his office. I remembered Jim Hanlon as the tough, serious-minded U.S. Attorney for the Northern Illinois district, but that seemed ages ago now.

Hanlon looked at both of us and shook his head. "So it's come to this," he said, swearing. "Oops, sorry Earl. I know you've got religion now. And Spence, you've always had it." Neither of us were in the mood to argue. The governor was in his down-home-buddy mode, relaxing his tone and grammar. No one ever heard him like this on the evening news.

He shook his head again. "Who would've ever thought my old and most trusted buddy would be the cause of my biggest political crisis?" Earl forced an apologetic smile to little effect. "Shoot!" the governor added.

Earl and I looked at each other and back at Hanlon when no one spoke for a moment. "So what do you propose?" the big man said.

Earl shrugged. "At this point, I think it's long since over. I'm ready to make it easy for you. As you know, my resignation is already written. All I have to do is haul it out and have the secretary type in the date."

Disconcertingly, Hanlon just stared bemusedly at his old friend. Then he turned to me. "What do you think, Spence? Should I let him off the hook so easily?"

I cleared my throat. "I don't think resigning under pressure is anything like being let off the hook, sir. I

81

think he's already suffered and that maybe if you're accepting his resignation, you should do it with reluctance publicly, even if you're glad to have it now."

Hanlon raised his eyebrows and cocked his head, smiling at Earl. "Well, I asked, didn't I? The kid speaks his mind. I like that. Liked it in you once, until you started speaking your mind to the wrong people."

Earl nodded as if surrendering in humiliation, and I felt for him. It was as if Hanlon was trying to rub it in. Earl had already acknowledged that he'd blown it twice. He had offered to resign. What was the purpose of dragging it all out again in this final meeting that could have been short and sweet and relatively painless?

"I've got a lot of less talented and more volatile people working for me all over Springfield, not to mention Chicago, Earl. You would have been way low on the list of those I would have figured might stir up trouble for me."

Earl had quit nodding. And smiling. Hanlon looked back at me. "No, sir. Best crime detection and prevention and law enforcement theorist I ever met. Good in the classroom and in management and on the street. You don't get that in any other single package anywhere. Only in Earl Haymeyer. Perfect candidate for a big national job if he stayed close to the right people."

A slight scowl played at Earl's mouth. I didn't know where Hanlon was going either. Was he going to keep digging and cutting, or had he shifted to compliments now to make the whole thing more palatable? And for whom? Himself? It obviously wasn't making anything easier for Earl.

Hanlon looked at Earl again and shook his head. "We were a good team for a lot of years, boy." Earl stiffened and didn't respond. "Never would have thought it would come to this."

Earl leaned forward, palms on his knees, and looked deep into the governor's eyes. "All right," he said, quietly but sharply. "For the third time, I blew it. We had some good times. There was no bureaucrat I respected more than you, because you cut through the red tape and did what had to be done. You were justice-minded and went by the book. I could have enjoyed a few more years with you, but I cooked that, so let's get this over with, OK? You're rubbing my nose in it in front of one of my men."

Just as I had feared, Hanlon had pushed Earl too far. But for some strange reason, it jumped out at me that Earl had never before referred to me as a man, let alone as one of his men. In the middle of a tense situation where the most powerful man in the state and possibly the future president of the United States had driven my boss to insubordination, I sat a little straighter and felt a little taller, proud to be considered one of Earl Haymeyer's men—especially by Earl himself.

The governor was still amused. "Having Spence join us was your idea, Earl. And not one of your better ones. But that kind of judgment is consistent with your performance lately. That's why we're here, isn't it?"

Earl sat back with a disgusted look, as if he was finished fighting. His best foray had failed, so he was giving up. "What do you want from me, Jim?"

"So, now it's Jim. You haven't called me Jim since

before you told the press what you thought of my decisions."

Earl rolled his eyes and crossed his arms across his chest. "Which I have already apologized for, probably more times than I should have."

"At least one more time than you should have," Hanlon said. "And to the wrong people."

Earl shrugged and spread his hands, as if to ask what he was supposed to say. What could he do if his old friend wouldn't even accept his apology? Earl looked at me, probably embarrassed by Hanlon and wondering if my impression of the governor was suffering. Of course it was—and I couldn't hide it.

"OK," Earl snapped. "Is this what you wanted, for me to lose my cool? I've lost it. You do what you want. You've got my resignation. You can accept it or you can fire me. There's no other option. Whatever makes you happy or furthers your political ambitions, you just do it." He stood to leave. My heart was pounding. "Coming?" he said.

I didn't know what to do. He had a reason to walk out on the governor. I felt as if I needed Hanlon's permission. I looked at him, my eyes wide.

"You leave too, Spence?"

"If I may, yes, sir."

"Oh, please stay. You want to know how this turns out, don't you? What I decide to do with old Earl?"

"I think Earl's already decided that," I said, rising. "I don't care to see it get any nastier."

"Then you won't get a chance to see us dance a jig together," Earl said, dead serious.

I blinked and shook my head. It was a nice shot, but I wasn't quite sure what he meant. I found out soon enough. He raised one eyebrow—something I've been trying to imitate since I first saw him do it years ago—then slipped past me and went around to the other side of the governor's desk. I wondered if they were going to come to blows.

Hanlon stood and held out his left arm, bent at the elbow. Earl hooked it with his own, and they swung around like square dancers, both singing a monotone Scottish ditty and laughing their heads off. Either this was a crazy dream, or I had gone over the edge. The intercom buzzed and Hanlon instantly grew serious. He pushed Earl toward his chair and motioned that I should sit back down too. The governor pointed into my face. "Get serious, look sad, quick, and I'll explain in a minute."

He reached for the intercom. "Yes, Loretta!"

"Your Coke, sir!"

"Bring it in."

Loretta scowled at me and peered at the three of us as she delivered the can and hurried out. It was all Hanlon and Earl could do to keep from laughing, but I was still in shock.

"So," the governor finally said, "what did you think I was up to, Spence?"

"Honestly?"

He nodded.

"At first I thought you were trying to rub Earl's nose in it, but that didn't seem like you. Then I thought maybe you were trying to get his dander up to see if he still had some spunk left and would be valuable if you decided to thumb your nose at the press and keep him on."

"And now?"

"Now I think I'll wake up and realize this has been a real corker."

Earl and Hanlon laughed again. "It's been a set up, Philip," Earl said. "From the beginning."

"From the beginning of what?"

"From my first indiscretion to the press."

"The whole thing?"

"Almost."

"There was no disagreement over the head of the local assistance?"

"Oh, yes," Hanlon said. "That was very real. Earl wanted to hire the guy back in some capacity. I didn't want to risk the chips. Earl told me frankly what he thought about it, just like he always does—which is what makes him the best ally I could have in this chair. He was mad and he said so. I told him I understood, but that was my decision. It was not unlike the heated arguments we always have at least once a week."

"I'm listening," I said.

"But we needed a reason to get Earl up to Chicago to work with you people on this Robinson case. The disappearance of Johnny Ray Robinson and the deaths of the other two men just fried my cookies. If we let them get away with it, it'll be like coddling terrorists, and I won't have it."

"So you staged an argument that would get Earl fired and free him up?"

"Not exactly," Earl said. "We did hit upon our last argument as the best vehicle for this, but it wasn't going to come down to a firing. That wouldn't help. That would leave me with no access to the technical equipment I need to do the job right."

"So you're not getting fired, and your resignation will not be accepted?"

"No. In fact, it's better and more creative than that."

"Yes," Governor Hanlon said. "And best of all, it will remove any suspicion that Earl is involved in an investigation of any magnitude, particularly the one he will be spearheading."

"What then?"

"You'll see."

"Feel a little used, Philip? " Earl said. I nodded. "Sorry," he added. "I really am. But I figured if I could convince you, I could convince anyone."

"Then none of it was true? The stuff about Gail Durning and your son?"

"Oh, yes!" Earl said, suddenly serious. "I couldn't have misled you about that." He turned to Hanlon. "That's something I need to talk to you about, Jim. They've moved little Earl, and I'm not at all happy about it."

Hanlon's eyes narrowed. "You just put in a memo whatever directive you want from me, and I'll sign it, Earl. You know that. Your son will be back where you want him within a week. You need anything else, just name it."

"Can you make Gail come back to me?"

"That I can't do. But from what you've told me about her, you'd better keep working on it." The governor smiled at Earl and chuckled at me as I sat there, no doubt pale, trying to make sense of it all. He pushed the intercom button again. "Get Wissy in here, will you Loretta? And have him bring the press secretary."

Within minutes, Wissy and a clone timidly entered and waited for Hanlon to assign them seats. "I want you boys to work on a message to the media," he said. "It's got to be something like this: 'Governor James Hanlon announced today the reassigning of Earl Haymeyer, Chief of the Illinois Department of Law Enforcement, to the position of Director of Support Services, a division of IDLE.

"'The current Support Services director, John Charles Close, will replace Haymeyer as head of IDLE and will carry the title Acting Chief until he is confirmed by the state legislature. Mr. Haymeyer will be headquartered at the Support field office in Schaumburg and will begin his new duties next Monday.

"'Haymeyer will supervise the work of six records experts and clerical workers and will continue to serve in a strategic role in this important aspect of the state's law enforcement community, blah blah blah,' you know, and dress it up."

"Did you want anything about his achievements during his abbreviated term as head of IDLE?" Wissy asked. "And something more on Close's background?"

"Yeah, sure, whatever," Hanlon said. "Give 'em the party line. They're all going to see through it anyway."

Wissy and the press secretary nodded gravely and sneaked a peek as Earl, who sat there as he had when I was feeling sorry for him, seemingly resigned to his fate and appreciative of the bone tossed his way by the benevolent governor he had irked.

By the afternoon rush hour, the late edition of the

Tribune and the *Sun-Times* would report the "stinging, punitive reassignment" and praise Earl for accepting it like a man. Both papers would also buy the entire package and comment on the menial administrative post he had been relegated to.

I was still shaking my head in disbelief at what I had witnessed in the governor's office, but Earl was busy. He cleaned out his office, spending the last half hour after his secretary left laboriously typing a memo to Hanlon on official stationery regarding his son.

Then he called Wally Festschrift to see if he had heard the news. "You did?" he said. "Nah. It's not all bad. Yeah, I'm going to take it for now. We'll talk about it when I get up there Friday."

He called John Close in Schaumburg to congratulate him. "Aren't you glad you didn't send that letter, John?" Earl asked. "You almost did? Ouch! A message for me? Oh, she was, there? In *person?* When was this, John? This morning? She didn't leave a number where I could reach her or say where she was staying? Thanks anyway, John, and congratulations again, man. I'm happy for you. Nah, I'm all right, John. It's OK, really."

Earl slammed the phone down and whirled to face me. "Gail was up there," he said, almost whining. "Who knows where she is now? Or what she wants?"

"Would she have looked for you at our office?"

"Might have, but Wally would have said something, wouldn't he?"

"Maybe he didn't know. He could have been out or something."

Earl dialed our office. "Wally! Me again. Any

messages for me? Yeah, yeah. I'll call him back. Bonnie said that? No name? What'd she look like? Where were you? Black hair? What'd Bonnie tell her?" Earl sighed.

"Gail had been there too," he said as he hung up. "Bonnie told Wally that a woman with black hair and perfect skin came asking for me. Said she was an old friend, but she didn't leave a name or number. Wally says Bonnie told her I was in Springfield for a few days. This isn't my day, Philip."

"Will she stay there and wait for you, or will she come straight back?"

"Who knows? I don't even know what she wants. She probably came to console me about the horrible things the press has been saying about me down there. Then she gets to Chicago and finds out I've been busted down a couple of ranks."

"What do we do now? Wait to see if she comes back?"

"No." He slowly ambled out and locked the door, pulling the key off his keyring and sliding it back under the door. "Let's get something to eat and then head for my place."

Chapter Ten

By late Thursday morning, busy-bee Earl had accomplished more than a younger man would attempt in a weekend. He had driven out at the crack of dawn to rent a trailer, and by the time I was up for breakfast, he had it hitched to the car, ready to load.

He had called Jim Hanlon and asked when he could pick up the signed directive, which told whoever needed to be told to do whatever it was Earl, Sr., wanted done with Earl, Jr. "We'll pick it up on our way out of town," Earl informed me. "Which should be no later than eleven if all goes well. Jim also reminded me that all my moving expenses would be covered by the state, but that he appreciated my doing it myself since he hated paying a moving company to move one apartment's worth of junk. I reminded him that this has been in the works for some time, so I've been rounding up boxes for days."

Earl had also determined that no one in Glencoe or Schaumburg or Springfield had heard from Gail since the day before, so his strategy was "to head back up and be there when she comes looking for me again."

"And what if she's on her way back down here?"

"Then I miss her. I can't stand sitting here not

knowing what to do. I have to do something. I don't know her well enough yet to know what she'll do. I'll take my chances."

I had trouble keeping up with Earl in wolfing down his homemade breakfast. "Gotta make a stop and see little Earl," he said, somehow rejuvenated since the night before when he had turned in early. "Wait till they see my letter from the governor."

"You gonna lay it on 'em right away?"

"Are you kidding? I'll give them a piece of my mind first and see how they react. I'll pull out the big guns when I need them. Lemon Juice Haines is there, did I tell you?"

"Who?"

"L. J. Haines, the guy who runs the home little Earl's been in for years. I always call him Lemon Juice—not to his face, of course—because he always looks like he just involuntarily swallowed some. I checked this morning to find out if I could see Earl, Jr., and to find out who was in charge. I was going to stop in and see Lemon Juice up north at the other facility, but they said he was going to be down here today. I'm glad."

"You think he'll see you?"

"Unless he runs when he finds out I want to see him. If he's there, I'll see him. Count on it." I *was* counting on it.

And I wasn't disappointed. Earl worked like a man being paid by the piece. It seemed he was passing me going in and coming out of his place all morning, loaded down with boxes and pieces of furniture. While I was scoping out the best way to turn a couch or bed to get it through a doorway, he was building boxes, taping them, filling them, and taping them some more.

We were done before eleven, just as he had predicted.

I confess I felt a little self-conscious sitting in front of the state capitol in a car pulling a big move-it-yourself trailer, but Earl didn't make me wait long. He trotted down the steps with his fist in the air, carrying a business-size envelope. It fluttered into my lap as he slid behind the wheel and pulled away.

The document, under a State of Illinois letterhead, read:

To: Lawrence Jay Haines
Re: Directive from Governor James A. Hanlon

Earl Haymeyer, Jr., is to be returned to the facility at which he has been cared for for more than ten years as soon as is humanly possible, no later than four working days from the date of this document. As soon as transportation can be arranged, I expect confirmation that this has been carried out. Any appeal of this decision or discussion related to it shall be deferred until after the transfer has been effected, and shall not be considered without the prior written notification of Earl Haymeyer, Sr.

Signed,

James A. Hanlon
Governor, State of Illinois

It was witnessed by Loretta M. Stephenson, notary public.

Earl drove to a facility on the outskirts of Springfield, near the interstate highway, and carefully backed the car and trailer into a tight spot between the last parking place and a high wire fence.

He was an imposing figure in the pullover shirt he had been working in all morning. And although he left his gun in the locked glove compartment of the car—and had me do the same with mine—he carried all the ammunition he needed in an envelope in the pocket of his trousers.

We had no trouble getting to see the administrator of the Springfield facility, but she told Earl that Mr. Haines regretted to inform him that he would be unavailable.

"But he *is* here?"

"Oh, yes, but he will not be able to see anyone today."

"He's in the auxiliary office at the end of the B wing?"

"Well, yes, but I—"

"You're wondering how I know that."

"Uh, yes."

"I checked this place out before, when I was first informed that they'd like to move little Earl here."

"I see. He's going to be fine here, you know."

"That may be, but he won't be here long."

"That's not my decision."

"I understand that, ma'am. I just want to see the man who thinks it's his."

"As I told you—"

"Yeah, all right. Can I see little Earl?"

"Certainly. Would you like me to join you?"

"That won't be necessary. If you could just point us

in the right direction—I won't stay with him longer than twenty minutes, and we'll find our way out."

The administrator led us to a long corridor and pointed. "Second from the end on the left," she said. "Private room." She smiled slightly, as if she thought that might make Earl happier. He had to admit that little Earl had never slept in a private room before.

"He's in there now?" Earl said.

"Why, yes."

"For lunch, you mean?"

"His lunch was served at 11:30 this morning, sir."

"Then what's he doing now?"

"Doing? He's, uh, doing what he always does, which is, you'll pardon my saying so, very little. Which is why he's here."

"Are you telling me he's in bed at this time of the day?"

"Where would you like him to be?"

"In some kind of activity where he's being stimulated—where there's something to play with, someone trying to reach him, to communicate with him."

"Mr. Haymeyer, this facility is not like the one your son has come from. We do not have the same size staff, yet we have more patients, and more are severely retarded. There is less activity, and there are fewer recreational facilities. This is almost totally custodial care. Your son is fed, bathed, and taken outside twice a day."

"That's it? No one talks to him?"

"Some of the volunteers talk to most of the patients until they've been here awhile."

"Until *who's* been here awhile? The patients or the volunteers?"

"The volunteers. They soon learn that the patients do not hear or understand and will not respond. I've been here more than fourteen years and have never seen a mistaken diagnosis. No patient ever admitted here was more responsive than his charts showed. Patients have been through years of tests and therapy before they come here."

"Before they're sentenced here, you mean."

"I won't argue that, Mr. Haymeyer. This is the end of the line for severely retarded children and adults, and for adolescent autistics who have shown no progress."

"So what do they get here?"

"I already outlined that."

"It sounds like solitary confinement."

"They don't know the difference, Mr. Haymeyer. It isn't as if they are sensitive to isolation."

Earl muttered under his breath, and it sounded like a vulgarity. "Excuse me," he said. "I know none of this is your fault."

Without another word, she walked away.

"I shouldn't hassle the underlings," Earl said as we moved down the hall.

"She's no underling," I said.

"Yeah, but she's not a decision maker. She might be able to run a different kind of place, but why duplicate efforts? The kind of place I think this should be is the one Lemon Juice runs up north."

All the way down the hall we could hear the moanings and wailings and screechings of children mostly between the ages of about nine and seventeen. I caught a glimpse of a few of them as we passsed the open doors of mainly shared rooms with three or four

96

beds in each. Only a couple of the rooms had just two beds, and very few had only one.

Several of the patients wore helmets for self-protection, and some sat hitting themselves on the head or banging their heads against the wall or the sides of their beds.

I was stunned, but apparently this was nothing new to Earl. "I helped take a group to a ball game once," he said. "It took us an inning or two to get in and get settled, another inning or two to get everybody to the bathroom and back, another inning or two to get everybody fed, and another inning or two to get them back out to the bus, with moving wheelchairs up and down steps and ramps and everything. And because we wanted to beat the crowd, we left in the eighth inning."

"Then you didn't see much of the ball game."

"None of it. But the kids loved being out and around and with a crowd of people. They knew something fun and different was happening."

Earl pushed open the wide, heavy door with "Haymeyer, Jr., E." printed on the card. The tiny room could not have accommodated another bed. Earl, Jr.'s bed was slightly raised at the pillow end, with rails raised high on both sides. There lay the long, lanky figure. Little Earl wasn't so little anymore, but the tiny legs tucked beneath the covers evidenced the atrophy caused by years without use.

His face was turned away from the sunlight streaming through the window. He rocked and hummed a guttural tone, staring at the cabinet next to the bed and crying, tears matting his hair and soaking the pillow.

Earl rushed to him and knelt by the bed, his hand resting gently on the boy's neck. "What's the matter, boy?" he said softly. "Can't figure this place out? I can't either." He stared into his son's eyes, but they seemed to look right through him. There was no break in the weeping and humming and rocking.

Earl turned to me. "He doesn't like changes in his environment," he said. "Never has. He even fights it when he's moved from a playroom to the cafeteria or to his bed. Moving all the way down here has him puzzled and angry and sad. They can't tell me he doesn't know what's going on."

He turned back to his son. "Don't worry, little Earl. We'll get you back where you belong. Here." He handed the boy his keyring, but little Earl didn't reach for it. Earl shook it before his eyes, then pulled the boy's hand up and closed his fingers around it.

Little Earl shook it and dropped it. His humming had stopped for an instant, but he cried out when the keys fell. Earl picked them up and dangled them in front of his face again, shaking them. Little Earl stopped rocking and stared. He wouldn't reach for the keys, but clearly he was captivated by their sound and shine.

"This is all I want," Earl said. "I want someone to find a way to reach him, to keep trying and not give up, to give him some pleasure." He looked around the room for something to attach the keys to. He tried fastening them to the bed rail, but it was too thick. Then he tried tying them to a string hanging from the bed sheet, but it was too thin.

He finally attached them to little Earl's wristband, then took the boy's forearm and shook it in front of his face. He stopped humming, crying, and rocking. He held his arm in front of his face as the keys swayed slowly before him, suspended at the wrist.

He shook his arm, shook it again, and then again, now harder. It was almost as if he were about to smile, but he didn't. He just shook his arm back and forth until he was tired, then he let his arm drop, and in a minute he started again.

Earl backed away from him. "Where's the B wing?" he said.

I pointed. "We passed it on the way here, as if you didn't know."

He smiled.

We looked both ways as we neared the intersection of the hallways and nonchalantly turned toward the auxiliary office. There was an empty desk in the outer office. "Must not have been expecting him today," Earl said. "They didn't assign a receptionist or secretary to him."

"So we wait here?"

"No. Too easy for him to spot us from down the hall. Come on."

Earl looked over my shoulder and then led me into the auxiliary office. "Earl!" I scolded, but followed orders.

"Sit down, Philip," he said, pointing to a side chair as if he owned the place. I sat. And so did he—in the chair behind the desk. He leaned back and put his hands behind his head. "Won't I be a nice surprise for someone?" he said.

We waited and chatted quietly for more than an hour until we heard footsteps in the hall. Earl held a finger to his lips and let the chair tilt forward until he was out of sight from the door. A man of about sixty, of medium height with a protruding stomach and low-riding pants, opened the door with one hand and clutched a portfolio bulging with papers in the other. His half glasses were perched precariously at the end of a long, generous nose.

He stopped dead and swore when he saw Earl in his chair, but he didn't turn to leave. "Do you mind?" he said.

"Oh, please, sit here," Earl said, rising quickly and moving next to me.

"I have a busy day," Mr. Haines said, letting his stack of papers plop on the desk. "I'd like to get back to my own facility before dark. I won't make it if I have to talk to you."

"Then you won't make it," Earl said.

Chapter Eleven

When Lawrence Jay Haines sat straight up in his chair, his white shirt showed at the belt line beneath his vest. He glared at Earl and wearily removed his half glasses, which he tossed atop his stack of papers. Clearly, he was not a happy man.

"Mr. Haymeyer," he began slowly, "I have never tried to claim that I can identify with every parent whose child has been placed under my care. I can't. I do not have a child who is a patient at a state facility, unless you call my daughter at Illinois State University an inmate. Her bills make *me* the prisoner."

He paused to see if that would elicit even a hint of a smile from Earl. It didn't.

"So, I won't try to tell you I know how you feel. I'll only tell you that you should trust us, the professionals. We don't do anything intentionally detrimental to the patients; we try to keep their safety and well-being uppermost in our minds."

"You run the facility my son was in, and you're sitting here today in the one he's in now," Earl said, "and you can tell me you have his best interest at heart?"

"I have the whole picture to be concerned with,"

Haines said. "I have to think of resources, equipment, budget, personnel, safety—"

"What is this safety business?" Earl asked. "It's come up before and nobody will explain it to me. Are you saying little Earl is a safety problem?"

"He could be."

"Now don't *you* start with the vague answers. Either he is or he isn't."

"He could be soon. He's not getting any smaller, you know."

"His legs are atrophied, L.J.! No one is working with him in physical therapy, no one tries to make him walk, no one massages him, no one does anything!"

Haines scowled and sighed, shaking his head slowly at Earl. "There comes a time in the history of every patient when the doctors and the therapists and the administrators must make difficult decisions."

"Apparently you've made one."

"You know we have. We've decided that Earl, Jr., is too big and too hard to handle in a facility that was designed for much younger children. His contemporaries have all been transferred; in fact, he was the oldest child by more than four years before we moved him here."

"That's what I really want to talk to you about, sir. We had discussed this many times, and I never gave permission for him to be moved."

Haines pursed his lips and said, just above a whisper, "Mr. Haymeyer, you know we don't need your permission. We held him in the previous facility much longer than we should have out of deference to you and your, um, position."

It was as if a light came on in Earl's mind. "And so what made you go ahead and ignore my wishes now?"

Haines stalled. "It, uh, became apparent that we simply couldn't wait any longer."

"But why? The boy can't walk! He can hardly sit up! All he does is sit and play with whatever object catches his attention. How could he be of any danger to anyone?"

"Frankly, he concerned some of the other visiting parents."

"He concerned them? How?"

"They would see him sitting in the middle of the floor, so much bigger than everyone else. And because he's maturing, he looks much older and less childish than the others. And they worry about him."

Earl slouched in his chair. When he spoke he was more subdued than before. "Why are we giving up on him?" he asked, almost pitifully.

"No one's giving—"

Earl interrupted, leaning forward to the edge of his chair. "Don't tell me you haven't given up on him, L.J.! He's here to rot! He's fed and bathed and clothed and taken outside like a pet. What's his future?"

Haines closed his eyes and leaned back in the chair, his face pointed to the ceiling. "His future," he said, "is the same as any other autistic who reaches adolescence without having shown any progress."

Earl said nothing, but he looked full into Haines's face, as if he was expecting him to continue.

"Are you aware," Haines said, "that it's very possible, in fact predictable, that your son will regress, beginning very soon?"

103

"In this asylum he certainly will."

Haines leaned forward and rested his elbows on the desk before him in a pose that reminded me of how Earl had addressed us in Wally's office Tuesday morning. "We've talked around this subject for so long, Earl," he said, and I wondered if he had ever referred to Earl by his first name before. "I guess it's time to put it on the table.

"Little Earl has been given more specialized treatment than any other patient I can think of in my years in the state system. He's unaware of his environment except as it catches his attention, and he is upset when it changes. This move did not make him happy, but within another day or two, he would cry if we moved him from where he is now.

"He will not improve. His awareness, his response, his potential—" Haines stopped and shrugged. "It's going or it's gone, Earl. What can I say? What can I tell you? The problem is, I think I know you better than you do."

Earl was taken aback. "You know *me* better than I do?"

Haines nodded confidently, but not without compassion. "You know it's true," he said. "You've known since the first time we discussed little Earl. I've been telling you the same things for years, and you've been on my case for just as long, pushing and prodding and hoping and praying and threatening and accusing. It hasn't been fun, Earl. But you've known all along. You've known down deep that I'm right, and the doctors are right, and the therapists are right.

"You could have taken your son out of our care

104

long ago, but you didn't. You could have pulled rank on me when you became an employee of the state and reported directly to the governor, but you didn't. That's not the kind of guy you are, Earl. You're just a dad, a dad who can't stand to lose his only son. And you lost him years ago when the first symptoms appeared.

"You know we're doing the right thing, Earl. I can't guarantee you that the people here will be as nice and pleasant and patient with little Earl as they were up north. Up there they are trained to talk to the children as if they can hear or understand, but when there is no evidence or response after ten years, they could just as easily quit talking to the patients. There are some here who can hear and understand a little, and they are talked to sympathetically and encouragingly. But not adolescent autistics, Earl.

"I know you don't want to hear this, but it doesn't make any difference to little Earl whether anyone talks to him or not. Like I say, there are some who will. The irony is, *I* can never quit talking to them. *I* talk to all the patients, regardless of age or condition, and *I* know better."

Earl raised his head as if to get a better look at Haines. "People make fun of me behind my back," Haines continued with a wry smile. "I know their nicknames for me. Mostly they think I'm an old softie who doesn't know when to give up on a kid, and that even if I have been realistic and reassigned someone to a custodial rather than a therapeutic facility, I still talk to the ones I know.

"Did you see your son today, Earl?" Earl nodded. "And did you talk to him?" Earl nodded again. "And did he respond?" Earl shook his head again. "Did he know you were there?" Earl shook his head. "Has he ever known you were there?" Earl looked down.

"I left my keys with him to play with," Earl said with difficulty.

"Did he look at you?" Haines said. "Say anything? Focus on the keys? Grasp them?" Earl continued shaking his head, his face contorted to keep from crying.

"I attached them to his wristband," he managed.

"And so now he shakes them in front of his face until his arm is tired, and it keeps him from humming and rocking and crying. Did it stop his crying, Earl?" Earl nodded. "That's good. I was hoping he'd get acclimated soon. I don't like to hear them cry for too long either."

Earl couldn't look at Haines. I got the feeling he had a whole new outlook on the man, as I did. All I had ever heard about Lemon Juice Haines was that he was a coldhearted administrator who cared only about dollars and employees and buildings and programs.

"Earl," he said, "I know you could pick up the phone and have your friend in the capitol order me to do whatever you want. I was sorry to hear of your reassignment, but my guess is your friendship runs deeper than that, and so Big Jim would love to make that up to you in some way, like this."

"You mean he might throw me a bone by overruling you on this decision?"

"Sure."

"You think Hanlon would do that?"

"It wouldn't be such a despicable thing to do after hearing only your side of it. You want to try?"

"You think I should?"

"Of course not."

"Because you're worried about your authority?"

"You know better than that, Earl. You may not want to admit it yet, but you know better. You know I'm thinking of little Earl first. He's where he belongs. The more comfortable he becomes, the happier he'll be. I'm a slow one to give up too, Earl, but Earl Haymeyer, Jr., is not going to be improving, and I want you to get realistic about it too. Let us take care of him the best way we know how. I'm not going to tell you we won't make any mistakes or that there won't be some insensitive staff people around. But I want you to let us leave him here. Come and see him whenever you want and ask about his progress. But don't take it out on us when there isn't any. We gave him the best chance an autistic child could have, every physical and mental stimulation we had at our disposal. That mind is locked up, Earl. Take comfort in the fact that except for confusion and anger over a change of scenery, little Earl doesn't really experience emotions to any extreme on either side of the spectrum."

Earl didn't answer, but the anger was gone from his face. He looked whipped, exhausted. "Guess we'd better get going," he said finally.

"You're going to let us keep him here?" Haines said.

Earl nodded.

Haines smiled kindly. "I don't need to worry about an irate call from the governor?"

" 'Course not."

"I didn't think so."

"I haven't totally given up on little Earl," Earl said.

"I'd be disappointed in you as a father if you had," Haines said. "Don't tell anybody, but I never *really* give up on any of them. That's totally unprofessional and leads to a lot of personal disappointment. But even though I'm realistic and have never seen any of the medical or psychological miracles I read and hear about, I'd have to get out of the profession if I ever got to the place where I didn't still hope to see one."

Earl glanced at me and stood. "Gotta get my keys," he said.

"May I come with you?" Haines said. And without even looking at the names on the doors, he led the way.

As we followed him into little Earl's room, L. J. raised an arm to silence us, and we slowed as we approached the bed. Little Earl was sleeping on his back, his forearms across his chest. When Haines tried to remove Earl's keyring from the boy's wristband, little Earl stirred and almost turned over, making the keys jangle and putting them out of Haines's reach.

He turned and smiled an apology, and Earl moved in front of him to try to remove them himself. He got the keys from little Earl but awakened him in the process. The boy seemed not to realize there was anyone in the room. I stepped back and leaned against the wall by the door.

Impulsively, Earl leaned over the high railings and drew the boy into his arms, embracing him and tucking his face in the boy's neck. The boy stiffened and hummed and began rocking, but obviously not in response to Earl. He was uncomfortable, his keys had been taken, he didn't recognize the room, and he felt restrained. Finally he broke free. Earl said something quietly to him and looked in his eyes, but there was no recognition coming the other way.

Earl pocketed his keys and hurried out and down the hall. I waved apologetically to Mr. Haines and left to follow Earl. Halfway down the hall, I felt I should say something to Haines, so I turned back and tiptoed into the room.

He was leaning over the railing in much the same manner Earl had, but he was not embracing little Earl. He merely had his hand on the boy's cheek and patted it lightly, murmuring something. He smoothed little Earl's hair back off his forehead, cocked his head to look in the boy's face, and patted his cheek once more. As he began to turn to leave, I slipped out and hurried to catch up with Earl at the main entrance.

As we walked to the car, Earl handed me the keys. In the car he tore the envelope and letter from the governor in half, rolled it into a tight ball, and deposited it in the litter bag. "Would you mind calling Hanlon's office and telling them to do the same with theirs?" he said, hardly able to speak.

I pulled the car and trailer out of the lot and toward the expressway. At a gas station just before the feeder ramp, I stopped and trotted to the pay phone. "Governor Hanlon's office, this is Mrs. Stephenson, may I help you?"

I asked her if she would, at Earl's request, destroy their copies of the directive related to his son.

"We made no copies, Mr. Spence," she said.

"Well?" Earl said when I returned to the car.

"No problem," I said.

Earl slept fitfully throughout the trip north to Glencoe.

Chapter Twelve

"Earl?" I said, gently touching his arm as we neared the office. He stirred. "You said you wanted me to take you to the office?"

"Huh?" he said, squinting into the darkness. "What time is it?"

"Pushing eight," I said. "We're here. You got an empty apartment in your building?"

"Yeah. Unless Wally's rented it right out from under me, there's one at the far end of the second floor, on the other side of the building from our office."

"How much rent are you going to charge yourself?"

"Plenty, but it won't be in dollars."

"You won't be rooming right next to Wally."

"I'm grateful for that. That guy would talk business all night if somebody didn't take the initiative to go home to bed."

"Wonder where everybody is," I said, as I pulled around to the side where Wally usually parked.

"Who knows? Let me get a look at the place and see what's the shortest way to take stuff up."

"There's no elevator?" I said.

"You know better than that. There're only two

111

floors, and the building was built before they were required."

"And you want to move everything in tonight?" I sighed, remembering the work from the morning, which had required no going up or down stairs.

"If it wasn't so late I'd even want to dump the trailer off tonight," he said. "You know me."

"Yes, unfortunately, I do. When can I go home and see my wife?"

"Good grief, Philip. How long have you been gone? Call her from the office and tell her you're here and that you'll be home in two or three hours."

"Sure, I'd be glad to help you, Earl. Thanks for asking."

He smiled. "I appreciate it, Philip. You know that."

"I'd appreciate it if you'd stay with us tonight, or check into a hotel and let us move you in in the morning."

"Can't do it. How could I ask anyone to help me on the day of Margo's big reunion? I'd rather have it all out of the way. The phone is going to be installed tomorrow."

"I keep forgetting you've had all this planned for weeks."

While Earl jogged up the steps to open his new apartment, I ducked into the office and called home. No answer. I was beginning to feel the way Earl did when he kept missing Gail. I moseyed over to Earl's apartment, and from twenty feet down the hall I could hear talking and laughter.

"You have no idea how long we've been waiting here," Margo said as she welcomed me. Bonnie and Wally were there too.

"I was kinda expectin' you by six or so," Wally said. "We finally ordered out some pizza, but there's nothin' left but some cold end pieces."

"No, thanks," Earl and I said in unison.

"Let's get this place furnished so I can take my husband home," Margo said. And within an hour, we were done. Wally gave up trying to navigate the stairs halfway through and became the unofficial supervisor inside the apartment. He would greet each carrier at the door, but instead of lightening their load, he would just direct them to the proper place.

When Margo and I left, Earl was starting his car. "Where are you going?" I asked.

"We got done so early," he said, "I think the trailer rental place is still open. I've got a thing about getting everything done as soon as possible."

"How well I know."

Late the next morning a call came to the office for Earl. It was Gail Durning, whom he'd been unable to reach at her number in Springfield. He'd been worried about her, because she had left messages at both our place and IDLE's Schaumburg office.

Earl took the call in Wally's office, and when he was through, he called us all in. Wally had asked him the night before if he was handling everything all right, "what with the news we heard about you." Earl had put him off then, but now he chose to set the record straight by telling Margo and Wally everything I had already heard, just so everyone would quit feeling sorry for him.

"So when this sting operation's over, you get your

old job back, right?" Wally said when Earl was finished.

"No, I couldn't let them do that to Close. I'll stay in that capacity until the end of Jim's first term. Then I'm coming back here full time."

"There goes my office," Wally said with a smile, obviously pleased with the news.

"Don't be too sure," Earl said. "I may float around here like a star consultant or something."

"I kind of thought you would be telling us about Gail," I ventured carefully, but I was not careful enough.

Earl grew cold. "Nothing to tell," he said. "We've spoken; that's all. I couldn't tell her the truth about why I'm up here, so she's just pitying me right now. I don't need that."

We sat there awkwardly for a moment. "So," Margo said brightly, "you want to hear how the reunion preparations are going?"

"Sure," Earl said. But we didn't believe him. Margo whipped through the plans quickly, just as she had done a few days before. Nothing had really changed, except the weather was threatening. "Larry and Shannon might be a little late," she said, "but I still think we might be able to get some time alone with them."

"We? *We* doesn't sound very alone."

"You mean we're not all going to be in on trying to talk Larry into this?"

"Margo," Earl said. "I told you that if he had to be talked into it, it was going to wear thin with him. It's only going to work if Larry's looking for something else. If he's happy where he is, I don't even want to bring it up."

114

"You're not even going to tell him what's happening?"

"No way."

"I don't understand that," Margo said, and I had to admit—if only to myself—that I didn't either. I mean, if we couldn't trust Larry Shipman, who could we trust?

"The point is," Wally said, coming to Earl's defense, "there are already too many people who know what's happening, as you put it. The basic problem is that we appear to have a leak within Internal Affairs itself. No one can know unless he has a crucial reason for knowing."

"Then how are you going to make him aware of the opportunity?"

"If he's lookin' for work, it'll be obvious. Otherwise, let's leave him and his wife and his career alone. Fair enough?"

I nodded. Margo didn't.

By midafternoon, Margo and Bonnie and Bonnie's granddaughter Erin were carting boxes to the park down the street. Margo had made and hung a colorful sign in the window of the downstairs entrance to our office to show latecomers where to go.

But at just after four, Wally stood at the window and hollered, "There goes the picnic. And from the looks of the sky, this one ain't gonna be blowing over." Earl and I tore down the steps to his car, trench coats pulled up over our heads. We raced to the park where Margo, Bonnie, and Erin were scrambling to cover the food and other paraphernalia.

The five of us were soaked and laughing by the time we had everything—including ourselves—in the

115

car. Not even Margo was disappointed that the party would have to be indoors. "Now nobody can claim they couldn't follow my directions," she said. "Once they show up at the office, they're here."

"Profound," I said, and she punched me.

Once everything was set up and all we had to do was wait, Bonnie embarrassed Erin by making her tell us all about the Olympic trials. It was obvious that Erin didn't really want to get into it. She had answered enough questions as an Olympic favorite, but she didn't want to disappoint her beaming grandmother.

It was amazing to see the maturity in the young woman we had met when she was a fourteen-year-old phenomenon. Now all the baby fat was gone, and the muscles, always tight, were defined and more taut, but not in an unfeminine way. She was really quite attractive, though not in the cute way we remembered when she was a high schooler.

She had been around the world, competed in the top levels, won the world's championship in two events, finished second in two others, and won the all-around the last two years in a row. She carried herself in a ladylike and self-assured manner, yet she wasn't cocky. In many ways she was still the shy, soft-spoken little girl we had met when her mother's illicit lover had been murdered.

It was a terribly difficult case for our agency, because it involved Bonnie and her family. Earl had always vowed that the agency would not deteriorate into domestic cases where we followed husbands or wives suspected of cheating on each other. But Bonnie had been so desperate and distraught over the condition of her daughter's marriage that she had asked that her son-in-law be tailed to prove that he was being unfaithful to Linda Gibbons, Bonnie's daughter.

Sadly, it was discovered that he was innocent, but that Linda Gibbons was seeing someone else—Johnny Bizell, a small-time operator with loose mob ties in Chicago. When he turned up murdered in his own car in the parking lot of a suburban high school where Erin had competed that very night, there were suspects galore. And because the dead man had connections to Chicago, Wally Festschrift—then a homicide detective sergeant—headed up the investigation.

Bonnie, her son-in-law Greg Gibbons, her daughter Linda, and even Margo had been at the gymnastics meet that night. Most of them had a motive to kill the home-wrecker, including, as it turned out, Linda herself, who had quickly soured on Bizell. So, Wally's investigation led right back to the detective agency of his former subordinate, then co-worker, and finally superior, Earl Haymeyer.

For all its trauma, it was a case that ended as well as could be expected. The people we cared about were cleared, and though there were emotional scars—particularly for Erin because she was acquainted with the murderer—it all turned out fairly well. Even Greg and Linda Gibbons got back together, and their marriage was solid enough to see Erin through high school.

They showed up at the reunion, and as Margo had predicted, Greg was very quiet. After shaking hands all around and being the genial sales type, he faded into the background and stayed close to his mother-in-law and daughter while Linda mixed a little more.

117

"Is it true," Linda asked Margo, "that Larry Shipman and his wife might make it?"

Assured that it was true, she said, "I'm eager to see him again. He was a kind and sensitive guy who really gave me some good advice. Who did he marry?"

Margo explained that Larry had married an old friend who had wound up as one of our clients. Talk about a bizarre case. Shannon Perry told Larry one time she was afraid she was being set up for murder because she had had at least some connection with every victim in a series of murders.

Larry enlisted the help of the agency to find out what was going on, and Shannon soon became a prime suspect of the Chicago Police Department and—guess who?—Wally. Her connection with the victims didn't elude that criminal mind (which, fortunately for all of us, is housed in a justice-minded body). When more murders took place with even more connections to Shannon, it became a race against time to find out if she was intended as a victim or only as a frame-up.

It was a fun but nerve-wracking case for me because I played a major part in the apprehension of the murderer. But not as big a part as Wally, who nearly crushed the man. We were all glad to see Larry hook up with Shannon, once they had determined that their attraction to each other was not based on pity from his side or admiration from hers.

Larry and Shannon moved to Indiana shortly after they were married so Shannon could elude some of the horror of what she had been through and so she could start building a new life away from the glare of the Chicago press. We hadn't seen much of them

118

since then, but Larry was always on our minds because of the unique contribution he'd made to the agency. We'd never been the same without him, though Wally's coming had filled a big hole.

Larry was first a journalist, so we shouldn't have been surprised when he gravitated that way after detective work. At first he was a freelancer on both sides of the fence. He had been stringing for newspapers and radio and television stations and working undercover jobs for Earl while he was a special investigator for then U.S. Attorney Jim Hanlon.

He added life and zest and street savvy to our operation, and he was always ahead of everyone, except maybe Wally, in trying to put himself into the mind of the criminal: His hunches were right more than anyone else's, except occasionally for Earl's. With all of them together, it'd be like an all-star team. I wondered if I would still fit in, but if they'd have me, I knew I would at least learn a lot. Margo was becoming a real pro, as Earl and Wally often enjoyed reminding me to keep me in my place.

I didn't mind their ribbing, and I couldn't argue that she was better than I was. I had a hunch I was better than they wanted me to think I was, but how would I even know? Margo tried to tell me I was, but she was prejudiced and probably feeling for me after seeing how they teased me about her expertise. I knew I liked detective work even better than illustration and painting, which had been the love of my life for years.

Amos Chakaris and Hilary Brice were the next to arrive, with Hilary announcing that Judge Pincham had indeed recessed early that afternoon, but still

119

they would be unable to stay long. Old Amos had to be in bed early, doctor's orders, and Hilary had an important meeting of the partners in the law firm that night.

It was good to see them again. Amos had defended Margo's mother in a murder trial that sent her to prison soon after Margo and I had met. He had served as secretary of state in Illinois a few decades before, and until his retirement he was a senior partner in the law firm Hilary practiced with.

Hilary had represented Margo's interest in her mother's estate upon her death in prison. Hilary and I once had to drive all the way out to California together because of an air strike, when we had to get a deposition from Margo's father. I'd have to say that Hilary was the most spiritually sensitive non-Christian I had ever met, and she wasn't offended in the least that I used her as a sounding board to try out different approaches to telling people about my faith.

"I'll be happy to let you know how I think a person would respond to your pitch," she would always say, "as long as you don't turn your guns on me."

I never did, either. At least not overtly. But there were many times when I would describe hypothetically a type of person in a certain stage in life and with certain values, and it was close enough to her that she had to listen to my approach from her own perspective. I learned more about talking to people about Christ from Hilary than from anyone else I ever knew.

"Still pitching religion?" she'd say whenever we met.

"You know better than that," I'd say. "It's not religion, it's—"

"I know, I know," she'd say. "I never would have bet you'd get through to Earl, let alone Wally. Just stay out of my backyard, hear?"

That made her such a challenge. I'd say, "You know, it wasn't Margo or me getting through to Earl and Wally. It was God. And nobody keeps Him out of their yard."

She smiled. "But if I keep you out, that's the first line of defense."

"God won't force Himself on you, Hilary. When you're ready, you'll find He's been there all the time."

"I like you, Spence," she'd say. "A little naive, not a great mind, kind of a sophisticated gumshoe—but likable. Keep pitching."

I was glad that Allyson and her soon-to-be husband made it before Amos and Hilary had to leave. He was all ears and short hair, but very pleasant and obviously head over heels for Allyson. She knew how to be appropriate around a former flame—me—by virtually ignoring me and spending a lot of time chatting with Margo, whom she won over in short order.

The room was getting crowded, and people were getting to know each other, but I could tell Earl and Wally were fidgety. Wally never liked parties and socializing that much, because he didn't feel comfortable practicing what few social graces he had garnered over the years. I knew Earl had many things on his mind, not the least of which was Johnny Ray Robinson. But there was also Gail, his son, and his move from Springfield, away from his church and the friends he had made in the three years he'd been

121

down there. Not to mention the fact that he couldn't tell anyone but his closest confidants that in reality he had not really been demoted for a protocol infraction.

I knew both he and Wally wanted very badly to talk to Larry Shipman about joining the new investigation and maybe rejoining the team for good. But they were dead serious about not pushing him; in fact, they were serious about not even raising the issue with him until they had a clue he might have a real interest in a change.

And their opportunity to talk with Larry seemed closer and closer the later it got, until the phone call came. Car trouble on the Chicago Skyway. Larry and Shannon were going to be late.

Chapter Thirteen

Amos Chakaris and Hilary Brice were the first to leave, of course. They were followed shortly by Greg and Linda Gibbons, though Erin stayed to help clean up. She would be staying with her grandmother that night anyway before joining her coach and teammates at a two-week training camp in Colorado beginning the following Monday.

The wedding couple stayed less than a half hour, but I think it was good for us to have interacted with them before their big day; there sure wouldn't be any time to chat with them the next day.

Bonnie and Erin finished up and then hung around for about another half hour as we shared what each had heard that the other didn't about the various old friends and acquaintances. "Greet Larry and Shannon for me, will you?" Bonnie said wistfully at about ten o'clock. "We really must get our world champion home to bed."

Erin rolled her eyes and said, "Oh, Grandma!" but it was obvious she appreciated being made over by her grandmother. She helped Bonnie with her coat, and Earl walked them down to their car. When he didn't return right away, Margo stepped to the window and looked down into the light drizzle.

She turned toward Wally and me and motioned with her head for us to join her. There in the soft pool of light afforded by the street lamp, Earl stood in the mist, staring into the darkness.

He looked tired. Maybe he was hoping Larry and Shannon would show up while he was down there, but it was getting cold, and he had not put on even his suit jacket. His hands were thrust deep into his pockets, and his shoulders were hunched against the wind.

Suddenly, as if he'd just thought of something or realized how cold he was, he turned and started back up the stairs while we separated from the window.

When he reached the top of the stairs and came through the double glass doors and saw us all sitting apart from each other and not talking, I had the idea he knew we'd been watching him. "You save some food for them?" he asked Margo.

She nodded. "It'll be cold, but it'll be good. Larry's favorite."

"Ribs!" Wally chortled. "I didn't know there were any ribs left!"

"There aren't," Margo said. "Only Larry and Shannon's."

"Maybe she's not a big eater," Wally said. "I think I'll tell her she looks like she's put on some weight, even if she hasn't."

We all laughed except for Earl. Wally turned toward him when he didn't get a response to his joke, and as if on cue, Earl said softly to no one in particular: "If anything happens to Johnny Ray Robinson, I'll never forgive myself."

It left us all quiet. The evening had been fun, but as we sat waiting for the most important guests, it hit Earl, and then us, what this was really all about. Earl's being here, our interest in Larry's returning, the charade of Earl's demotion—everything pointed to the worst type of problem a law enforcement agency could have.

Bad cops are not a new story. That's why there's an Internal Affairs Division in the first place. But what kind of bureau do you create when you have dishonest cops in your IAD? And then what do you do if you can't trust the people in your super bureau to check out IAD? Start another double agent force? Where does it end?

"Let's put all the chairs back where they belong and get the desks organized again," Earl said, evidencing his neatness fetish again. I'm sure Margo thought they'd made great strides by having everything else tidied up and put away.

Without enthusiasm we shuffled about, sliding desks, rolling chairs, and rearranging until within a few minutes the office looked the way it had looked before the party. "Looks like we missed the whole thing!" Larry said, pushing through the doors with Shannon at his side. We hadn't even heard them on the stairs, let alone their car.

There was so much hugging and how-are-you-ing that I almost hugged Wally. Larry hadn't changed much, but then his best attribute had always been that he looked like the guy next door. Of average height and build, he was now a little fuller in the face, with maybe a strand or two of grey peeking through his hair. There was still a little of his perky old self there despite the hour, but clearly he'd rather have been in bed, and he said so.

"We almost went straight to the hotel. But we had a feeling you might be waiting up for us."

Shannon looked radiant, though weary. Her hair was much longer, and she seemed more quiet and peaceful than I had remembered her. But letting a cold night wind blow your hair while standing on the Chicago Skyway is nothing compared to living in terror of a mass murderer.

She seemed genuinely pleased to see all of us and happy that Larry was back among his old, good friends. Margo and I took their coats and led them to chairs, where Margo then brought the ribs. "You didn't have to save us anything," Shannon said, moved.

"I'm glad you did," Larry said.

"I'm just glad you didn't make us wait until tomorrow to see you," Margo said, passing along everyone's greetings, asking them about their car trouble, and filling them in on how the party went. "You'll see most of the people at the wedding tomorrow."

"This place hasn't changed much," Larry said, wiping his mouth with a napkin. "Still got a vacant desk for a broken-down old P.I.?"

"P.I.?" Shannon said, her mouth full.

"Private investigator," Margo said, looking expectantly at Earl. But Earl just laughed at Larry's joke and eyed Margo carefully to be sure she hadn't read too much into it.

Shannon didn't scowl, but her face quickly lost its

animation. She obviously had not been amused at Larry's comment. "Can anyone help me finish these ribs?" she said. Wally was moving toward her before the last syllable was out.

"Just here to serve," he said.

"So what's happening around here?" Larry said. "What're you guys working on?"

"You wouldn't believe it," Margo said, realizing immediately that she shouldn't have said it. "I mean, actually, believe it or not, we're between cases right now. There's just not that much going on."

"How about you, Lar?" Earl said. "What's going on in your life?"

"Oh, pretty much the same as usual. I'm managing editor now, you know."

"Yeah, that's great, isn't it?"

Larry shrugged.

"That bad, huh?" Margo said, again trying to read more into his comments than he might have intended. Earl glared at her. "Uh, what does your new job entail, Larry?"

"Nine to five," Shannon said. "Which I love."

"And which I hate," Larry said.

"You don't like getting home at a decent hour every night?" Wally asked. "I mean, I'm not one to talk 'cause I never have gotten home before six myself, but I would think a young family man like yourself, why—"

"Oh, I like having some free evenings," Larry said, "and the more time I spend with Shannon, the better it is for both of us. What I don't like is the routine of the job, the distance from the part of the work I like the best."

127

"The dangerous part," Shannon said flatly.

"There's no danger in newspaper work," Larry said. "Not even on the police beat. But at least when I was city editor I could run out now and then and supervise the coverage of the big stories. Now I just supervise the supervisors and sit in with the brass on the overall planning."

"It's not you, right Larry?" Margo pressed.

"Takes some getting used to, like all of our jobs do, I suppose," Earl cut in quickly. "I faced a lot of the same frustration, as you can imagine."

"Oh, I would think even more so," Larry said. "From frontline detective work to bureaucratic politics, whew!"

"Well, it wasn't quite that bad. But it did take me out of the action."

"You're talking in the past tense, Earl," Larry said, revealing the attention to detail that so endeared him to Earl. "Why?"

"Well, I'm getting out a little more than I used to. Get some occasional action."

"He sure does," Margo said, still trying to steer the conversation.

"One of the perks of being the boss, huh, Earl?" Larry said.

Earl nodded. "But you're basically happy in your job situation then, Larry?"

Larry looked at Shannon, who returned his gaze but didn't say anything. "It's all right," he said. "It's OK."

"That's all?" Margo said.

"That's enough," Earl said. "Isn't it, Larry?"

"It's almost enough. It's not quite enough. But then

I have several other interests and responsibilities that demand my time. It's fine."

We all sat looking at each other with polite, close-mouthed grins, some of us realizing there was sparring going on, others—or at least Shannon—having no idea there was another level of meaning flying back and forth.

"He hates it," she said suddenly, without emotion.

"I don't hate it," he said.

"You hate it."

"I've never said I hated it."

"I know you, Larry. You don't have to say anything. You tell me every night when you drag yourself home by five-thirty and sit listlessly, unchallenged and unmotivated. If you can't tell your old friends or your wife, who can you tell? You hate it."

Larry threw his head back and laughed loudly. "You're right! I hate it!" He draped his arm around her and drew her close. She smiled. "Thanks for noticing," he said.

"Talk about actions speaking louder than words," she said.

Earl was glaring at Margo, daring her to say anything. She was nearly bursting, wanting to jump right in with the solution, the answer, the alternative. Her mouth was half-open, and her breath had been drawn, but Earl's look froze her into submission. She wasn't going to speak until the subject had been broached, and apparently Earl was reserving the right.

"So, how serious is it, Larry?" he said. "Do your superiors know your feelings?"

"No. They're insensitive to it. They wouldn't

believe it anyway. They won't believe it until I walk out the door. I can't ask for my old position back, because no one would believe I wasn't demoted, not that that would bother me. But my colleagues can't imagine anyone who's *made* it wanting to go backward in his career. There's nothing I would like more."

"Than to go back to city editor," Earl suggested.

"He wants to go back further than that," Shannon said, and Margo nearly fell off her chair.

"What're you saying?" Larry said. "We haven't even discussed this."

"Tell me you wouldn't rather be back on the street with your little spiral notebook, chasing policemen and firemen and getting the story, the human interest, all that. When you talk about *those* good old days, that's what you're talking about, and *that's* what gets you going."

"You liked those days even better than your days in full-time detective work?" Margo asked, unable to help herself. She ignored Earl's glare.

Larry looked embarrassed, Shannon preoccupied. Larry leaned forward toward Margo and spoke softly, but we could all hear. "You see, Margo, I don't talk detective work with Shannon. Understand?"

"Sure. I'm sorry."

"It's all right," Shannon said. "But I don't need any reminders of what I went through up here. In fact, I know that's why Larry talks so enthusiastically about his police beat stringer days. He'd really rather be talking about the days he was knocking around here, tracking down clues in murder cases. Talking about the old police beat is as close as he can get to that."

"If you feel that way about it, Shannon," Earl said, "I don't suppose there's ever a chance that Larry would feel free to get back into that line of work."

"I can't speak for him," she said. "I can't imagine worrying about him putting his life on the line. On the last case he worked with you guys, my case, he could have easily been killed."

"Shannon!" Wally scolded. "You forget that Philip and Earl and I were within feet of him every second."

"But if anything had gone wrong—"

"If there had been a problem with any one of us, the other would have handled it."

"But if the murderer had been quicker—"

"We knew his method of operation. If you'll recall, he never got a bullet in the chamber."

"I'd rather not talk about it."

"I understand. I'm sorry."

"What've you got cooking?" Shannon said, suddenly suspicious. "A little weekend distraction? A little danger Larry can dip into now that he's been out of the profession long enough to have lost his edge, his timing, his reflexes? Is that what this is all about? Seeing if he wants just another little something to involve himself in so I can lose him to the nightmare that's been plaguing me for months?"

"No," Earl said. "Nothing like that. Nothing like that at all. We just wanted to know how things were going for you two. If you were happy and settled. It sounds like maybe you are."

"It does?" she said. "We just revealed more to each other in ten minutes than we have in the past year. It sounds to me like we aren't settled at all. It sounds to me like I've made a prisoner of my husband, and he has lovingly locked himself in."

"I'm happy," Larry insisted, grasping her hand with both of his. "All I want is for you to be happy."

"I'm happy when you're moving up in your profession to a job that you hate, a schedule that bores you, and a routine that's going to drive you crazy. What kind of a wife am I?"

"You've been through a lot," Larry said. "I knew that when I got involved."

"That I would be a special case, requiring fragile handling? When am I going to grow up, Larry? When can I be treated as an equal and not as a cracked egg shell? If you want out of your job, then I want you out of your job. I want you happy even if I'm forced to grow up a little."

"How about if it meant growing up a lot?" Earl tried gently.

"Meaning?"

"For instance, Larry getting involved in putting murderers in jail again, the same kind who terrorized you and murdered your acquaintances and even one of your friends. Is that a valid life's work?"

She stared evenly at him. Larry spoke. "You really think I've lost something since I've been off the street?"

She couldn't hide a smile. "Got to you with that, did I?"

"Yeah. If you really think I've lost a step or an inch or an ounce, I'll go a few rounds with you right here, right now."

"You wanna step outside?" she said, smiling.

"I want some sleep," he said.

"Me too," she said.

"We'll have time to chat about this, Earl," Larry said.

"We will?"

"Yup. I get three weeks vacation. The first two started today. I wanted time to get away and think and bounce a few things off you and Shannon. I didn't exactly expect it would begin tonight, but here we are. Are you serious that there's something here for me if I want it?"

"Did I say that?" Earl said. "Or did I say that we had nothing cooking like Shannon suggested?"

"All I suggested was a part-time, weekend fling for an old detective," Shannon said.

"I'm old?" Larry said, pained. "I'm thirty-five! And I look thirty! And if Earl has something for me to consider, I want to consider it. But only if you are open to it."

"Let's sleep on it," Earl suggested. And we all nodded wearily.

Chapter Fourteen

There were loose ends, things that puzzled us, knowledge we hadn't shared with each other, and all manner of reasons to talk rather than sleep that night. But Margo and I were both so tired that we had little choice.

Our subconscious minds must have been working overtime while we slept though, because by the time we were up and showered and dressed and ready for breakfast, we were also ready to talk. And when we're both in the mood, there's probably more talking than listening going on.

"Were you there when Gail Durning came looking for Earl?" I asked.

"Yes! Who is she?"

I told her what I knew.

"Doesn't sound like she's too eager to keep the cooling-off period cold," Margo said. "Driving all the way up here?"

"That's what I thought, but apparently they didn't get anything resolved when Earl finally got hold of her by phone. He's decided that she's just feeling sorry for him because of the misfortunes in his career."

"If she only knew."

I nodded. "Any idea why Earl feels so personally responsible for Johnny Ray Robinson?"

She shook her head. "Except that I'm sure he took part in assuring Johnny Ray that he was doing the right thing by exposing his co-workers. And, of course, Earl has his wife and daughters and mother hidden away somewhere. I'm guessing they're around here somewhere so he can keep an eye on them."

"You may be right," I said. "I never thought of that. Can you imagine being responsible for the most important family members in a person's life?"

"Yeah. And not knowing where that person is, or even whether he's dead or alive?"

"It really has Earl preoccupied. As if he has nothing else to worry about right now." I told Margo about little Earl.

"Do you think Earl's going to be able to accept Mr. Haines's evaluation?" she asked.

"Emotionally, no. But I think he accepted it intellectually and proved it by not producing the governor's directive. Margo, if you could have seen Haines, that old administrator that Earl has made out to be such a scoundrel, speaking softly to Earl, Jr., and touching his face . . ."

The conversation turned and weaved and covered the many old friends we had seen the night before, and before we knew it, we were talking about Allyson. "I assume she's out of our systems," I said.

"She was never in *my* system," Margo said.

"You used to adore her," I said.

"So did you," she said, hitting where it hurt.

"Margo, it's over and you know it. I fell for her when I thought you were through with me."

"I was."

"Then how can I be punished for feeling I was available?"

"Who's punishing you?"

"You make me feel guilty."

"I've said or done nothing to make you feel guilty. If you feel guilty, you must *be* guilty. But of what? Still enamored with her?"

"She's beautiful," I admitted.

"You'd have to be blind not to see that," Margo said, "but then I gave up competing with beautiful women a long time ago."

"You're the most beautiful woman I've ever seen, Margo."

"Then quit thinking about Allyson. You're losing her today."

"I lost her years ago. I realized I was wrong to have given up on you so easily, and in the long run, that was best for Allyson, too."

"You think she prefers her CPA over you?"

"I'm afraid so."

"I think she does too," Margo said, a twinkle in her eye. "That must be what's bothering you. You didn't break her heart. She just started looking for something better. And she found it in a numbers man!"

Margo was laughing. I was taking it. "I won't be crying at the wedding."

"I should hope not," she said. "But I'll bet Allyson will be."

"You mean you think she'd rather have me?"

"Nah. She probably has herself convinced that

136

money is more important than character. She knew when she lost you, she lost a character. Good grief, Philip. You should be glad you missed out on a girl with the kind of taste that prefers a CPA to a P.I."

"And you, Margo? What do you prefer?"

"I prefer teasing my husband mercilessly because he's so self-conscious about having dumped a raving beauty for a plain Jane like me, and he's cute when he's embarrassed."

"Nobody anywhere would call you a plain Jane," I said. "I get comments about you all the time, and so do you."

"I don't turn heads the way Allyson does. Admit it. You and Larry used to watch from the upstairs window when she walked down the street to lunch, for Pete's sake."

"So did you and Bonnie!"

"Guilty. See? She even turns women's heads."

"I'd rather watch you walk to lunch than anybody else in the world."

She smiled victoriously. "And don't you forget it."

Margo needs mock arguments like that every once in awhile for her self-image. They don't do much for mine, but she enjoys them. She knows well that she has no competition in my eyes, but she gets a kick out of seeing me squirm.

After an hour or so of our Saturday morning custom—reading aloud to each other from books or magazines or the Bible—we went for a long walk. And the conversation turned to Larry and Shannon.

"Your gut feeling," I requested.

"I want him back with us."

"No kidding! We all do, and we kinda did get that

drift from you, if you know what I mean. I want to know if you think it's going to happen."

"For this case or for the long term?"

"Can't have both. There's no way he could participate in this sting operation and get his old job back. His decision is going to have to be on the whole ball of wax, not just one—admittedly large—case."

Margo always walked faster when she could smell the water. We had gone east almost as far as we could. She led the way up a grassy area into some trees where we could sit in the cool darkness they provided, our backs to their trunks, and still get a good view of Lake Michigan, with ships passing in the distance and waves slapping at the rocks below.

"I don't think he'll do it," Margo said.

"Really? I would have thought you hadn't given up on him yet."

"Oh, it isn't him," she said. "I think Larry would come in a minute. But I've been trying to empathize with Shannon. I tend to think it's still too soon for her to be thrust back into a world of danger and suspicion. Tension. Violence."

"I can't argue with that. *He* sure seemed ready though, didn't he?"

"That's just it, Philip," she said, snuggling close, "so did she."

"You said you didn't think she'd let him."

"I don't. I can't see how she could. And yet she almost seemed open to it last night, going on about if he was happy, she'd be happy. But he has to leave it up to her, doesn't he?"

"*I* sure would."

"You would?"

138

"Of course. I couldn't do something that made you miserable, no matter how happy it made me."

"But she said she'd be happy if he was. It's so confusing."

"It's not that confusing, Margo. She'd be happy *that* he was happy, but she wouldn't be happy happy."

"Happy happy? You're telling me it's not confusing, and you prove it by telling me she'll be happy but not *happy happy*?"

"You know what I mean."

"I certainly do not."

"I mean she'll be happy that he's happy, but—"

"Here we go again."

"Hear me out. But she won't be happy generally."

"Uh-huh. So, what's *your* gut feeling, Philip?"

"I don't think she'll let him do it either. Wanna jog home?"

"I would, but then I'd have to shower again before the wedding."

We walked. "See how the husband does what the wife wants just to keep peace?" I said.

"Give me a break," she said. "You're so glad I didn't want to jog that you can't stand it. If I'd wanted to, you'd have had to because you suggested it. But you're so lazy—"

"You got that right," I admitted, slowing my walk.

When we got back to the apartment, I was fixing us a light lunch when Mrs. May, our neighbor across the hall, rang the bell. "There was a very large man snooping around here while you were gone," she said. "A very large, very sloppy, fat man in a trench coat. He looked distraught."

"Distraught?" Margo said. "How could you tell?"

"He kept running his hand through his hair and pacing around. When he didn't get any results from ringing the bell, he knocked loudly, waking up all the late sleepers, no doubt. He knocked several times and then put his ear up to the door for who knows what. Then he walked up and down the hall, looking this way and that and out the window, I guess to see if you were out in the courtyard. Where were you, anyway? Never mind. None of my business. Which he wasn't either, except he looked like such an unsavory sort."

"Did you tell him we were out?"

"Well, I didn't know you were out. I mean, I knew it, but I just happened to know it because I just happened to be near my front door when yours opened and I, you know, heard, or saw, you and Mr. Spence, you know, leaving. Otherwise, how would I know whether you were here or not or coming or going or what? Anyway, I wasn't about to speak to that man. He was very large and fat and—"

"Thank you, Mrs. May," Margo said, shutting the door. "Thank you very much."

And from the hall we heard, "—and unsavory! A bum type of a person! I'd be careful!"

Margo called the office. No answer. She called Wally's. No answer. She called Earl's. No answer. "Everybody's out doing their last minute wedding present shopping or laundry or something," she guessed.

She called Bonnie's. Success. "Strange," she said, hanging up a few minutes later. "That wasn't like

140

Bonnie at all. Have you ever known Bonnie to keep a confidence?"

"No!" I said, setting fresh fruit and a grilled cheese sandwich before Margo. We prayed.

"She said Wally had received some bad news and wanted to talk to us. I asked her what it was, and she said he said he wanted to tell us himself, if she didn't mind. But that's never stopped her before."

"I'll bet he didn't tell her then," I said.

"You're probably right. I know she would have told me if he had told her."

"What can it be?"

"I can't imagine. Not much rattles Wally. Nothing that would make him want to talk to us, anyway. Why doesn't he talk to Earl?"

"Maybe he has."

The phone rang. I answered. "Where've you two been?" Wally demanded. "I've been calling everywhere lookin' for ya!"

"I'm sorry, Wally. We'd have stayed home if we'd known you wanted us."

"I gotta talk to you!"

"What is it, Wal?"

"I wanna see you in person. Can I?"

"Sure, but—"

"I'll be right over."

"Wally!"

"Yeah?"

"Is it something about Earl? His son, his lady friend?"

"I wish it was."

"Johnny Ray Robinson?"

"Nah. I'll tell ya when I get there."

We had just enough time to finish our lunch and get the dishes put away when we heard heavy footsteps in the hallway and Mrs. May's singsong voice from the little bit she opened her door. "He's back again!"

"Mind yer own business, you ol'—" Wally said, and we heard her door slam.

"You've got to know she's got her eye pressed up against that peephole," Margo said. "Watch this."

As soon as our bell rang, she threw the door open and rushed to embrace Wally. "Dad!" she cried. And we thought we heard Mrs. May fall against her wall.

It was all Margo could do to drag the scowling Wally Festschrift through the door. He was clearly not in the mood, but Margo and I could have laughed till we cried.

"That was cute," he muttered. "Who'd we nail with that little ruse?"

Margo was doubled over to keep from laughing out loud. All she could do was point toward Mrs. May's door.

Chapter Fifteen

Wally lowered his bulk onto one end of our couch before beginning his coat-shedding operation. He scowled at us until we were through laughing, which wasn't as soon as it should have been.

As he wriggled out of his trench coat and suit jacket at the same time, I sat across from him in an overstuffed chair, and Margo sat on the floor between my feet.

Wally balled up the mountain of coat and set it on the couch next to him. He laboriously drew one ham hock of a leg up and leaned heavily on one elbow. He shook his head slowly. "If you can make bad news fit into bein' a Christian, you're a better man than I am—or better woman."

"You got some bad news, Wally?" Margo asked, stating the obvious.

"Two scoops," Wally said. "I wish I still swore without thinking twice about it. It's work not to on a day like this."

"This should be a happy day," Margo said. "Shannon's wedding and everything."

Wally winced. "Wrong thing to bring up," he said.

"You're not going?" Margo said. "We were hoping you'd sit with us."

"I don't know. Don't feel much like it. Probably will. Nothin' else to do."

"You wanna talk about it?"

" 'Course! That's why I'm here."

"We're listening."

"Like I say, the bad news came in two scoops. At least it came from the same pail. The wife calls and says, 'Woofer, we need to talk.' Philip, you knew she called me Woofer, 'cause I think I told ya that. It's because of my initials bein' W.F., Margo." She nodded.

"Anyway, she says we need to talk, and I go, 'OK, shoot,' and she goes, 'Not on the phone.' Now for the last few years, she never once has asked to see me. I talk her into seein' me; at least that way I know how I stand and don't get my hopes up like I used to about us gettin' together again.

"I says, 'Ethel, it's not about Clarence, is it?' and she says, 'Partly.' And I know I got trouble. See, Clarence is the youngest of the four boys and the only one in the family who isn't divorced, including me. Between the five men in the family—and I use the term lightly—we've been divorced six times. One for me, two for the oldest, one for the next, two for the next, and none for Clarence, but then he's never been married, either. You got any Coke?"

"Only diet," Margo said.

"Yuck. I'll take a tall, cool one."

Margo went to get it, and Wally continued. "So, you know, Clarence is livin' at home, moochin' off his mother—and me 'cause I'm still payin' alimony—and he's a shoveler in the barns at Arlington Park. I think the only good thing since he got out of Joliet Stateville Prison is that I don't think he does drugs anymore. Ethel thinks he doesn't either, but I don't think she'd know grass if she smelled it. He's always floatin' around in what seems to me to be a marijuana-type daze, but I'm willing to give him the benefit of the doubt.

"So, I'm thinkin' Clarence is in trouble again. I remember when he first was up for parole. He had done pretty good in the pen, and they asked him what job he thought he could get if he got out, and he told 'em of his friends at Arlington. The parole board didn't think that was such a good idea—and I agreed with 'em—and they said he should try to get something more gainful or something like that. He told 'em—brilliant kid that he is—that if they didn't mind, he'd rather serve his time so when he was out he wouldn't have to answer to them anymore and could get the kind of job he really wanted.

"And that's what he did, and that's what he got. Well, as I've always said, I didn't think it made sense for a former stickup man—who embarrassed his cop father to death by gettin' busted enough times to be sentenced—to get a job where he's that close to betting and gangsters and all that. But he had served his time and paid his dues. He still had to check in with the parole board, which bugged him to no end. But at least they weren't telling him where to work after he had served his time.

"So, I'm wonderin' what has Clarence got himself into this time, and worse than that, what's Ethel mean by 'partly'? Clarence is bad enough. There's more?"

Wally took a long drink of his diet cola, coughed a cough that was clearer than the coughs we used to endure when he was a three-pack-a-day man, folded his arms across his chest, and took a deep breath. "I tell Ethel I'll be right over, and she says, 'No, meet me at the diner.' I mean, what is that? I can't go over to my own former wife's house, which I've been payin' on for more'n twenty-five years?

"Why in the world wouldn't she want me there? All I can think of is that what she wants to tell me is gonna get me so riled that I might make a scene in the house that I wouldn't make in the diner, so my mind is goin' a mile a minute. But what can I say? I agree to meet her.

"I'd already had breakfast, but nobody in the world makes a better breaded veal cutlet than the Saturday morning man at the Round the Clock, and it was close enough to noon—I'd say pushin' ten-thirty, anyway—so I order that before Ethel gets into her sob story. She starts with Clarence, just to keep me in suspense. If she'd started with the other, I might have actually let the meal get cold. I can eat and hear about Clarence. It didn't make me any too happy, but at least it wasn't totally new.

"Disappointing, though. Seems he got hooked up with some guys who wanted him to help 'em break into the executive offices and look at the files or steal some horse medicine or something. All he had to do for 'em was leave certain gates and doors open and make it look routine. Which, unfortunately, he's pretty good at. He forgets a lot of stuff anyway, so he had a built-in excuse. Even if he got caught and it looked like he helped them, he could say, 'Yeah, it

146

was my job to secure that gate, but I musta forgot.' A million character witnesses would vouch for that story, myself included."

"Who were these guys who wanted him to help them?" I asked.

"Hoodlums. I mean, they were associated with certain stables, owned a couple dozen horses in the barns there; but any time you get guys who want to see files or get into medical stuff, you're talking about your real lowlifes.

"So, Clarence sets it up with these dudes that he's gonna do what they say for a certain amount of money—which, I hate to admit, wasn't what the job was worth, not that I would ever condone such a thing even if the money *was* good. Which it wasn't. I think he was gonna make something like four or five hundred dollars if they got what they wanted, which was supposed to help them either get something dirty on another stable's owners or help their horses win or something.

"Well, Clarence pulls off his part of the operation and doesn't get caught. These guys send two or three of their better inside men into the place and get files and some other stuff—I don't know if they got any horse dope or not. I guess not. Well, Clarence waits a coupla weeks and never gets a dime, so he starts makin' noise that they're a bunch of creeps and shouldn't they be comin' across with some cash.

"They tell him that the money will come out of the winnings that result from the edge they got on their competition from what they found in the files. But whoever was behind it—whoever sent them in—didn't

147

think they found much of any value and chewed 'em out and told 'em they blew it or whatever.

"Anyway, nothing good for their horses came from the break-in, so they told Clarence he wasn't going to be getting any money. And they also told him that he should be glad because now he was totally in the clear. No one had suspected he was the one who made it easy for them to get in, and since he got no payoff for it, they could all just forget it, and he could sleep easier.

"What they don't know is that Clarence sleeps easy whether he's just pulled a crime or had a glass of warm milk. He just wanted the money for his trouble and started strong-armin' these guys a little."

"Threatening them?" Margo asked.

"In a way. Saying they weren't gonna get away with it and that he could still squeal on 'em, tell the authorities that he was forced or scared into helping. And since he took no money, he would pass a lie detector test about being in on it. That's what he thought, anyway. All the polygraph guy would have to do was to ask him if he felt he was in danger if he didn't help them, and if he was in on the caper to begin with, and he'd have flunked with flying colors."

"How did they react to his threats?"

"They believed him. He scared 'em, which was dumb on their parts. They should have known he wouldn't want to draw attention to himself and risk gettin' sent back to the slam. Anyway, to beat him to the punch they turned the tables on him and sent anonymous notes to the security staff, fingering him in aiding the break-in.

"When security double-checked the locations of the

locks that had not been forced and the timing of Clarence's shift and his work assignments that night, they came around and asked him some pointed questions. Questions that convinced him he had been set up.

"He talked his way out of the frame, which really wasn't a frame, of course. I mean, he was guilty, but he was still being set up by the guys he was working for. But he just flatly denied the whole thing, and he should have stuck with that story. You understand, I'm not saying that I would have lied and stuck with it, or that I would have thought he'd be morally right in sticking with it, but once he got into it, he could have pulled it off."

"You mean he waffled on his story?"

"Not exactly. What I mean is, he should have let his denial be his revenge. They would have gotten no satisfaction out of trying to implicate him, because it wouldn't have worked. But no, that wasn't enough revenge for big Clarence. He wanted to stick it to 'em, make 'em regret they did that, make 'em pay in another way if they weren't going to pay in cash."

"Do we want to know what he did?"

"Let me just say that I'm glad I had just sopped up the last of the gravy with my bread crusts when Ethel dropped the bomb. It was all I could do to horse down the apple pie after hearin' what dumbo did."

"So what'd he do?"

"He set fire to their barns."

"You're kidding."

"I'm serious."

"That big fire the other night—"

"Was set by Clarence Festschrift, son of the former you-know-who who's now a you-know-what."

"That'll come out in the papers?"

"If it doesn't, somebody ain't doin' his job, 'cause Clarence did it all right. He admitted it, told why, and is throwing himself on the mercy of the courts."

"Why?"

"Probably thinks there's enough corruption at the track that they'll give him immunity if he fingers some more people."

"Will they?"

"Nah! He can't come close to givin' 'em the kinds of guys they'd really like to put away. These two-bit amateurs were such small-time bunglers, they aren't worth lettin' an ex-con arsonist go. Anyway, the public would destroy a judge who'd be lenient on a horse killer."

"How many horses died in that fire?"

"Only two, thankfully, and I know that bothered Clarence because he never figured on that. I gotta hand that to him; the man loves horses."

"Then why burn down their barns?"

"He wouldn't have done it in the winter. It was a nice, warm, spring night, remember."

"And he shooed the horses away first?"

"Yeah, and none of the horses in the crooks' stables were injured. Problem was, he didn't figure on the wind and the kind of fire created by hay and stubble and the kind of wood they build those rickety barns out of. The fire spread quickly, and by the time he called in the alarm, two horses were dead, and he was scattering fifty or sixty others to save their lives."

"What's going to happen to him, Wally?"

The big man guzzled the last of his cola and let a huge ice cube lodge between his teeth and his cheek.

It affected his speech. "Back to Joliet," he said. "He confessed early this morning, and he'll be behind bars by Monday night. But the sentence will be tougher this time. He'll get five to ten, I'm sure."

"Ouch."

"Yeah, it hurts. I'm embarrassed, disappointed. I kind of feel sorry for the kid, even though I know I shouldn't. He's old enough to know better."

Wally grew emotional and almost couldn't speak. "That's not it at all," he said disgustedly. "The problem with Clarence is the same problem his brothers and his mother had. The problem is me. I never had time for 'em; I was the justice freak. The city couldn't function without Wally Festschrift out there makin' things tough on the murderers. The thing is, I never thought anybody at home minded. I thought hollerin' and screamin' and hatin' one another was a typical family. It was the way I was raised, and I figured I turned out all right. I was honest, hardworking, knew right from wrong. I knew I was no socialite, no fashion plate, a bit odd, a slob—all right, I knew. But it was only when the family started fallin' apart that I knew."

Wally was distressed. "You can't blame yourself," Margo said.

He glared at her. "You know, Mar," he said, "I wanted to talk to you because I've got some hard questions, and I've always found you and Philip to have some pretty good answers. But that wasn't a very good start. You know good and well that I have to take most of the blame for the rotten shape my family is in. Now that I'm a Christian I see it even more clearly.

151

"The worst part is, it's now that I really want to make good. I want to give of myself. If there's one thing that sticks out in my new life, you know, it's that God did so much for me. He personally gave so much for us that that's what we should want to do.

"There's nobody left for me to give myself to or for, you know what I mean?"

We nodded.

"Clarence. Hey, I lost Clarence years ago, and I haven't been able to reach him since. Especially not since I've become a Christian. He doesn't want to hear about that at *all*. And the older three? They tolerate me. They give me little shots now and then, compare alimony payments, say they should have learned from my example instead of following it. That kind of stuff."

"But you can still try to communicate with them."

"Sure. Sure."

"And you can be of help to Ethel. She'll be lonely. She'll probably need you more than ever. This must be a difficult time for her."

"Nope," Wally said, shifting his weight. His shirt was wrinkled, and his tie was greasy and spotted and creased. He was sweating, and his hair was matted. "That's the other part of my problem. That's why Clarence and his stupid move and his certain conviction and sentence were only 'partly' what Ethel wanted to talk to me about."

I looked at my watch and knew that within an hour and a half we would have to be ready to go to the wedding. I told Wally. "You guys can go ahead and get changed, and I can still talk to ya, OK? Luckily, I'm ready."

152

Chapter Sixteen

"You sure you wanna take time to keep listening to me?" Wally asked.

"Are you kidding?" Margo said. "Wally, we're your friends."

He looked at her thoughtfully and for once didn't react immediately. Slowly, deliberately, he said, "Ya know, Margo, I believe that. And you may be the only ones I got."

"C'mon, Wal," I said, "how 'bout Earl and Larry and Bonnie?"

"Bonnie knows I'm a slob. Larry only knows me professionally. Maybe respects me, but he isn't my friend. Earl, yeah, we're friends, but it's hard for me to talk to Earl about, you know, personal things. He worked for me once, ya know. And then I worked with him and for him and against him and now for him again. We've got a good relationship, I think, but not the kind that can take me cryin' on his shoulder. I don't wanna do that, you understand?"

We nodded. "You want to cry on *our* shoulders?"

"I never felt more like cryin' in my life. I won't, though. Learned a long time ago that men don't cry. My boys never cried, 'cept the second one when his wife divorced him. You know, none of my kids have remarried after their last divorce. Five guys in the family and we're all bachelors. But, yeah, he cried and said he didn't care what I thought about him cryin'. Almost made me cry, and I didn't chew him out for it. In a way I was kinda proud of him, and I worried about myself that I'd grown so hard over the years.

"He's the only boy I got who's workin' right now, 'cept Clarence, and he's not really workin' 'cause he won't ever be back to those barns again. The number two son, he runs a delivery service, works day and night. Wishes he could find another wife or get the old one back, but he knows it's over."

"That *is* sad," Margo said. "All those broken marriages and homes and families."

"We're not much for family reunions," Wally said. "All we do is head for the house, Ethel puts on a crock pot of barbecued hamburger meat, and we each bring a pack of buns and a six-pack. At least we each used to bring six-packs. Now just the boys do. I been tryin' to quit drinkin' beer, you know, since I, you know."

"Since you became a Christian, Wally," Margo said. "You can say it, can't you?"

"Yeah, but you know what I mean."

"I know, but it's good for you to get comfortable talking about what you did and what God did for you, and what happened to you—the transaction, the event."

"I know," he said, but he averted his eyes. "Anyway, we had one of those little reunions a coupla weeks ago, and the boys all show up with their beer and buns, and they're watchin' me, ya know, to see if

154

I'm gonna break down and have a beer. Which I hate to admit I did. I mean, I been tryin' to quit, and I never drink it in public and hadn't drank anything in front of the wife or the boys in a long time.

"But at my apartment, sometimes I get the hankerin', and I go out and buy like two cold ones, not a six-pack, 'cause I know how I'm gonna feel afterward anyway. But I'll stop somewhere and get a couple of sixteen-ouncers and nurse 'em during a ball game on TV or somethin'. Then I feel all mellow, but guilty."

"Wally," I said, "did anyone tell you that you had to give up beer to be a Christian?"

"No, not really. But I never see anybody from church or you guys or any other Christian people I know drinkin'. I guess I just know it's part of the package."

"It's not *really* part of the package, you know."

"Yeah, I guess I know that. I know it doesn't mean I'm not really a Christian or that God doesn't love me or that I lose anything. I just know that every few weeks when I get tired and need to really relax, I just can't talk myself out of it, even though I feel guilty when I stop to buy it, and I feel worse when it's gone. Every time, I vow I'm not gonna do it again, and then I do it anyway. At least I didn't do it in front of anyone, but I lived in fear that you might drop in on me and notice the cans in the trash or something."

We smiled. "We wouldn't have said anything," I said.

"Yeah, you probably wouldn't have," he said. "But what would you have thought?"

"We never thought about it," Margo said. "You

155

never drank that much in front of us anyway. I didn't know if quitting drinking beer should be your first priority as a new Christian or not."

"I guess it kinda was, but I haven't done too well."

"But you feel you failed in front of your sons?"

"Well, it was that first hot day the weekend before we got onto the vagrant case."

"I remember it," Margo said. "We were actually sunning at the beach."

"Yeah, well, that was the kind of day it was," Wally said. "Me and the boys are all sittin' around the portable TV lookin' for some early season baseball or somethin' and wishin' we had the neighbors' pool. They got one of these Olympic-size jobs that they've never invited any of us to fall into since they moved in.

"But anyway, we're sittin' there gettin' hotter and hotter by the minute as the sun rises in the sky, and Ethel's laughin' at our crazy stories and memories, 'cause we've softened up since when we used to holler at each other all the time. We just remember the fights and embellish 'em and get her going, and we can forget that we're not really a family anymore, and that Mom and Dad are divorced and none of the boys are married.

"My sons are all guzzlin' the brews, ya know, and I gotta admit it starts lookin' pretty tasty. And when Ethel, who sips a beer maybe twice a year, pulls a frosty can out of the tub of ice and pops the top, I really start gettin' the taste. We men have all got our shirts off by now, and we're sweatin' and burnin' from the sun, but we don't wanna go inside and sit in front of a fan. There's nothin' like sittin' with the guys

156

and swappin' tall tales in front of the TV on a hot day.

"Ethel swallows down a few big gulps and sees me eyeing the can with that longing look of mine, and she hands it to me. I hesitate for a second and look at the guys, and they aren't even paying any attention. I take a long draw on that can, and it goes down smooth and sharp against the thirst at the same time. I go to hand it back, and she just nods at me like she wants me to finish it, so I throw it down in a few more swallows.

"But when I look up, the guys are all lookin' at me sideways as if they're disappointed or something. I don't know what to say. They kinda set their cans down and go back to watchin' the game, and I feel like I've disapointed 'em somehow. I mean, I didn't know what I was supposed to feel.

"I was angry at 'em, I'll admit that. I wasn't angry with Ethel. She knew I wasn't drinkin' much any-more, but she doesn't know any better than to hand me a cold one. She thought she was doin' me a favor; I coulda refused it. I can't blame anybody but myself. But here are my own sons who have, all but the sec-ond one, made fun of me gettin' religion, and they're livin' off the government or pickin' up odd jobs or shovelin' manure at the race track, and they wanna look at me like I did something wrong?

"I wanted to holler at 'em, to call 'em hypocrites, everything. But then I realized that that was what they were thinkin' about me. That I had come on kinda strong with my new life. I never told 'em I was gonna quit drinkin', and I agree with you, Margo, that it's not the number one thing on God's hit parade of worries about Wally Festschrift, but I couldn't shake the guilt. I knew that right or wrong, they expected something different from me because of the way I'd been talking to them the past several months. I wanted to ask 'em what their problem was and why they were judging me, but I knew that just because they had given me a hard time in the past, they *were* watching me to look for differences.

"They had to notice a change in my language. It wasn't easy, especially hanging around kids who learned swearing from me, but I was pretty good about it. And you remember that I quit smoking almost immediately. I didn't talk too much about that, though, because that wasn't something I even felt strongly about.

"I wasn't praying to quit or thinking that it was a terribly filthy habit; I didn't even know that business about the body of the Christian bein' the temple of God or however that goes. I just lost my craving, and smoking didn't seem right or necessary. But I wasn't about to start preachin' about it, because if I use that body/temple idea, somebody's bound to bring up my weight, which is something I haven't seen change yet. In fact, without smoking, if anything I eat more."

By now I would have guessed that the second part of Wally's bad news for the day was that Ethel told him he had really offended his sons by showing some inconsistency by breaking down and enjoying a beer on a hot day. But I was wrong. He got back on track by summarizing his reunion story.

"But I guess those days are past," he said.

"They're past?"

"No more reunions. At least not with all of us. Just me and the boys, I guess."

"Ethel doesn't want to have them anymore?"

"Doesn't think it would be appropriate under the circumstances."

"With Clarence back in prison?"

"Nah! She's gettin' married."

We stared at him, speechless. Ethel, married? She had let him know in no uncertain terms that she was not interested in getting back together with him, but he had never given up hope. And he certainly never suspected she was interested in anyone else.

"To top it all off," he said, "she reaches over and puts her hand on mine while I'm polishin' off the last of my chocolate shake at the Round the Clock. Now Ethel's no spring chicken. She's almost a female version of me, only she's a little better preserved. No siren, but I like to touch her arm or hug her when I see her or put my arm around her and remember. I always wanted to get back together. I've tried to hold her hand, you know, and she never lets me. And that's all right. Only now, she gently touches my hand, and I almost choke. I mean, I know she's about to give me the second barrel of this bad news shotgun, but why does she want to touch me after all this time?

"I wanted to grab her hand and hang on, but I didn't have the nerve. And she says, 'Woofer, you said once that we oughta get hitched again, and I said yeah, we oughta.' I was dyin', trying to put together this change of gear with whatever the bad news was supposed to be. 'But you read too much into it, remember?' she says, and I nod. 'But I did agree with you. Only I don't think we should marry each other. I think we both need to be married again, but not to each other.'

"Now my fingers are frozen to the metal container in one hand, my other hand's sweatin' under hers, and I'm wishing she would squeeze it and tell me she's been wrong and that we belong to each other. But no, she's layin' somethin' else on me, and I'm not gettin' it yet. I say, 'Ethel, it's you or nobody. I don't want anybody else.'

"And she says, 'I know that, Woofers, but I do.' And I can't talk. I mean, what am I supposed to say to that? My throat gets tight, and I force out, 'You mean you've got somebody already picked out?' I thought I was in a nightmare. I know she had never given me any reason to be hopeful, and she was always careful to shut me down if I started assuming too much, but marryin' somebody else? How could she do that to me?"

Wally's shoulders sagged, and his elbows rested between his knees. His feet were crossed at the ankles, and all his weight was on the front edge of the couch, giving the frame a true test.

"So she tells me, 'No, Woofers, it isn't that I have somebody already picked out, but somebody already has me picked out.' Now, I know this is crazy, but for some fool reason, I was still thinkin' she was tryin' to tell me some good news. I says, 'I know somebody's got you picked out. I do.' 'I know,' she says, 'but so does somebody else, and I've agreed to marry him.'

"I don't know what I looked like at that point, but I'll tell ya, I could have broken down and cried. It was like she kicked me in the stomach, but if I had known what was coming next, I would have thought that

160

news was mild. She says, 'I'm marryin' Slim Stepanik.' I don't know how I even got it out, but I says, *'Slim Stepanik! You're kiddin'!'* "

"Who is he?"

"Who *is* he? Only one of our best friends from the early days of our marriage. He and his dad ran a little grocery store on the west side in the late forties, but when the neighborhood got bad and the old man retired with a coupla heart attacks, ol' Slim takes the profits and borrows enough to buy an eight-lane bowlin' alley, the Kegler Palace on West Madison, not far from skid row."

Wally got that faraway look that accompanies good memories. "I remember wakin' up Ethel when I came home from work at about eleven-thirty, almost every night before we had kids. She was working at a bank in the Loop during the day, so she'd go to sleep after supper and be ready to go out in the middle of the night.

"We'd go over to the Palace for a steak sandwich with Slim and his wife, Myrtle, who was the best female bowler in the state back then. Averaged almost a hundred and eightly or some crazy thing, not far below where Slim was. 'Course he came by his name honest enough. Was almost six-four and couldn't have weighed his bowlin' average. But he could crank it up, boy. I saw him roll a two-ninety one night in his own place. Record stood for years till one of the pros came in and rolled a perfect game in fifty-nine or so. Ol' Slim spared in the first and then struck out, eleven straight. What a night. Mixed doubles. Myrtle had a six-hundred series that night, but Slim's two-ninety got all the attention. You know, those silly people had Ethel and me actually bowlin' in a league for a coupla years. I never averaged more than a hundred and forty, but I loved it."

Wally fell silent and appeared almost ready to cry. "I'll never forget when Myrtle died," he said. "Some kinda complications with her first baby. Lost the kid, too. Slim didn't bowl after that, and even though we kept in touch with him, it was never the same."

"You never suspected anything was going on between Ethel and him back then?"

"Oh, no. Nothing was. I would have known. He was totally dedicated to Myrtle, and after she died he kind of rebounded, probably a little too fast, and married one of the bar waitresses in his place. They were divorced inside two years, and he never married again. We kept in touch a little over the years, but not much."

"When did Ethel start seeing him?"

"That's just it; it wasn't that long ago. She ran into him. She was shopping or something downtown and found herself in the neighborhood. So she stopped in to see if he was around, which he always is. He lives over the bowling alley. Well, he was glad to see her and she hadn't changed a bit and blah, blah, blah, and then he starts with the how-come-a-good-lookin'-woman-like-you-never-got-married-again routine, and she gets to gigglin', and he asks her out just for fun. Here it is a couple of months later and they're gonna get married. You'll love this part. He tells her they gotta break the news to me and get my blessing. They want me at the wedding. That'll never happen."

"I'm sorry, Wally."

"You're sorry? How do you think I feel? I don't

have anything against Slim. He'll take good care of her. But if she wanted an old, run-down, no-account, divorced man from her past, she already had one."

Chapter Seventeen

Wally turned and stared out the window, obviously through talking for awhile, but not entirely finished with his story. "We're going to get changed for the wedding, Wally," I said. "OK?"

He nodded, and we slipped out. As we dressed, Margo and I hardly communicated except to look at each other with bewildered expressions, wondering what in the world we could say to Wally to console or counsel him. Did he really want advice, or just sympathy? It *was* a story that demanded sympathy, but somehow we sensed he needed more than that.

When we returned to the living room, he was standing by the window with his arms folded and his back to us. He turned halfway around to acknowledge our presence, but then he turned back to the window. When he started talking again, we had to edge close to hear him.

"I knew it would never be the same," he said softly. "I guess I just hoped and prayed that maybe it could even be better. I've been tryin' to help the boys get work and tryin' to make up for all the years when I was working and didn't have time for them and only talked to 'em when I was threatening them because they did something stupid. I thought I was gettin' somewhere with them, because when we get together at the house once in awhile, it's been better.

"At least up until a few weeks ago, that is. I haven't heard from any of 'em since. Usually I hear from one of them every few days, but no. They don't need or want anything from their old man anymore. They never acted like they did, even though I knew all of them were having a rough go of it."

"You think you disappointed them that much?" Margo said. "I can't imagine it was that bad. Maybe they expected something different from you than drinking beer again, but would they write you off just because of that?"

"I don't know," he said. "I would have thought they'd be relieved to see it, in a way. I think they were put off by my different lifestyle. I mean, it wasn't as totally different as it maybe should have been, but let's face it, I spoke differently, I didn't smoke, I was nicer to them, I was helpin' them, I was nicer to their mother and more interested than ever in gettin' back together, and I never missed an alimony payment. They probably thought I was off booze completely, too. Maybe it threw 'em."

"Maybe. Or maybe they just knew about their mother and Slim, uh—"

"Stepanik."

"Right."

"Maybe," Wally said. "All I know is, I feel like I've lost my sons and my wife, even though I guess I lost her when we first got separated years ago. You know, I never really believed it was over with her until today. Never. Not from the first time she walked out on me. She walked out on me the first three times, and I begged her to come back, and she always did. When she kicked me out a couple times, I almost didn't go, but I didn't wanna create a big scene and have one of my co-workers have to be assigned to come and roust me out.

"Then, by the time she wanted a separation, I was good and ready for one too. But not for long. We were gonna try it for six weeks. Four days later I'm on the phone, beggin' and makin' promises, you name it. She let me come back after two weeks, and three days later said she would leave if I didn't. We haven't lived together since. That's been a lot of years. We were separated for probably two and a half years before she finally filed for divorce. Cost me a lot of money over the years, but I never minded.

"There were years when I treated her rotten, mostly because I was hurt. And I'd let the payments slide awhile, knowing she was having a tough time raising the boys. They never gave me the time of day from the time I left home until they graduated from high school. Then they expected all the stuff the other dads were givin' their kids. Forget that noise. I told 'em so, too. Told 'em, 'You make it on your own just like I made it on my own.' Know what my oldest said to me then? He says, 'Yeah, I hope I'm as big a spectacular success of makin' a mess of my life as you've been.'

"That hurt, but you know what? He's made a bigger mess of his. Bankrupt once, divorced twice, and sued for alimony."

"You can't totally blame yourself," I said. "He's an adult."

Wally turned and faced me with the same look of

frustration he'd flashed at Margo when she first suggested that. "I don't buy it," he said, his voice thick with emotion. "I was a lousy husband and father, and I got no one to blame but myself. What I can't figure out is how come now that I'm getting a few things together, feel better about myself, feel I've got something to offer my family, they're gone. I guess turnabout is fair play. I wasn't there when they needed me, and now they're not there when I need them."

"They need you too, Wally," Margo said.

"I know that, and you know that, but do they know that? And their needing me is just what *I* need! I really feel like I've got something to offer them but I'm not going to get a chance to prove it."

"Are you sure it's not just temporary?" I suggested. "Maybe you surprised them a little or disappointed them, but they'll realize it and want to get back together with you."

Wally returned to the couch and picked up the empty Coke glass, swirling the two dying ice cubes around in the bottom. He looked at the glass and then imploringly at Margo, and she jumped up to get him a refill. He was as close to tears as I'd ever seen him, and I wondered if he'd break down with Margo out of the room.

But he waited with the rest of his story until she returned. "My boys may want to forgive me," he said. "But I don't know if I can forgive them."

"For what? Being disappointed in you? Or for saying so?"

"They're gonna stand up for Slim at the wedding." He shook his head slowly. "I don't know if I can take that. I'll tell you one thing. I won't be within a hundred miles of the wedding that day."

"They're actually standing up for Slim?"

"Yeah! Can you beat that? I don't understand it. They hardly ever knew the man. In fact, I don't remember that they ever knew him at all. But I guess they're so glad their mother found an alternative to me, a man with a business and a nice guy, that they're gonna show their support or something. They couldn't hurt me more deeply."

And finally, for the first time since we'd known him, and maybe for the first time since he'd been an adult, Wally Festschrift broke down and sobbed. He buried his face in his hands, and his shoulders heaved. Margo embraced him, but he turned away. She didn't give up on him though, and she sat next to the big man with her arm draped around his shoulders. He would tell me later it was the most meaningful gesture she could offer him, and it convinced him we were truly his friends.

I caught Margo's eye and pointed at my watch. If we were going to be on time, we'd have to be in the car within a few minutes. Allyson's church was way up north off Route 41. Wally rubbed his eyes hard with his fists and dragged a broad palm across his mouth.

"I can't go to a wedding today," he whispered. "I just can't. They won't miss me. I never knew Allyson except to say hi to her in the building now and then. Think they'll understand?"

"If you're sure, Wally," Margo said. "I'll just tell them you couldn't make it and that you're sorry."

He nodded. "I might catch a little nap here if you

168

don't mind. When Ethel was finished with all her news, I felt drained. I just sat there staring at her, slowing putting down the empty shake can. She was rubbin' my hand, but I didn't like that anymore, and I pulled it away and just put my hands in my lap.

"I couldn't move; I couldn't talk; I couldn't take my eyes off her. She was sayin' something she thought was nice and comforting about me not havin' to pay alimony anymore or something, but I didn't hear it. Finally I just pulled out a twenty and left it on the table and stood up, pulling my coat on. She says, 'Woofers, you gotta tell me if we got your blessing?' I says, 'Ethel, don't ever call me Woofers anymore. And yeah, you got my blessing. Anything you want, you got. I'd never stand in your way.' But honestly, I don't know how I got that to come outa my mouth, because I didn't mean a word of it."

He kicked his shoes off and rolled to his back, putting his feet up at the other end of the couch. He grunted loud and put his hands behind his head, closing his eyes. "Maybe later you'll tell me how all this fits in," he said.

"We don't have all the answers," Margo called from the front closet where she was getting down a light blanket. "All we can tell you is that God knows and cares and still loves you," she said, floating the blanket down over him and shutting the drapes to keep the sun from his face. "Just ignore the phone and the doorbell."

Wally didn't respond. He was breathing heavily and, we assumed, would shortly be sound asleep.

In most weddings—Margo's and mine included—

the bride is so radiant she makes the groom look either anemic or invisible. In Allyson's wedding, the same was true. The groom would have done better to send a stand-in. Anybody paying any attention to him missed the best part of the show—the bride.

Allyson's red hair was long and luxurious beneath her veil, and she glowed. When her tiny German father walked her nervously down the aisle, he kept getting ahead of her. She deftly kept him with her without making a big show of it. After he responded "Her mother and I do" to "Who gives this woman?" he misfired twice in trying to raise her veil, so she raised it for him and kissed him on the cheek. He blushed and looked as if he didn't know where to go or what to do. Mrs. Scheel finally reached out and tugged him into the pew next to her.

Margo and I sat on the right, two rows back and a couple of places to the right of Earl, Larry, and Shannon, so I had a perfect view of them as we watched the ceremony. Larry looked very somber and tired. Shannon looked tired too, and I got the impression they had talked until much later than they should have after their hectic day and evening the day before.

Occasionally, Shannon would turn to Larry as if to get his attention, and it was obvious he could see her, but he never turned to acknowledge it. Maybe she wanted eye contact, maybe a smile; maybe she wanted to tell him something. But he never turned to her, never said a word to her. And as far as I could tell, he never touched her during the entire time.

I didn't know what to make of that. My mind was racing, wondering if he had tried to talk her into letting him come back to the agency, and maybe she had said no and wanted to make sure that didn't hurt him too much.

Margo pointed out Bonnie, who beamed when Erin walked down the aisle. Bonnie was lovely in a cream dress with dark brown accessories. Her row was dismissed before ours and Earl's, and when she passed she bent to whisper loudly, "Where's Wally?"

Earl shrugged and looked back at us and we told her, "Couldn't make it. Not feeling up to it."

Later, in the parking lot, the six of us decided we should get together for dinner, since—as Wally would say—we were all dressed up with nowhere to go. I told them Wally was at our place, without going into detail, and suggested they come over for a couple of hours since "it'll be that long before we'll be hungry again."

Margo ran to a phone to let Wally know, but when she returned she said there was no answer. "We'll find him," Earl said. "He can't be too many places. Maybe at his wife's place or at the office or at his apartment. If he's feeling better, I know he'll want to join us."

Margo and I looked at each other. "He was lying down when we left him," she said. "And I told him to ignore the phone and the door, so he could still be there."

We all came traipsing down the hall, trying not to be too noisy for our across-the-hall neighbor. I carefully unlocked the door and tiptoed in. Wally was sound asleep on the couch, lying on his stomach with his face toward the back of the couch.

There aren't a lot of alternatives in our apartment for entertaining a half-dozen people, so we all just sat quietly and whispered as Wally slept on. But no matter how quiet you try to be, of course, when the body heat makes the room temperature rise, the muffled murmuring tends to eventually pierce the subconscious mind.

"Hey, hey," Wally said thickly, rolling over and rubbing his eyes. He squinted as Margo opened the drapes and didn't look terribly thrilled to see Earl and Larry and Shannon and Bonnie. Come to think of it, he wasn't that thrilled to see Margo or me, either. "What's shakin'?"

We asked if he was interested in dinner.

"Am I interested in dinner?" he said, sitting up. "Does a duck have lips?" He stood and motioned with a nod that I should follow him into the kitchen. On the way he slowed as he passed Bonnie. "Bon! You look great!" She nearly fell off the chair. "Listen," he said in the kitchen, "I'm not done talkin' to you and Margo, hear?"

I nodded.

"It's not that I think everything has to go right for me because I'm a Christian now or anything like that. I do wonder what God's tryin' to do or tell me or whatever, but I may wonder that the rest of my life. It's just that the whole change He's made in me has to be for a purpose, and if it's not for puttin' my family back together, for allowin' me to somehow start giving to people I took so much from over the years, what's it for?"

"Well, why don't you plan on coming back over after dinner, and we can talk some more. But I can tell you the reason for the change in you is to evidence the greatness of God. That's why we're changed. To be like Him. When people see the change in you, God gets the glory."

"Ouch. All that makes me think of is what the boys must have thought when they saw me drinkin' that beer."

"I don't know, and neither do you, for sure. But you were there and I wasn't, and if you think they seemed disappointed, maybe they were. But on the other hand, maybe it gives you a reason to talk to them about it. Be honest. Tell 'em how you feel. Tell them God *can* take that desire away too. Then trust Him for it if that's what you truly believe He wants you to do."

Wally nodded slowly, but more to acknowledge that he'd consider it than that he agreed. "My biggest problem is I'm full of the wonderful stuff God has given me, and now I want to do some giving. I can't do much in the church because I'm not trained. I give money, sure, but everybody does that."

"Don't be too sure."

"Well, if they don't—ah, anyway, I want to give something back. I know you can't earn God's favor, and I'm not tryin' to. I just want to do what He did a little. I want to give. I want to give me, Wally Festschrift. Isn't there some one or some thing I can give myself to? I thought it would be to my wife and my boys, but now I think I've lost 'em both."

"Shall we join the others?"

"Might as well. If nothing else I want to badger Larry into comin' back. I'm tired of playin' games about it. Either he's in or he's out, huh?"

173

Chapter Eighteen

Dinner was not at all as wonderful as we might have hoped. Seven is just too many to be able to enjoy real togetherness and conversation. We had some fun, especially teasing Earl about his standard order, two fresh bananas and the biggest steak in the house. But in the end, I think most of us wished we had just stayed at our place for pizza.

Bonnie excused herself shortly after dark, saying she hated to drive at night and that the later it got, the more she dreaded it. I was hoping Wally would volunteer to run her home, to give himself a break. But Margo jumped in and admitted that she wasn't feeling well and would be happy to drive Bonnie's car as far as our place, if Bonnie could get the rest of the way herself.

I tried to get from Margo what was wrong because I hadn't realized she was ailing, but she wasn't saying much.

With just five of us left, there weren't any distracting side conversations. Earl worked the subject around to Larry and the case he might help us with. "I don't want to put any pressure on you," he said. "But if you're not happy where you are, and if *both* you and Shannon—and that's very important to us, Shannon—would be happier back here, let's go to the office and talk it over."

Larry looked at Shannon for what seemed to be the first time all night. I may have missed a glance earlier, but I don't think so. He had ignored her at the wedding and at dinner, even though they sat next to each other. I didn't know if they were feuding, if they already knew what each other was thinking, or what. They smiled at each other now, and that confused me even more.

"There's a bit of irony here, Earl," Larry said. "You see, Shannon is a couple of steps ahead of me. All we did this morning was talk about it, and we're at a very confusing point. We don't know what to do."

"*He* doesn't know what to do," Shannon cut in. "I have very definite opinions. Only he doesn't believe me."

"I sure don't."

"You gonna keep us in suspense all night?" Wally said. "Or are you gonna tell us which one wants to come, and which one wants to stay in Fort Wayne?"

They pointed at each other, which made everyone laugh. Earl paid the check, and we rode back toward the office. Shannon insisted that she be dropped off at the hotel. "I just can't take another long night," she said. "I'll be worthless tomorrow. Anyway, Larry can represent my position, whether he agrees with it or believes me or not. Whatever he decides will be all right with me, as long as he doesn't base it on how he *thinks* I feel rather than on what I told him all morning. Promise, Larry?"

175

He nodded unconvincingly and kissed her goodbye.

So it was just the four of us at the office, and we were down to the nitty-gritty. Wally was impatient. "Forgive me, Earl," he said, "but can I recommend that we get on with it? I don't wanna be talkin' and talkin' about this psychological baloney. Let's tell Larry the whole story and find out if he wants in."

"That would be all right," Earl said carefully, "but it's not quite that simple. I have to know whether Larry wants in—as you put it—*before* I can tell him the whole story. I wish it were otherwise, but it isn't. It's not that I don't trust you, Larry, but you *are* a newspaperman, after all."

"Not according to my wife, I'm not," he said. "She thinks I'm a detective, born and bred. That I'll never be happy until I'm back in the game."

"And what do you think?"

"I think she has me figured pretty well. But I don't think she knows herself too well."

"See what I mean?" Wally grumbled. "This sounds like a quiz from the *Ladies Home Journal.*"

"Let him talk," Earl said, not too kindly, apparently tiring of Wally's complaining.

"I know what you mean, Wally," Larry said. "But you have to understand that this is not an easy decision. Last night I left here wondering if there might be a reason to leave Fort Wayne, get out of journalism, and get back into detective work. But I knew beyond a doubt that Shannon would be terrified by it. You remember the situation with her case and what a nightmare that was."

Wally nodded.

"Well, we get back to the hotel, and she tells me she knows what I'm thinking. And she proceeds to prove it, right down to my worrying about her and how she won't be able to handle it. And she picks up where she left off last night with her argument that she has to grow up and get back into life and quit babying herself, and how I have to do the same. All of a sudden I find myself arguing her points and her arguing mine."

"What's she sayin' now?" Wally said. "That you should come?"

"It's better—or worse, as the case may be—than that. She's convinced I should find out if you'd take me back, and if so, I should quit by phone and let her go back to Fort Wayne and handle everything. She would sublet our apartment, get a U-Haul trailer, get us packed and loaded, drive here, look for an apartment, look for a job for herself, and get us settled while I'm getting my feet wet."

"Then do it," Wally said. "What more can a guy ask for?"

"Not so fast," Earl said. "Larry's not sure she's being realistic."

"That's a mild way of putting it, Earl," Larry said, smiling. He grew serious quickly. "The fact is, I wonder if she's flipped out."

"Did you tell her that?"

"Yes."

"What'd she say?"

"She assured me she hadn't, and that if she felt she was on the edge, she would tell me. If she couldn't handle my being back in a dangerous profession and

177

her being back in Chicago and reliving some of the terror, she said she'd tell me."

Earl scratched the back of his head. "Doesn't sound irrational to me," he said. "But her offer is mighty generous."

"I know, but I'd feel guilty about letting her do all that."

"Wait a minute," Wally said. "I don't wanna get into any details, but I gotta tell you from personal experience that if I'd made that offer, I wouldn't wanna be denied the privilege of making good on it. Now don't look so puzzled, Larry. I know what I'm saying. Think about it. If she starts with all those chores, she'll know right away if she's gonna be able to handle this. The living in Chicago and worryin' about you will seem easy after she's spent a couple weeks doin' all that stuff a couple of hundred miles away."

"But what if she's only doing it to please me, and she isn't sincere or doesn't know herself well enough to know her true motives?"

"There you go with that psycho-babble again. I must be gettin' old. C'mon! She's in her thirties, and she's lived with herself from birth. Maybe you oughta introduce her to herself."

Larry smiled sympathetically. "I hear what you're saying, but I also feel Shannon is a very complex person. If I'm worrying about her worrying about me, I'm not going to be very effective."

"You lost me," Wally said, "but I think you should take her at her word. What else can you do?"

"Even if I did, should I quit a responsible position

at the paper without showing up in person? Quit by not coming back from vacation?"

"If they can get along without ya for two weeks," Wally said, "why can't they keep rollin' without you at all?"

"We *do* have a problem there," Earl said. "I'd be surprised—in fact, astounded—if the case we want to talk to you about is wrapped up in two weeks. So, in deciding on this one, you're at least deciding on a leave of absence."

"I wouldn't do that. I'd rather resign by phone and mail. I'm high enough on the totem pole that I don't make that much difference anymore. I guess that's why Shannon has seen through my phony enthusiasm and satisfaction."

"You know," I said, "Margo had to deal with trauma similar to Shannon's. In her case, her life was threatened. It may not have been quite as mysterious as Shannon's danger, but it was traumatic anyway. Her own mother wanted her killed, her family broke up—the whole bit. She came back from Atlanta to live in Chicago and had to face surroundings and people that reminded her of some very painful days. You remember her case."

"Do I remember it?" Larry said, incredulous. "Do you remember my role in it?"

"You had several," Earl said.

"But the big one—when U.S. Attorney Hanlon approved your request to have me put in jail in the same cell with that hitman, Salerno."

"I remember that," Wally said. "And I wasn't even in on that case. I just read about it later. A classic.

That's the kind of thing that would be involved in this case."

"Wally!" Earl scolded. "Please."

Wally held up both palms in apology and surrender. "You gotta tell him sometime, boss."

Earl turned to Larry. "Where are you, kid?" he said.

"Half-tempted," he admitted.

"It's your decision. I must say, I tend to agree with Wally that letting Shannon follow through with her plans will be the best test you could give. If she's sincere, and if it's going to work out, she'll be able to handle all that. I know you hate to dump it on her, but it wasn't your idea. It was hers. She offered. She really wants to. And she may need to, Larry, for her own therapy. Philip's right, Margo came through her problems a stronger person. And it was *she* who became a detective, not just a detective's wife. Imagine what Margo must have gone through in the early days, carrying a weapon and dealing with murders and murderers."

"She still goes through it now and then," I said. "But she has become a whole, healed person."

"And you think Shannon will too?" Larry asked.

We all nodded, but Earl cautioned, "No guarantees. And remember, the best voice for your wife's side is your wife, and she's in bed. All of us want you to come back to the agency so bad we can taste it."

"You do?"

"We do, but I shouldn't have said that. I really shouldn't have, because that shouldn't have anything to do with your decision."

"You're kidding. You just *made* my decision by telling me that."

"Shoot," Earl said, genuinely disgusted with himself.

"It's all right, Earl," Larry said. "Let me tell you a quick story and you'll see why. There's a guy at the paper who goes by Toots. I don't even know his real first name, but he's Toots Fallon. He's one of these unbelievably talented, but condescending and cocky, young, upwardly mobile professionals who makes everyone above and below him sick. He has succeeded, with his insensitivity, in alienating most everyone.

"But the problem is, he's made everyone competitive with him and with one another. I can hardly take it anymore. I don't care who is above or below me, who contributes more to the front page than the feature page, or who has a summer place or a boat or three cars or more money or more potential. I miss the camaraderie, the fun, the sense of family and belonging. I want to be where people want me, not where they size me up and decide whether I'm a threat or not. I want out of there so badly."

"We *do* want you, Larry," Earl said. "And you'll always be family here. But you have to make your decision based on what's best for you and Shannon. We'll understand totally either way. No pressure."

"Yeah, there's pressure," Wally said. "I won't understand if you don't come!"

We all laughed, and it was just what we needed right then. "You don't have to decide tonight," Earl said. "Take your time."

"But you won't tell me about the current case until I decide, right?"

"Right."

"And if I decide against coming, you won't tell me about it at all."

"Right again."

"That alone is enough to make me decide."

"Don't let it be."

"Oh, I won't. But there is one other thing."

"Go."

"I feel like a real pagan in this crowd."

None of us spoke. He had broached the subject and put the ball into play, lobbing it into our court, and now he saw it dribble past the end line. None of us even took a swipe at it. So he continued.

"I used to get the religion pitch from Philip all the time, and I took great comfort in the fact that I wasn't the only one who felt it was better to leave well enough alone. You've-got-your-beliefs-and-I've-got-mine was my philosophy. As long as Earl could stand up under the gentle pressure, so could I.

"Now, Philip, I know it's not religion. We've been over and over that. And I'll admit that you never pressured me or preached at me or badgered me. But you did come after me in your own humble, subtle ways. It's what makes you you, and I respect that. I never told you off, and I never would, but you can see how it's a different issue now.

"Earl, both you and Wally have come after me a bit in your letters. That makes Shannon real nervous, and it makes me nervous too. I don't begrudge you your beliefs, as long as you respect me and mine, or my lack of 'em."

"We'll go easy on you," Earl said.

"Oh, don't be afraid of me. I know enough about your relig—ah, beliefs to know that telling other people about it and trying to convert them is what you're supposed to do. But I do want to be clear about how you're going to treat me and what you'll think of me if you can't bring me into the fold. Will I never be fully accepted as part of the team? Will I feel like an outsider? Will I be the sinner among the saints?"

"You will always be family," Earl said. "Can we never even ask you to church?"

"Ask all you want. I'd be disappointed if you didn't. But don't take it personally if I refuse too often for you. And don't give up on me. Just don't judge me."

"How about tomorrow?" I asked. "Will you and Shannon join Margo and me?"

Larry smiled and shook his head in mild amazement. "Why not?"

"You tell us to back off if we come on too strong," Earl said. "And remember, we never bring it up because we think you're inferior to us, or because we think we have something over you. We care about you."

"I know you do," Larry said. "That's why I want to come back."

"Is that your answer?"

"Conditionally."

"Here we go again."

"No, it's just that I can only commit myself to this one case. If it's obvious that Shannon can't handle it, I'll try to find other work here in Chicago or somewhere else. I'll be burning the bridge at the newspaper, and I wouldn't want to go back there anyway."

"When can you tell me whether it's permanent or not?" Earl said.

"Two weeks from today, whether this case is over or not."

"It won't be."

"Really?" Larry said. "Tell me about it."

Something told me Wally and I were not going to be finishing our earlier conversation that night.

Chapter Nineteen

Margo was still feeling queasy from dinner the night before, so she stayed home from church Sunday morning. She assured me she'd be OK by dinner time, when Wally was to join us so we could come to some conclusion from the previous day's discussions.

Larry called me early and informed me that Shannon had already left for Fort Wayne. "She doesn't mess around," I said.

"She's really into this. I don't know what to think."

"Margo's not well this morning; you still wanna go to church with me?"

"Uh, I think not, Philip, if you don't mind."

"It'd just be the two of us."

"Divide and conquer, huh?"

"You know better than that."

"Yeah, sorry. I think I'll just relax this morning, if that's all right."

"Whatever you say, Larry. It's great to have you back on the team."

"On probation, you mean."

"We're on probation," I said. "You're not. We know what you can do. Shannon is our parole board."

He laughed. "Mine too," he said. "Hope I'm pardoned from the corporate jungle."

As much as I love my church and the people, and as much as I appreciate the pastor and the music and all that, I have to admit I feel out of place in church alone. I felt distracted and eager to get home to my wife. It wasn't that I didn't benefit from going, but I sure wished she could have been there.

Margo was much better, but not hungry, when I returned, so her big turkey dinner was going to be wasted on just Wally and me. We suffered through. "I like Earl's old church," Wally said. "I'll bet he's glad to be back up here for that alone."

"I didn't know you were going with him today," Margo said.

"Neither did I until early this morning," Wally said. "I think he was tryin' to get Bonnie and me to the same place for some reason. Fortunately, she couldn't come, or she didn't want to, anyway. Boy, I hope he's not tryin' to matchmake us."

Margo laughed. "Wally! Haven't you noticed what Bonnie's like when she's around you? She's enamored with you!"

"Baloney! She thinks I'm a slob, and she's right. She's kind of a classy lady in her own perfumy sort of way. We don't fit together any more than night and day."

"You should have seen her when you complimented her yesterday! I thought she was going to faint."

"When did I compliment her?"

"About her outfit or something, remember?"

"You mean when I said she looked great? That was

no compliment; that was a shot. What I really meant was, why couldn't she look like that in the office every day. Anyway, I had just woke up!"

"She *does* look nice in the office every day, if you'd just notice. But yesterday she looked better than nice, she looked great, and you noticed. Admit it."

He waved Margo off. "I have no interest in an older woman, as nice as she might be."

"Wally! If she's older than you, it couldn't be by more than two years. And at your advanced age, that's a small percentage!"

"Gimme a break; I didn't come here to talk about Bonnie. I came to talk about me."

"I know," Margo said carefully. "And if you really want friendly counsel, I need to tell you that that might be part of your problem right now."

Wally stared at her warily, his mouth full. "Meaning?" he mumbled.

"You're feeling sorry for yourself, and—"

"Of course I'm feeling sorry for myself! Don't I have a right once in awhile? Doesn't anything make a person qualify for a little self-pity?"

"Sure, but—"

"But not this? Not losing your kids and then your former wife to one of your old best friends?"

"Yes, but the prob—"

"The problem, Margo, is that you're not understanding me. I'm not just being selfish. I really want to be able to serve God, and I can't think of a better way than to give myself to my family. Now my chance is gone. You know what our pastor preached about a couple weeks ago? That verse in the Old Testament that talks about the man who troubles his own house inheriting the wind. I don't even know what that means, but I can tell you I don't want it, whatever it is. But the fact is, I have troubled my own house. Now I'm in a position to do something about it, but there's no chance."

"We can only do what we can, where we can," Margo said.

Wally looked frustrated. "That's profound," he said. "But I'm not. You wanna try that one again?"

"Just that you can only do what you can do," she repeated. "If one door of service is closed to you—which I'm not totally convinced of yet—then look for another."

"What do you mean, you're not convinced yet? What do I have to say to convince you that even if I hadn't disappointed my sons a few weeks ago, and even if my wife wasn't marryin' Slim Stepanik, I lost my family years ago? I was the reason. I blew it. I missed my chance."

"But you're going to talk to your sons, right? About the very incident you're so worried about. Who knows what might come of that conversation? And do you realize that if you react calmly to this new marriage, as painful as it is, you could someday be instrumental in leading both your wife and your old friend to Christ."

"I'm not as idealistic as you are."

"You mean you don't have enough faith yet? I wouldn't either, if I hadn't seen two old professional cops come to Christ because of the hesitant, almost incoherent witness of two young people."

Wally put his fork down, sat back, and smiled at Margo. "You've always been hard to argue with.

188

Have you found that, Philip?" I nodded. "You're a special lady, Margo," he added. "I'm still skeptical, but I gotta tell you, this is the reason I wanted to keep talkin' to you two."

"To us two?" I said. "I haven't offered much."

"That's true," he said, winking. "But that's always true."

"Anyway," Margo said, "we're not finished. I just want you to consider for a minute that you might fail with your family."

"Consider it—?"

"Hear me out. It's a very real possibility. But think of the other people in your life you can give to. I think your need, your desire to give, is wonderful and God-given. It's a perfect reaction—like you said—to what has been given to you and done for you. But there are more people in your life than your family; we all need you."

"What can I give *you?*"

"Yourself. And you do, every day. Until you started feeling sorry for yourself."

"And now I'm a burden."

"Close," she said, but she smiled.

"So, what have I got to give you?"

"Your cheerful, happy, upbeat, optimistic, earthy self," Margo said. "You don't have to fake it. And we'll understand moodiness the day your wife gets married. Or disappointment if you're not successful in reestablishing a relationship with your sons. But we need you, Wally. You're a miracle of God, and we need the encouragement of seeing Wally, the genius, doing his thing. Who knows what impact you could have on Larry and Shannon and Bonnie?"

189

"That's just it, Margo. I want to make a difference to them, but I feel like there's nothing I can do but talk to them. I want to be able to show them somehow that I'm willing to give myself for them, so they can get an idea what that means. You and Philip being so generous with me in giving your time and your concern really helped me see what Christianity was all about. How can I show them if I can't even pull my family together?"

"I don't know," Margo admitted. "But I know that if you're willing and available, God will show you ways."

The next morning Earl, Wally, Larry, Margo, and I entered the second floor of the Schaumburg office of the Illinois Department of Law Enforcement. It was a fairly warm day, which means that Earl wore his lightweight pin-striped suit, Wally wore his trench coat without the lining and no suit jacket, and Margo wore a sweater-vest outfit.

Larry, as had always been his custom, wore construction shoes, faded blue jeans, a flannel shirt, and a sleeveless insulated vest.

"Ain't you hot?" Wally asked. "Why can't you dress like Philip with a button-down shirt and slacks? I'm not sayin' you need a tie, but—"

"Just want to be ready for action," Larry said. "I haven't worn this outfit since I left. Brought it along just in case." He rubbed his hands together and tried to suppress a grin as he surveyed the computer technology Earl was explaining.

"I want each of us to learn how to use this stuff,"

Earl said. "That way there'll be no slowdown or stoppage just because the right person is unavailable."

"No way," Wally said. "I can't even type, let alone worry about one of these monsters."

"I was thinking particularly of you, Wally," Earl said. "Since you can't be on the street in this operation, you and I will be here more than anyone. I'll teach you."

"That'll be the day."

"It's not that difficult."

"Gimme a break."

"You'll be enjoying it by this evening."

Wally shook his head, and Earl began recapping the case as it stood to that moment. We'd all heard it before, some more recently than others. When he finished, Earl said, "Larry, you've heard it, but you've never responded to it except to say that you wanted to be involved. Give me an outsider's—that is, a newcomer's—view of what you heard."

Larry had a way of speaking softly but earnestly, using his hands a lot, and staring anywhere but into anyone's eyes when he was addressing the group. He edged forward in his chair and spread his knees so he could fold his hands between them. They didn't stay there for long, but when he was good and comfortable he stared at the floor and began. He made us all wonder how we had gotten along without him. He was brief, analytical, summarial, and organized. All without notes.

"Seems to me," he said, "we have three main objectives in this order of priority: One, find Johnny Ray Robinson, a.k.a. Willie Banks. Two, find the leak in the Chicago Police Department's Internal Affairs

Division. And three, bust up the illegal fencing operation."

"I agree," Wally said, " 'cept for one problem. Robinson's safety is top on the list, but you may have to find the leak before you can get close to him. And you may have to infiltrate the fencing ring before you can find the leak."

"So the priorities are reversed," Larry said.

"Yeah, well, the method might be reversed, but I can't quarrel with your order of importance. Obviously, the man's life is tops, if we're not too late already. Anybody here think we're gonna find this man alive?"

We all shook our heads except for Earl. "I still maintain that if they'd killed him, they'd have made hay with it already and used him as an example."

"He's still an example," Wally insisted. "If he's alive, he's living proof that even if you're given a new name and location and identity and career, you can be found and snatched from your family, leaving everything in turmoil. You can be sure if we don't find him soon, we're gonna find a dead man."

"I know," Larry said. "But I sure hope you're right, Earl. I don't know why they're keeping him alive, unless he's been abducted by somebody other than the ones who killed the first two. But why would he have been?"

"He wouldn't," Earl said. "I'm not ruling it out completely, because we have to stay open to all possibilities, but I think we have to proceed under the assumption that the same people who murdered the first two informants are the ones who have Johnny Ray now. So, where do we start?"

"Any leads at all on Johnny Ray?" Larry asked.

Earl responded by swiveling around in his seat to face the console keyboard. He turned on the electricity and gave it a few seconds to reach maximum power. Then he punched in the details of the missing person—name, address, aliases, former occupation, where last seen—everything.

What appeared on the video display terminal within the next few minutes had been mostly composed and dispatched by Earl in the first place, but now it was coming from the National Crime Information Center in Washington, D.C., and appeared in staccato narrative style. It was the story we had just heard from Earl, along with several warnings of dire consequences for anyone reading, transmitting, or disseminating any of the information illegally or without classified security authority.

"Leads?" Earl asked. "Zip. There is, in essence, an underground all-points bulletin out for him."

"Those terms are contradictory, aren't they, Earl?" Margo asked.

"Normally, yes. But obviously we can't put out a standard APB on Johnny Ray Robinson without every newsman in the country picking up on it. If his abductors don't want to publicize his kidnapping, we don't either. When they get ready to go public, he'll probably be dead. Of course, not even they want it to appear that policemen did it. So, this APB is only on the crime network. It ties together covert teams like ours, all working toward the same goal but in contact only by computer and otherwise basically unaware of each other."

"It's exciting," Larry said.

"It's also dangerous," Wally said. "I don't like it. I like to know who I'm workin' with, be able to look 'em in the face and tell 'em what I got and find out what they got. Know what I mean?"

We nodded. "But you can see how much more dangerous that would be in this situation, can't you, Wally?" Margo asked.

"I guess."

Earl said we had to plug in the name, social security number, and other pertinent personal information of everyone on the task force. "I'm calling it Operation Baseball," he said. "And I'd like to get all our information transmitted to the central computer before Bubba gets here."

"Jasper Buchanan's coming here this morning?" Larry asked.

Earl nodded.

"Wonderful," Wally said miserably. "One of my favorite people."

"He may be by the end of this," Earl said. "Anyway, you said you wanted to be face-to-face with your colleagues."

"Yeah, sure. Just tell me how you named this case."

"You can't figure it out?"

"Should I be able to?"

"Of course. They always have special meanings. And an old pro like you?"

"Hm. Give me a minute."

"I have it," Margo said.

"So do I," Larry said.

"I don't," I said.

"Me either," Wally said. "But if you let one of

these punks spill it before I figure it out, I'll never speak to you again."

"Here's a clue," Margo said. "Ernie Mays."

Larry laughed loudly.

"I get it now," I said.

"I don't!" Wally said. "And no more clues. Oh, OK. Mays, Banks. That's Robinson's alias. You took Willie Mays's first name and Ernie Banks's last. Not too tricky, Earl."

"Tricky enough to trip you up without help from a young woman," Earl deadpanned.

There was a knock at the door.

Chapter Twenty

Due to years of training and apparently some close calls in clandestine operations, Jasper "Bubba" Buchanan moved back two steps after knocking and squinted into the room for a familiar face as I opened the door.

"Bubba!" Earl called out in a friendly tone, and the big black man was introduced all around. He appeared to be Wally's age, but there were major differences other than color. Buchanan was a classy, conservative dresser, shedding a black wool overcoat to reveal a charcoal two-piece suit, a pale blue shirt, and a darker blue stick-pinned tie.

He was a tall, broad man, only a few pounds overweight, and jowly, with high cheekbones. He had small eyes that might have been beady had it not been for their pale brown color, and his salt-and-pepper hair was between cuts. He wore a ring on each long and almost delicate hand, and I had to wonder how he handled the mean-looking, snub-nosed weapon strapped to his ribs inside his suit jacket.

Buchanan was pleasant enough during the introductions, but he was not a happy man. He eyed us all warily and scowled when Wally offered an unenthusiastic and deadly silent handshake. Without a word, Buchanan accepted the chair Earl rolled over to him, then sat and looked expectantly at Earl.

Earl did a quick rundown of everyone in the room except Wally, explaining who we were, how long we'd been with him, and what he assumed our roles would be in the investigation. Bubba reacted without expression until Earl got to Wally. Then he interrupted in a voice that seemed too soft for the size of the man.

Earl was reminding Buchanan that Wally would have to remain behind the scenes because he was too well-known among Chicago cops. "There's outside work for Festschrift," Buchanan managed huskily. "I've got bad news."

"Like what?" Wally said. "You runnin' this thing now, or what?"

Buchanan pursed his lips and looked disgusted. He turned to Earl. "Doesn't your assistant know that I'm the pivot man on this operation?"

"Of course," Earl said. "C'mon, Wally, give the man a chance."

"A chance to what, slap some wrists when he finds out who's been killin' his informants? No thanks."

Buchanan straightened. "You know, Wally, I had hoped it wouldn't come to this in front of the people you work with, but if that's the way you want it, that's the way you'll get it. I don't know what your problem is. I've always had nothing but respect for you and your work. I knew you'd be cleared when you got in trouble with the department, because I knew you'd never do anything underhanded. That's why I was always on you to become an IAD man. You'd have been perfect for it. But you—"

"But I never thought you guys did enough to the ones you did catch. I hate a bad cop as much as anybody, but with you guys it was always by the book, by the book, by the book. Nobody ever suffered the way he should have."

"Wally! It was never *our* job to mete out justice to these men! Our job was to ferret them out, present evidence against them, and bring them before either the inside or outside review committees or before a court of law."

"And how often were they prosecuted for crimes that a civilian would have gone to jail for?"

"I don't know."

"Of course you do! You know as well as I do that what happens to bad cops is that they get suspended or fired or sometimes have to pay fines. That's it. You have to be a real bad guy to go to jail, but if we caught a civilian doin' the same thing, he'd be in the slam so fast it'd make your head swim."

"OK, all right, Wally. You're right. That happens more often than not. Don't you think it eats away at me, too? But don't you also know that the justice part of it is out of my hands?"

"Then how could you stay in it? Why didn't you fight it? Why can't you say to your boss, hey, this isn't right? These people ought to suffer; they ought to go to jail. The guys who killed these cops ought to be put to death."

"You *know* I would settle for nothing less than that."

"Do I?"

"Every day I do just what you've been suggesting, Wally. I fight, I argue, I tussle with the brass. They tell me to just keep bringing the bad cops to justice and to let the city or the state or the feds worry about the sentences."

Wally shook his head, almost as if in resignation. "I know it can't be all your fault, Bubba," he said. "But you can also see how I couldn't be part of it. I think you should have authorized your guys to do a little justice of their own, 'specially when they caught one of those creeps red-handed."

"You mean like roughing them up in the squad car on their way downtown? Or taking them out into an alley somewhere and administering the only sentence they may ever receive?"

Wally nodded, staring at Buchanan.

"Yeah, I know how you feel, Wally. And don't think there weren't times when I would have liked to have done that work myself. But I have to tell you, I'm surprised to hear you still feel that way, now that you've got religion. Or is that just another rumor? What I'm hearing today sounds like it's coming from a man who still has a lot of bitterness and vindictiveness in his heart, not to mention a lack of understanding for me, a man who's trying to do his best under impossible circumstances."

Wally's face lost its color. He was speechless. To bail him out of an obviously embarrassing situation, Earl cut in. "What's the bad news you said you had, Bubba? The news that provides outside work for Wally."

Buchanan was having trouble getting back on track. He didn't seem to be a man who enjoyed verbal sparring, especially with someone he respected but could neither understand nor reach. "Yeah, uh, the news is this. I've been studying the reports of the investigation in Tallahassee, and I don't like them."

"So you want me to go down there and double check interviews by local detectives?" Wally said. "Sounds challenging."

"It'll take more than one person," Buchanan said, "and I'm surprised no one else has noticed the discrepancies in the findings down there. Wally, I can't think of anybody better than you to head that up."

"It's not that we didn't see the discrepancies, Bubba," Earl said. "We hadn't really gone over the reports in detail yet. I can have them printed out from the NCIC network."

"Probably should," Buchanan said. "Did you see what I saw in them, Earl?"

"I can't say I was ready to assign a couple people to run down there, but I know the local guys didn't turn up anything of value."

"That's just it, Earl. I think they did but that they—and most everyone else who has read their report—missed it. There are some very revealing findings there, findings that should be followed up."

"And you, crime detection wizard that you are, found them," Wally said, "even though no one else did." His comment was dripping with such sarcasm that it made all of us, even Larry, turn and glare at him. It seemed so out of character, especially when he had just been put in his place about his new faith—or "religion," as Jasper Buchanan had called it.

No one spoke, so the attention was turned back to Earl. It seemed we always waited for him to make something out of disorder or stalemates. Even Buchanan looked appealingly to Earl.

"I think it's a good idea," he said. "Wally, I'd like you to plan on getting down there as soon as possible and taking Philip with you." And when Wally made a face and shook his head, Earl added, "And I'd like to see you in the other room for a moment."

A few minutes later, Earl emerged alone and asked that Margo and Larry and I step into the other room with Wally. Earl stayed in the outer office with Buchanan.

"Earl tells me I'm making a fool of myself," Wally told us. "That I'm not giving a good cop the benefit of the doubt. He tells me that Bubba's logic should have blown me away even before his shot about my religion did. And he said that Bubba *is* a crime detection wizard, and that if I wasn't embarrassed for myself for not having found what Bubba found in the Tallahassee report, Earl was embarrassed for himself, anyway."

Wally looked glum, staring at the floor and speaking softly, but still in a rapid-fire monotone. "I told Earl I would apologize to Bubba if even one of you thinks I was out of line. So, what do you think?"

We looked at each other. Finally Margo spoke. "Earl's right," Margo said. "You want specifics?"

Wally shook his head. "How about you two?"

Larry shrugged. I nodded. "That's all I need," Wally said, and we followed him out.

Wally took Bubba Buchanan off to the side and spoke to him in low tones, gesturing earnestly. When it was over, Buchanan was smiling and apparently kidding Wally. They shook hands.

"The basics are these," Bubba resumed when we were all back together. "I smell a rat in Tallahassee.

None of our men were out of the state the day Robinson was abducted."

"How do you know there was IAD involvement at all?" Larry asked.

"You mean from the beginning?"

"Right."

"There were so few people who knew where any of our informants had been moved or what identities they had received, there had to be a leak at a very high level. Frankly, we have narrowed it down to four people, none of which know we suspect them. The problem is, of course, that they were so carefully screened and are professionals of such high reputation and character that Earl and I together have ruled out each of them."

"I don't follow."

"Well, you know how you say, 'All right, it *has* to be one of these four, but it can't be this one'? We have each done that for two of the four. According to the two of us, none of them could have done it."

"But one of them did," Earl said. "Unless either Bubba or I did."

"When you say having done it, you mean revealing to someone the whereabouts of the relocated informants," Larry said. "The ones who were killed."

"And Robinson," Bubba said.

"You know for sure that only six of you knew where the informants were being relocated?"

"Fewer than that," Earl said. "I knew none of the new identities and only a general area of the country before the men turned up dead."

"Are you ready for this?" Buchanan said. "*I* didn't even know. I didn't want to know."

"Then who knew?" Larry said.

"Only two men in IAD. The rest of the information was classified, hidden in other documents in general files. Only someone who really knew what he was doing could have discovered it and deciphered it."

"Maybe this is a naive question," I said, "but why don't you put these men on a lie detector or get them involved in this investigation so we can all get next to them and see what we think?"

"We've thought about both, Mr. Spence," Buchanan said, "but these men are so well-versed in the law that they would either not submit to a lie test—knowing that refusal cannot harm them in the least—or they would submit, and if they failed they would know enough not to break down and confess anything. We couldn't use the result in court, and they know it. The only time a lie test is useful is with people who will confess rather than face it or might confess in the wake of a poor result.

"As for involving them in this investigation, we're trying to give them a false sense of security by not involving them. As far as they know, it's a federal matter that we have turned over to the FBI. In fact, only the law enforcement agencies in the towns where the murders and the abduction were committed are involved. And they are looking for the killers and kidnappers of the men under their pseudonyms."

"Except for us."

"Exactly right. Except that we must use only the pseudonym too. I can't emphasize how important that is."

"So how are the four suspects responding to the news of the deaths and the abduction?"

"Just as you'd expect. They're outraged, wanting to be involved, ready with suggestions—you name it."

"But you're not listening?"

"Not without suspicion, I'm not."

"Any one of them stand out as a more likely candidate than the others?"

Bubba looked to Earl, who shook his head, smiling. "Only some that seem less likely than others," he said. "And you can't accuse someone on the basis of a process of elimination."

"You can't?" Wally said. "I do it all the time."

"So do I," Larry said. "But I can see how it's more difficult in this case. What do we do now?"

"We make assignments," Earl said. "The printout will come soon on the findings in Tallahassee. Then Wally and Philip will head down there. Larry and Margo will set up a phony fencing shop. Bubba and I will hold down the fort here."

"Where are we supposed to do this?" Larry asked.

"Close enough to where the cops have theirs that we can figure out who's behind it and what connections they might have—however slight— to IAD."

"And what are we going to fence?"

"You name it. Whatever they want. Appliances, high tech, auto parts, whatever."

"What will our individual roles be?" Larry said. "Margo's and mine, I mean?"

"You'll be partners, with her husband coming back in a few days to be in on the scheme. Or the scam, as the case may be."

"Whew," Larry said. "No time to even think about it."

Earl smiled. "Welcome back to the big leagues, cowboy."

Chapter Twenty-One

Earl called Bonnie and asked if she would arrange for two will-call tickets to Tallahassee at O'Hare for Wally and me. "Get them into Tallahassee early this evening and leave the return flight open," he said. "They're going to pack, and then we'll go to lunch. Then we'll be reachable at the Holiday Inn on West Madison only in the case of an emergency. Have them ring Sandy Gibson's room."

"You've got Robinson's family holed up in Chicago?" Wally asked, incredulous. Buchanan and Earl nodded. "How'd you figure that out?" Earl said.

"You changed the name again, but it's still Operation Baseball, isn't it?"

"Uh-huh," Earl said.

"Only this time you mixed pitchers' names. Sandy Koufax and Bob Gibson. It took me awhile on the first one, but not this time."

Neither Wally nor I had any idea how much to pack, so we each took one suitcase. During lunch Earl explained that we would park some distance from the Holiday Inn and make our way individually to the lobby, heading for a phone or a magazine rack and looking as if we were either guests or belonged there.

Then we were to somehow casually get to the elevator or the stairs and head for suite 405-407, a three-room, end-of-the-hall complex with only one entrance. "Five knocks in about two seconds, with a steady cadence, will get you in," Buchanan explained, demonstrating on the table. "But let's not all show up at once. Let Earl and me get in there and give us a few minutes."

It went off without a hitch, but Margo and I agreed we'd never been in a colder room, regardless of the temperature. Only Johnny Ray Robinson's mother was hospitable. His wife was like a caged animal.

The eldest daughter, a sleepy-looking girl with heavy eyelids, sat staring at cartoons on television and didn't acknowledge anyone else's presence. The middle daughter, wearing a bright red sweater and jeans, lay sleeping on the couch, not ten feet from the loud TV.

"Where's the baby?" Earl asked. Alicia Robinson, a small, thick, pretty, fast-talking black woman in her mid-twenties, wasn't speaking to Earl. She just looked disgusted and turned her back to him.

"She's in the crib," the older Mrs. Robinson told him, pointing to the other room.

Earl felt the need to explain why Johnny Ray's wife was being so hostile. "Mrs. Robinson is rightfully upset," he said, "because we have nothing new on finding her husband."

"And now you're sending someone to Tallahassee," she fired back, turning around to face him. "Which is where me and my girls ought to be."

"You know we feel it's too dangerous for you there," Earl said. "Until we know who took your husband and why, it wouldn't make sense to send you back there."

"In fact," she said, "we won't never be able to go back there, will we?"

"Possibly."

"Don't give me possibly! If we go back there at all it'll be to pack to move somewhere else, so we'll keep runnin' and hidin' and worryin'."

"You're worried more about your own comfort than about finding Johnny Ray," her mother-in-law said softly.

"How can you say that?" the younger woman said. "You see?" she said, turning to Earl again. "You see what's happenin' here? You're turning family against family."

"We were never that close to begin with, Alicia," Mrs. Robinson said.

"Oh, sure! Well, why don't you tell the man everything? That's what he wants, anyway."

"All I want," Earl said, "is for you to give Mr. Festschrift and Mr. Spence here another rundown on everything, just the way it happened before Johnny Ray disappeared."

"And I wanna fight with my mother-in-law, all right? I think you should separate us."

"Alicia," Mrs. Robinson said soothingly, "you need me to help with the girls."

"I don't need nothin', 'cept to get out of here."

"And find your husband?"

Alicia glared at her.

"Well?" the old woman pressed.

"Of course I want to find my husband, if for no other reason than to divorce him!"

"That's the first I've heard of that," Bubba Buchanan said. "You want to talk about it?"

"To all five of you? Sure! I can't think of anything I'd like better! Just get out of here and leave us alone. This is all your fault in the first place. You push a man and push a man until he tells you what you want, never mind about his safety or his family. Then when you realize he's in trouble, you mess up his whole life, family and all, and move him where you don't have to worry about him anymore. Big deal!"

"Can we sit down somewhere?" Earl asked awkwardly.

When Alicia Robinson didn't respond, Mrs. Robinson invited us to the kitchenette, where she rounded up every chair and stool she could. The younger Mrs. Robinson reluctantly joined us, then began telling us what had happened, starting with the conversation.

"I got a call from Judy, the physical education secretary."

"Judy Prewitt."

"Yeah. And she says, 'Willie told me to tell you IAD.' And I says, 'What?' and she repeats it, and I say, 'What's he mean by that?' and she says, 'He said you'd know.' I ask her if she's kiddin' or if he is, and she says, 'No, I don't think he's kiddin'.'"

"What did you think about all that?" I asked.

"I didn't know what to think. I thought about calling her back or calling Johnny Ray and just seeing what he was trying to tell me, but I figured if he wanted to talk to me he could call me himself."

"You weren't worried?" Margo said. "You didn't

put the IAD message together with his former work and wonder if he was in trouble?"

She shook her head. "You got to know Johnny Ray to know why I wouldn't do that. He's a strange man. He does strange things, sometimes just to see what you'll do. I thought maybe it was supposed to be a joke or a funny message, or that he wanted me to worry or something."

"But you and he were carefully instructed not to talk about police work or Chicago or—especially— IAD with anyone at anytime in Florida," Buchanan said.

"I know. That's why I thought maybe he was just trying to mess my mind by having said IAD to the secretary. I didn't know what she was going to do with that message. I mean, it didn't mean nothing to her. She said she didn't know what it meant, and I believed her. I thought he just wanted me to know he'd been right on the verge of saying something he shouldn't have and wanted to see what I'd do."

"I guess I'm kind of surprised you didn't call Miss Prewitt back at the end of the day," Margo said.

"What are you sayin'?" Alicia Robinson challenged.

"I'm not implying anything," Margo assured her. "I'm just putting myself in your place, and I think if my husband didn't come home at the usual time, I'd call the secretary back."

"Well, I did. But it wasn't until a lot later, and he was already gone."

"I don't think I was aware of that," Buchanan said. "All I knew was that you had talked to the secretary only once."

210

"That was true. But I tried to talk to her again. When Johnny Ray didn't come home for supper, I didn't think much about it because he sometimes had things to do at school later. He was coaching some sport, I don't remember what."

"You didn't go to any of the games?"

"Me? No. No interest. He wouldn't have wanted me to, anyway."

"How do you know?"

"He never asked me."

"So you thought he was coaching after school?"

"Yeah. I thought a little about him callin' me with that message, but not much. Not until it was almost getting dark and he still wasn't home. Then I called The Talon, that's his favorite bar. Nobody had seen him. Then I called Miss Prewitt's number again."

"And you talked to whom?" Buchanan asked.

"I let it ring and ring and ring and finally some kid answered it, a white boy."

"How did you know that?"

"From the way he talked. I can always tell. Real whiny, you know." We suppressed grins. "He said nobody was around 'cept the intramural basketball players and that he didn't think Mr. Banks was anywhere. I asked would he check around and he said sure, but he never came back to the phone. I hung up and called back a lot of times and it was always busy. That fool left the phone off the hook for a half an hour or more. Later I called and it rang, but no one ever answered it."

"Then you did what?" Bubba said.

"I called you. I knew I shouldn't call no local police."

"So nothing else happened between the time you thought Johnny Ray was too late getting home and the time you called us?"

"Like what?"

"Any other phone calls for him or anything?"

"Not that I remember."

"Is there a reason the story you're telling us today is a little different than the one you told me on the phone that night?" Bubba asked.

"Different how?"

"I never knew you called the school back and talked to an intramural basketball player."

"Is it important?"

"It might be. Everything might be important. Even your wish to divorce your husband."

"What's that got to do with anything?"

"We didn't know it before."

"It was none of your business."

"But your husband represented the marriage in an opposite fashion."

"In a what?"

"He thought he had a good marriage."

"*He* does! *I* don't."

"Does he know that?"

"What do you think?"

"I think you've probably expressed it to him."

"You got that right, Jack."

"Are you not worried about him?"

"I don't know what I am. I know I can't sleep and that I wonder where he is and whether he's alive or dead, but I can't say I care that much, except for his mother and for his daughters."

"That bad, huh?"

She nodded. "I'm not in love with the man anymore. I have trouble answering the girls' questions, and I know Mrs. Robinson is worried sick, but I'm not going to stay married to Johnny Ray no matter what happens."

"Can I ask why?" Bubba said.

"I don't want to talk about it."

"Don't you see how it's important to us?"

"No!"

"We need to know what was going on in his head before he disappeared."

"Good luck. I never knew."

"Is the reason you don't want to talk about your problems with him because it centers around one incident? Something embarrassing or distasteful to discuss?"

"No. It's been on the rocks for a long time."

"Why?"

"I'd rather not talk about it! And I don't think it's important to you for finding him or for anything else. It's our business, and the sooner you find him, the sooner we'll get it over with."

"So you want us to find him so you can sue him for divorce."

"And alimony. And child support."

"Does he know you feel this way?"

"Probably not, but he should. I've tried to tell him enough times."

"This is going to make things difficult, you know," Earl said. "I don't know what kind of survival instinct he'll have in a tough situation if he knows he doesn't have a wife waiting for him."

"Oh, he'll be all right. Viet Nam prepared him for

everything, he said. Anyways, he still loves his mama and his daughters, and they all want him back. I want him back too, but for a different reason. It don't make too much difference to me. I'll make out either way."

"What are you saying?" Wally asked, an edge to his voice.

"Even if Johnny Ray turns up dead, I stand to see a lot of money."

Old Mrs. Robinson bolted from the room in tears. Margo shook her head. Wally glared at Alicia. "That was a rotten thing to say. We won't be able to live with ourselves if we can't find him and keep him alive. He sacrificed himself for the sake of the law and the good of the police department and the city of Chicago."

"And he paid for that with his family," she said. "I'm sorry, but you're not gonna get me to say that I'd miss him. I don't miss him yet. I get tired of trying to answer the girls' questions, and I get tired of his mother crying all over the place. And I guess I don't wish him any harm, really. I'm just sayin' that money-wise, he's almost better dead than alive to me."

"Do you realize," Bubba said, his face flushed, "that comments like that could make you a prime suspect in a man's disappearance or murder?"

"No," she said quickly and without emotion. "I didn't know that. So am I a suspect?"

"Of course not. I was just saying—"

"You were just trying to mess my mind," she said. "Just like Johnny Ray. Just like all cops, just like all men."

We stood as if one, and that startled her, if only a

little. Wally and I had been glancing at our watches every few minutes, but everyone was glad to be leaving that place. Mrs. Robinson was weeping softly in the living room with the second daughter, now awake, on her lap.

The older daughter was still glued to the TV, unaware of anything else. As we left, we heard the baby crying from the back room.

"That woman is something else," Buchanan muttered on our way down the hall.

"A real piece of work," Wally agreed. "And her attitude complicates the whole investigation."

We took separate elevators and the stairs, but we all headed for the same car down the block. Less than an hour later, I was kissing Margo goodbye at the airport, and Wally and I were boarding a flight to Florida.

Chapter Twenty-Two

Wally spent almost the entire flight alternately chastising himself and apologizing for the way he had treated Bubba Buchanan that morning. I wanted to tell him it was all right and that I understood, but the fact was that it wasn't, and I hadn't. All I could say was, "I'm glad Earl called you on it," but I don't think that made him too happy either.

I was a little surprised he didn't spend a lot of time grousing about Johnny Ray Robinson's wife and how cold she was about him even while he was missing and could be dead. On the other hand, Wally spent whatever time he wasn't using for eating or talking about his feud with Buchanan writing copious notes in his grimy little spiral notebook.

"You wanna switch places with me for landing?" he asked as the announcement of our descent toward Tallahassee Municipal Airport was announced. "I ain't real big on scenery, let alone landings."

It must have been something for the people behind us to see Wally and me trading places. Every move a picture. It was still light out, though, so it was worth the effort for me. I had never been to Florida by air before, having only driven in a few times from Atlanta when I lived there.

From the air I could see the Gulf of Mexico about twenty miles to the south of the city, and the pilot said that in the night you could see the lights of Jacksonville about a hundred and fifty miles to the east on the Pacific coast. But we weren't high enough to see it during the daytime. Wally said he thought we'd have a better chance of seeing Mobile, Alabama, to the west, but I couldn't make it out.

Just as I was asking if he knew what the giant trees were that covered the rolling hills surrounding the city and hemmed in the many rail beds running into town, the flight attendant said they were magnolias and oaks with Spanish moss hanging from them.

The pilot mentioned other landmarks, such as the governor's mansion and some plantations, but I knew we wouldn't have time to see any of them—not even the famous Grove, a plantation built by a former state governor in the early 1800s.

" 'Bout the only thing we'll get to see is one of the universities," Wally said, looking at his printout from the National Criminal Information Center. "Looks like this junior high school is down the street from a high school, which is sort of like an orbital part of one of the universities. Question is, which one?"

He asked the flight attendant. "If it's a big one," she said, "it would have to be either FSU or FAMU."

"I'm not a native," he said, chuckling. "You wanna try those in English?"

"Sorry. Florida State or Florida Agricultural and Mechanical, better known as A & M."

Wally couldn't imagine an agricultural and

mechanical university having a high school and junior high nearby, and after we were checked into our hotel, he proved himself correct with a quick look in the phone book.

In the morning we rented a car and visited Carl Fisher Junior High, not far from Seminole High School, which had a huge campus with a giant mockingbird logo representing its mascot gracing the front lawn. "Why in the world would Seminole High School not have an Indian as its mascot?" I wondered aloud.

"Who knows?" Wally said. "I was wonderin' why you'd name a junior high school after a guy nobody's heard of."

"Just because we haven't heard of him doesn't mean he's not famous down here," I said.

"Ask a student or two," he predicted. "I'll bet not one of ten knows who Carl Fisher was."

"How will you know if they make something up?"

"I won't," he said, laughing.

It was the last laughing he did for several hours. When we entered the Fisher Junior High School and began asking where to find Miss Prewitt, we were stalled so quickly it was almost as if they knew we were coming.

We were hustled into the principal's office, where a Mrs. June Kolesar showed not the slightest intimidation at our credentials. "What makes you think private investigators from Illinois have any business in a junior high school in Florida?" she asked. "How do I know you're private investigators? Anyone would say you look like a cop, Mr., uh—"

"Festschrift, ma'am."

"Festschrift. But you, young man, you could be one of our teachers. Are you really a private investigator? Don't tell me, because I won't believe you. Even if I did, and even if you were from this state and had an office down the street, I wouldn't let you come waltzing in here, expecting to be introduced to just anyone you wanted."

"Speaking of down the street," Wally said, hoping to win her over, "can you tell me why they'd name a high school Seminole and—"

"Because of the Seminole wars early in this state's history, I presume," she said. "Not that hard to figure, really. There were more Seminoles here than in any other part of America."

"OK, fine, but why not call yourselves the Indians or the Seminoles then? Why the Mockingbirds?"

"You mean the high school's nickname? I really don't have time to get into it, Mr. Festschrift. I—"

"We'll go, but if you didn't notice, I'm the curious type, and—"

"The fact is, sir, that the team used to be called the Warriors. Some of the modern day Indians were offended by that, though it had been that way for more than forty years. So they changed their mascot to the state bird. Don't ask me why."

"Can't you tell from my curious nature that I'm the real article? That I have reason to be investigating this case? That I need to talk to these people before they head home because I'll have no way of looking them up?"

"You're an engaging fellow, but you're not going to violate my policies. The local law enforcement agencies are investigating the disappearance of Mr. Banks, and our hope is that no harm has come to him. Our students enjoyed him during his brief stay here, and he was an excellent soccer coach, too."

"What would it take for me to get permission to nose around here a little?"

"I'm afraid there's nothing you can do, short of convincing the local police department that you can be of some assistance. You know that business better than I do, but my guess would be that you will not get far, being from Chicago. I hope the entire trip wasn't wasted and that you gentlemen will be able to do a little sightseeing. Unless you're up to no good, and then I don't care if you head straight back for Illinois."

"I like you, June," Wally said, making her wince. "I like your style. I'm going to have to see what I can do about getting permission to come back here today, because I don't have a lot of time, and I do need to ask a lot of people a lot of questions. I'd like to think your local police department could handle this, but up until now they haven't done much, have they?"

"They've been here almost every day."

"Almost every day since Mr. Banks has been missing, you mean?"

"Yes."

"And has he returned?"

"Mr. Banks? No, of course not."

"Unsuccessful, I'd say."

"Perhaps."

"Even worse, they haven't gotten two stories to corroborate each other."

Mrs. Kolesar looked strangely at Wally. "That's the first thing you've said that makes me think you might have any inside knowledge about this case. But that's not enough. I'll give you the name of the chief investigator here, and if you get police permission to come back, you've got mine."

"A tough bird, huh?" Wally said.

"You'll find Inspector Rogers interesting," she said.

"Impossible to crack?"

"Well, at least impossible to charm. You'll either convince the inspector that you're legitimate, or you'll be in trouble for even asking."

"May I use your phone?"

"No, sir."

"For a credit card call?"

"No, sir."

"Do I remember seeing a pay phone in the hall?"

I nodded.

"For students, faculty, staff, and invited guests only, sir."

"Meaning I can't use it."

"That's right."

"Pay phone near the building anywhere?"

"I wouldn't know."

"Are you angry with me, June?"

"I'm getting there."

"We're leaving."

"Thank you."

"We'll be back."

"We'll see."

"Whew!" Wally said in the car as he headed for a phone booth. "I don't think she likes me."

"Funny," I said. "I think she did. I really do. I

think she'll be impressed if we get back in there today."

"If?"

"You think there'll be no problem?"

"The only problem will be time," Wally said. "Remember, we're in the state capital."

"Meaning?"

"Watch."

He pulled up to a phone on the shoulder of the expressway, then leaned out and grabbed the phone. He could barely reach far enough to punch in his credit card number. "Hi, Bon. You gotta get Earl for me, ASAP. No, nothing like that; we're fine. Hurry, Bon, huh?" He waited.

"Huh? Yeah, have him call me." He gave her the number, then kept the car near the phone so no one else could use it. About ten minutes later, Earl called. Apprised of the situation, he told Wally to hang on while he called the governor. It was more than a half hour before he came back on the line and told Wally that Hanlon was trying to get hold of the governor of Florida. He asked Wally who the inspector was that needed to be made aware of our legitimacy.

"Rogers," Wally said. "Tallahassee P.D."

"Hang on," Earl said.

We waited again. Several minutes later, Earl was back. "Hanlon's office has talked to the Florida governor's office. They're trying to figure a way to get the word to the local police department without giving away our whole plan. Call me in an hour and I'll tell you what to do."

We cooled our heels in a coffee shop, but there was no way Wally could wait an hour. It probably wasn't

222

forty minutes before he called Earl again. He gave me a thumbs-up sign. "All they have to do now is have Rogers call Mrs. Kolesar, and we're in."

"How will we know when that's been done?" I asked. "Earl won't know that, will he?"

"No. We've got to call Rogers in a half hour and see if the call's been made to the school."

Wally must have eaten another four jelly donuts waiting to make that call, but again, I don't think he lasted the full half hour.

"Inspector Rogers, please. Wally Festschrift, EH Detective Agency. There? I don't understand. Well, could you—? You couldn't? Well, how do we get there?" He told whoever it was he was talking to exactly where we were and jotted the directions in his notebook.

He was disgusted as we hurried to the car. "Rogers wants to meet us first," he muttered. "For cryin' out loud, what does he want? To see if we're human beings, or what?"

"Maybe he's a little offended that we're horning in?" I suggested.

"Oh, probably. But if they'd done their job properly, we wouldn't be here. He got an edict or whatever from his governor, so why can't he just call the school and tell 'em it's OK for us to come?"

We waited outside Inspector Rogers' office for nearly an hour, with Wally steaming enough to want to call Earl every few minutes. I was able to talk him out of it. Finally, the door opened and an assistant emerged, asking us to come in. She went out and shut the door, and we turned to face Inspector Rogers.

Inspector Mae Rogers. She could have been a sister to our own Bonnie.

"Well, Miss Rogers," Wally said, unable to hide his surprise.

"*Inspector* Rogers to you, Festschrift," she said, not unkindly.

"Yes, ma'am," he said, waiting for her to sit down before sitting himself and introducing me.

"We were just wondering if we'd been cleared with Mrs. Kolesar at the junior high, that's all."

"That's all? How do you think it makes me feel to have a private agency from Illinois come into my jurisdiction with state-level clearance?"

Wally didn't answer at first. He just looked at her, expressionless. "Let me say this as courteously as you just corrected me on how to address you, Inspector," he said. "I don't guess it matters much what I think or how you feel about it, does it?"

She glared back, defeated.

"The fact is," he continued, "we have it, and we're here, and—"

"The fact is," she said, "I want to know why you're here. Who are you, who are you working for, and what are you looking for? What does Illinois have to do with this? Our records show Willie Banks moved here from Biloxi, Mississippi, to teach junior high. We don't know where he is or why he's gone, or whether he left on his own or was abducted."

"All I can tell you is that we work for the EH Detective Agency in Glencoe, Illinois, and we have been assigned by our boss to come here and interview people who last saw Willie Banks."

"We've already done that. Who is your boss?"

"Name's Earl Haymeyer."

"And he owns your agency, so that accounts for the initials EH, right?"

Wally nodded and raised his eyebrows. "I can see how you got where you are," he said.

"Don't be cute, Festschrift. I'm not a big fan of private detectives, as you can imagine. If you'd ever been a cop, you'd know why."

"Our agency is different."

"The only thing different about your agency is that you somehow have connections with our state government. That doesn't do much for me, either."

"Mr. Festschrift was a Chicago policeman," I said, feeling the need to defend Wally if he wasn't going to himself. "He was a homicide detective sergeant for years."

Wally held up his hand to stop me. He told me later he was afraid I was going to spell out Earl's full credentials too and spill the beans.

"So you think this is a homicide, Mr. Festschrift?"

"I sure hope not."

"So do I, but that doesn't answer my questions about why you're here."

"No disrespect, ma'am, but I don't really have to answer your questions, do I?"

"Not unless you want access to our evidence."

"You have evidence? I wouldn't call the typed transcripts to a couple dozen personal interviews evidence."

"It's all we have, as you'd find out if you read them."

"I don't need them. I've read them."

She was clearly peeved now. "Will you be sharing with us anything further that you find?"

"I don't know. Depends on how nice you are to us, I guess."

"You won't mind having me or someone I assign go along with you? All brothers and sisters under the blue, right?"

"We're not all under the blue anymore, Inspector Rogers, remember? I'm private now, and you don't like that because you're a cop. I don't need your transcripts or anyone from your office tailing along. You've been in that junior high, and you think you've picked it clean. Sad to say, you must have missed something because they've still got a big hole in their physical education staff. We're just going to see what we can see and dig up what we can dig up. You stay out of our hair, and we'll stay out of yours. If we turn up Willie Banks, we'll let you know."

Inspector Rogers pulled a small, hand-written note from under the blotter on her desk, pushed an intercom button, and said, "Get the Fisher principal on the line for me, please." When the buzzer sounded, she picked up the phone.

"June, it's Mae Rogers," she said. Then, reading from the note, she said, "You will be visited by two gentlemen named Festschrift and Spence. They come under our auspices, and you should show them every courtesy you would show us." She looked toward the ceiling. "I'm not at liberty to tell you anything more, June. Thank you. I appreciate it. We'll talk."

Chapter Twenty-Three

It was midafternoon and hot by the time we returned to the Carl Fisher Junior High School. Wally, knowing when to rub it in and when not to, was more than civil to Mrs. Kolesar.

"I suppose you want me to beg your pardon, Mr. Festschrift," she said.

"Only if you think it necessary," he said.

"I do not," she said. "I would do the same again, even though you apparently are legitimate. Now, how can I help you?"

"First of all," he said, "you were so kind with the answers about the high school, I was wondering if you knew why this school was named after this guy, Carl Fisher."

"I do, but it's not a pleasant subject. In fact, if a citizens group wants to get up in arms about using inappropriate names for schools, they ought to fight to have this one changed."

"Really? What was he, a gangster or something?"

"I couldn't speak to that," she said. "All I know is that he is famous for having made Miami Beach what it is today."

"A tourist trap?"

"You said it; I didn't. And they name a school after him."

"What is your mascot?"

"We're the Flamingoes, which is just about as bad. Even the Falcons would have been better, if they had to match the F in Fisher." She stood. "I'd better help you get started. Where would you like to begin, where everyone else does? With Miss Prewitt?"

Wally nodded, and she led us to the gym.

From a distance we could tell that the head of the physical education program was upset at having to let his secretary go for another few hours. The tall, thin, green-eyed, and homely Miss Prewitt wasn't thrilled about it herself. "How many times do I have to go through this?" she asked in the teachers' lounge a few minutes later.

"I don't know, ma'am," Wally said. "This may not be the last time. This is taking the time of a lot of people every day, as you can imagine. The time isn't as important as bringing back Mr. Banks, is it?"

"I guess not, but I'd just as soon put my recollections on tape and let you all hear them at once or as many times as you want. My story never changes, and it doesn't mean that much."

"But someone hearing it might hear something different than someone else," Wally said.

"That could happen on tape, too," she said. "It's just—"

But Wally had already had enough hassle in one day. He interrupted. "If I hear something different from what the last guy heard, I can ask you to clarify it," he said coldly. "I can't do that if I'm reading your comments or listening to them in Illinois, now can I?"

"Illinois? Has Willie, uh, Mr. Banks, been seen in Illinois?"

"No, ma'am."

"Well, I *thought* Mrs. Kolesar said you were from Illinois, and you just now confirmed it, so if he isn't in Illinois, what are you doing here?"

"If he *was* in Illinois, we *wouldn't* be here," Wally said. "Now how about lettin' *us* ask the questions."

"Go ahead," she said, bored. "Surprise me with a new one."

"All right," Wally said. "Anybody ask you if you were havin' an affair with Banks?"

She shot him a double take. "Wha—? You're kidding! He's a black man, and this is Florida! I mean, this may be the 1980s, mister, but that simply does not go down here." She shook her head and touched her neck with her fingers. "I'll admit you surprised me with a question no one had asked before."

"And I'm noting that you haven't denied it," he said.

"Haven't denied what?" she said, giggling. "That you surprised me?"

"That you had an affair with Willie Banks."

"You put down whatever you want," she said. "I don't have to sit here and take this."

"According to your boss and his boss, apparently you do, ma'am. Now could you run down the events on the day of Willie's disappearance?"

"Well, first of all, I hardly knew the man. He's not been here that long, you know. He's funny, a fast-talker, a favorite of the kids. I've called his wife a few times for him when he's going to be late and can't take the time to talk to her. That's it. So this one day

229

he tells me to call his wife and tell her IAD. Now at first I didn't catch that he was saying three initials. I thought he was saying something about something he ate, and I told him I wasn't going to call his wife with some silly joke. He tells me, 'It's no joke, Judy,' or maybe he called me Miss Prewitt, I don't remember. He says, 'Just tell her I said IAD. Can you do that?' Beat that, he asks me if I can do that. I say, 'I can do anything I want. It's will I or won't I.' And he pleads with me to do that for him."

"What do you mean, he pleaded with you?"

"You know what pleading means. He begged me. He said please. He said, 'Please do this for me, Judy. I'll owe you one.' "

"He *did* call you by your first name then?"

"Yeah, but don't make any big deal outa that. It didn't mean a thing."

"How bad was his relationship with his wife?"

"What do you mean? How should I know? Who says it was bad at all?"

"I did."

"How do you know?"

"I don't. I'm askin' you."

"And I'm saying I don't know."

"Why did he have you call her? Why didn't he call himself?"

"I already told you."

"C'mon, Judy. The man has time to tell you the message, so why doesn't he have time to call himself?"

"I wondered that myself a couple of times. You know, when he would say, 'Gotta stay tonight, could you call Alicia and tell her?' And I'd say yeah, but I wondered why he didn't want to call. I wouldn't want that news comin' from someone else who couldn't explain it or smooth it over. That's the only clue I had that their marriage might not be perfect, but then what do I know? I'm not married."

"Was it also true in this case? Should he have had time to call his wife for himself?"

"By the time I got through givin' him a hard time, he could have, yes. But when he first asked me, he was in a hurry, and like I said, I thought it was a joke. Then, by the time I figure out that he's serious, I mean dead serious, he's really almost in a panic. So by the time he got out of the office, I was calling her."

"How did she react, Judy?"

"That's the second time you've called me Judy, sir. Are we having an affair?"

"Not funny."

"Not intended to be. Were you intending to be when you asked me the same thing?"

"Just tell me how Mrs. Banks reacted."

"I don't really remember. I think she was irritated."

"You mean upset?"

"When I'm irritated, I'm upset."

"I mean, was she worried, or did she sound irritated?"

"I said she sounded irritated."

"Why would she be irritated?"

"Why is there air? I still don't know what IAD means, so how should I know why it upset her or irritated her?"

"Was she just irritated that the call came from you and not her husband?"

"Who knows? I suppose."

231

"You're not being very helpful, Miss Prewitt."

"I'm answering everything you're asking."

"Was that the last you saw of Mr. Banks?"

"Yes, sir."

"Did anyone ask about him?"

"What do you mean?"

"Well, when did you realize he wasn't coming back?"

"I still don't know that, do I?"

"C'mon! When did you know he was missing?"

"When the boss asked if I'd seen him."

"When was this?"

"About ten minutes into his two oh-five class."

"Two oh-five. Is that a number or a time?"

"Time. Five after two in the afternoon. He has a class."

"And when he didn't show, the boss came looking for him."

"Right."

"And you told him what?"

"I told him I had seen him before lunch, and that was all."

"You didn't tell him about the message for his wife?"

"No, I didn't even think about it right then."

"So you had no idea that Mr. Banks might be in trouble when he told you to give that message to his wife?"

"None at all."

"When did you think it might have some significance?"

"I'm still not sure. When they started asking me all

the questions, I just remembered it, that's all. Is it significant? No one will tell me."

"Yes, it is."

"Can you tell me why?"

"No, I'm sorry."

Miss Prewitt swore, then apologized.

"Don't apologize for your language, Miss Prewitt," Wally said. "If you want to apologize, apologize for your memory."

"What do you mean?"

Wally pulled a sheaf of computer printouts from his case and began paging through them. "Your story has been pretty consistent up until now," he said. "You've told everyone almost the same story, but now you're fudging on us a little, and I can't figure out why. Maybe it's nothing. Maybe it really is just your memory. Or maybe you know more than you're telling."

She sat staring at him, silent.

"You told the police on two different occasions that Willie told you to tell his wife IAD as if it was a practical joke."

"And isn't that what I just told you?"

"Not quite. You told me *you* thought it was a joke, but that he convinced you he was serious, desperate, in a hurry, and that he would owe you one."

"OK, all right. That's what I think. That's not so much different, is it?"

"You told the police that his wife asked if that was all there was to the message, you assured her it was, she asked to talk to him, you looked for him, and you couldn't find him."

"And I would have told you the same thing."

233

"Would you? You told me you didn't realize he was actually missing until his boss came looking for him at 2:05."

"I forgot."

"It's not been three weeks yet, Miss Prewitt."

"Am I on trial?"

"You may be eventually, if your memory doesn't clear up. Didn't you tell the police that his wife sounded alarmed?"

"Alarmed?"

"That very word."

"They may have put that word in my mouth."

"What do you mean? You mean they asked you if she sounded alarmed by the message, rather than asking *you* to describe how she sounded?"

"That's right."

"Are you sure?"

"No."

"I'm glad, because that would be even sloppier interviewing than I thought they'd done on this case so far."

"I thought you were on their side."

"Believe me, I am. Whose side are you on, Miss Prewitt?"

"I'm on Judy Prewitt's side," she said. "And it's getting a little lonely over here."

"You have nothing to fear by telling the truth, especially if you had nothing to do with Willie Banks' disappearance."

"Give me a break."

"Ma'am?"

"You couldn't possibly think that."

"I worry about your creative memory, Judy. That's

234

all. Did you tell the police that you told Mrs. Banks, in fact that you *promised* Mrs. Banks, that you'd find Willie and have him call her?"

"I may have."

"How did you happen to forget that here?"

"Is it that important?"

"Everything is important. It's important that we find this man before harm comes to him."

"How do you know he didn't leave on his own?"

"Why would he?"

"How should I know? *You're* the one who said he had a bad marriage. Nobody around here knew him well enough to know if he was stable. All we knew was that he taught in Biloxi and moved here. And I knew he liked phys. ed. better than civics, which is the straight course he taught, and I'm oh, so sorry I forgot to mention that before. I hope that doesn't make you think I murdered him and buried him under my garage."

"I'm not amused."

"Neither am I, sir. Anything else?"

"Not right now. Thanks for your time."

"Oh, my pleasure. I've got nothing better to do."

As Wally and I trudged back to the office, I asked him if he really thought she was involved. "Don't you?" he said.

"Not in the least," I said.

"Me either. But I want the word getting around that tough interviews are ahead. And unless I have her misjudged, the word is already "spreading.""

235

Chapter Twenty-Four

Wally was unable to reach Earl that night. The word was that he had left Bubba in charge until Wednesday afternoon, when Earl would return from Springfield.

Neither of us could imagine why he had to return to Springfield so quickly, and we spent most of our dinner hour speculating. Was it something with the governor? Something with his son? I wondered if it had to do with Gail Durning, but not knowing whether Earl had broached that subject with Wally—and not hearing Wally even hint that he knew any-thing—I said nothing.

"Even though I guess me and Bubba have sorta reconciled," Wally said, "I wasn't too crazy about tellin' him all the details about today, but what could I do? He took it all right, I guess."

"What'd he advise?" I asked. "Anything useful?" As soon as I said it I could see I had wounded Wally's pride. It wasn't that he was above advice from an old veteran, but I sensed he was hurt that I assumed Buchanan would have even thought to advise him.

He just shook his head as if he'd never considered such an idea. "Oh, he said something about trying not to alienate the local department, but hey, I know better'n that, don't I?"

I cocked my head. "You *were* a little rough on Mae Rogers," I said.

"*Inspector* Rogers to you, boy," he said, laughing louder than the line was worth. "Hey, know what else? Buchanan said an Ethel called for me late this afternoon, over at the Glencoe office. *An* Ethel, can you beat that? As if there's more than one in my life."

"She showed up in person, you mean?"

"Nah. On the phone. Bonnie told her I was out of town, but she wanted to talk to Earl or to someone who knew where to reach me."

"So did you call her?"

"Tried. No answer at her place. I tried the boys, and none of 'em have seen her or heard from her, but I'm glad I talked to 'em. They didn't want to talk about the marriage, I could tell. I asked them what they thought of it, and they all said the same thing, as if they'd rehearsed it. Glad for her, you know. I says, 'What about me?' And they said, 'What about you?' "

"That must have hurt."

"A little, but I laughed it off. They all sounded, ah, cordial, know what I mean? Like they weren't mad at me or disappointed in me or holdin' a grudge or anything like that. They were even a little excited about gettin' a long distance call from me down here, and they wanted to know what I was up to and all that."

"Did you talk to all four of them?"

Wally shook his head and looked away. He held up three fingers.

"The oldest three?" I said.

He nodded again.

"Was Clarence indicted yesterday?"

He pressed his lips tight, nodding only slightly. "Maybe that's what Ethel wanted," he said. "How's your London broil?"

Later he told me that Bubba had reported good progress on the setting up of our sting operation. Thousands of dollars worth of stolen property was being appropriated from the Chicago Police Department pound and delivered quietly to an abandoned warehouse in Oak Park that had been sold to the city a few weeks before.

"Larry and Margo are looking for the right clothes for themselves and trying to come up with the personas that will fool the victims."

"Hope it works," I said.

"Hope nothin'. It has to. You'll be in on it too, soon as we get back."

I sighed. "Goody."

"They're trying to come up with a front, too."

"Like what?"

"I don't know. Usually your front is dictated by your facility."

"Come again?"

"What kind of building you have limits what kind of phony business you can set up to hide your operation."

"What are they considering?"

"I don't know," Wally said. "I told Bubba that maybe a secondhand store—clothes and appliances and stuff like that—might work. He sounded like he agreed."

"So, how would they attract the attention of the operation the crooked cops are running?"

"By bein' in the area. And one of 'em would have to try to take his car to the phony garage, ask the right questions, have the right stuff showing on the back seat, that kind of thing. They'll be ready for you and Larry to try that 'bout the time we get back."

"You're kidding. That early?"

"They're not messin' around, man. The warehouse will be full and they'll be open for business with phony permits and everything by tomorrow."

Early Wednesday morning Wally was troubled. He had not been able to reach his wife even very late the night before, and he wondered if he should call and have someone look for her. "I'd been sort of hoping that she had good news for me," he said. "Like maybe she was changin' her mind or something, or that she couldn't do this to me. But now I'm afraid if I called the right number, she'd answer."

"Or Slim would," I said.

He pointed at me, wordless.

After breakfast we were back in the office of June Kolesar, principal of Carl Fisher Junior High School, Tallahassee, Florida. Wally was in his glory. He had just showered, as was his custom, but he was already working up a day-long sweat.

He had left his trench coat in his hotel room for the first time since arriving, but he kept his tie and suit coat on, which made him stand out in the hot climate. Now he was poring through a giant stack of continuous sheet computer printouts with the transcripts of all the interviews conducted surrounding the case of the disappearing physics teacher/soccer coach Willie Banks, a.k.a. Johnny Ray Robinson—which we had both been careful not to mention or even allow into our minds during the discussions in Florida.

By now Mrs. Kolesar was resigned to our presence and not a little intrigued with the earnest, slightly sloppy detective and his young cohort. Wally seemed the last person who would know anything about computer forms, but he had a way of digging until he found just the quote, just the description, just the fact he wanted, and then he'd ask questions about it.

"You sure you got time for this?" he said, looking up as several pages slipped loose and billowed out and down to the floor. Of course, since they were all hooked together, it was no major disaster, but I did wonder how Mrs. Kolesar kept a straight face.

"Certainly," she said. "I blocked out some time because you have clearance, and because I want to get to the bottom of this as quickly as you do."

"Did you know Mr. Banks personally?" Wally asked.

"No, sir, I didn't. In fact, I hate to say it, but if someone had given me his name and described him as the new black physics teacher and soccer coach, I don't think his face would have come to mind. But, of course, his photograph was in the papers for several days running, and I do remember having interviewed him briefly before his hiring and then seeing him around occasionally. He was not a noisy or flashy person, Mr. Festschrift, and we do have several young, athletic black men teaching and coaching here."

"So you didn't come to any conclusions when he turned up missing?"

"Just the usual. I wondered if there'd be a story at

240

home that would explain it, as there often is. Usually when a teacher disappears during the school day, he or she is discovered at home, trying to solve some domestic problem. It's a serious offense, but forgivable, and generally a relief. When that kind of situation didn't arise for Mr. Banks, I just got a terrible feeling that harm had come to him."

"Why? Couldn't he have just been under pressure, felt the wanderlust, whatever?"

"I don't know. He could have, of course. But with a wife and three young daughters, a new, secure job, and a seeming sense of adjustment unusual to a new resident—"

"You knew all that?"

"Only from what I read in the papers."

Wally looked back to his stack of printouts and rifled through them again. "From what I read in *these* papers," he said, "there are a couple of people who saw Willie Banks on his last day here who need to be questioned again."

"Because their stories don't add up?"

"The opposite. They come close to corroborating each other, even though they saw him at different times in different places. They're remarkably similar, and for some reason they avoid all the wild speculation that some of these other kids engaged in."

"Like what?"

"Like this girl, for instance, saying she 'just knew Mr. Banks was in trouble because he looked so pale.' So pale? Willie Banks is a very dark man. If he looked pale, we do have a problem. Of course, she couldn't even describe accurately what *he* was wearing, let alone his two companions."

"Who was that girl?" Mrs. Kolesar asked.

"Uh, let's see, Regina Wehmeyer, a fourteen-year-old eighth-grader."

When Wally looked up, the principal was smiling and nodding. "How do the kids say it?" she said, thinking aloud. "A real airhead."

"Says here she's a cheerleader," Wally said.

"Right. Good thing the cheers rhyme."

"Here, now. Here's the kid I wanna know something about," Wally said. "Fifteen-year-old eighth-grader, objective about this to the point of being bored. Told what he saw with no speculation, very clear and direct. He's one of only two who noticed that the taller of the two visitors was white, had sandy, long hair, was late forties or fifty, and wore tan, ankle-height boots and a leather or vinyl jacket that looked too warm for the day. What intrigues me is this kid notices that the guy had a tight, white and green check pattern in his pants."

"But Mr. Festschrift, you have dozens of interviews there, with some that corroborate and some that don't—and most don't. There are more that agree on other things, but how in the world can you determine who's right and who isn't? I was under the impression that the local police had given up hope on the student interviews."

"Tell ya what, June," Wally said, and she caught her breath. "If this guy and the seventh-grader whose account I'll find in a minute here, are—what did you call them? Airheads?—we'll give up on 'em and go to something else too. Fair enough?"

"Names?"

"Lewis Milton." He looked up for a response and

received none. He looked back down and fished through more paper. "And, uh, Joaquin Capilla. Spanish, I assume." Mrs. Kolesar smiled at his understatement. "You familiar with either of 'em? I know you got a big school here."

She stood and reached out to shake his hand. He was startled, but she was still smiling. "Is this good-bye?" he asked.

"No, sir, this is congratulations."

He stood and moved forward, taking her hand in one of his and protecting his papers with the other. "What'd I do?" he asked as they sat back down.

"If you put those two boys in the same category without ever having seen them, but just by reading those printouts of the transcripts of their interviews, you are indeed a detective of the highest order."

Wally tried to suppress a smile. He looked almost embarrassed. Almost. "They're friends?" he said.

"No. They hardly know each other except for one activity. They run in different circles. Joaquin lives in a trailer park. Lewis is what the students here would call a rich kid, but he's also a nerd."

"A nerd?"

"Out of it. Tacky dresser. Concerned only with studies, not with sports or with who's in or out. Serious-minded."

"That's a nerd?"

"That's a nerd."

"And the Cuban?"

"Mexican."

"Sorry."

"That's all right. Joaquin is not a nerd, but he's a

bit of an outcast in his own right. He's a little flashy, a little streetwise."

"Forgive me, ma'am, but what's so impressive about my putting them in the same category? I shoulda known from their names that they're not the same kind of kids."

"Mr. Festschrift, those two are the brightest students who have ever attended this school, bar none. Next year both will be sophomores in the high school down the street."

"But one of 'em is only in seventh—"

"And the other is in eighth. If I had my way, they would be in the high school now. State and national testing have shown that they could compete academically at the college level, and both have appeared on television with the *high school* academic quiz team. What drew you to them in the interviews?"

"I dunno," Wally admitted. "Just lucky, I guess. Seemed kinda easy, though. They were the only two who spoke in complete sentences."

I may have been mistaken, but to me it appeared that Mrs. Kolesar was looking at Wally as if she wondered how he would know the difference. "Both of them are almost straight-A students."

"Almost?"

"Lewis can't stand physical education. Gets a C every time. Joaquin hates industrial arts—has even received D's in it. A's in everything else. Tell me, do their stories match?"

"Not totally," Wally said. "I'd be a little suspicious if they did. But Joaquin saw some things Lewis didn't, and vice versa. Both were very observant and not excited. With their different vantage points and their fairly consistent stories, I guess I was just hoping they were good, smart kids."

"If that's what you were looking for, you hit the jackpot with these two. Would you like to speak with them now?"

"The sooner the better."

"In any particular order?"

"Yeah," Wally said, laughing. "Let's start with the nerd."

"One moment."

Mrs. Kolesar stepped out to speak to her secretary. "I'm sorry," she said when she returned, "Lewis is unavailable right now. Shall we start with Joaquin?"

Chapter Twenty-Five

The brilliant Mexican seventh-grader looked nothing like what I expected. He looked much older, maybe sixteen or seventeen. He wore almost all black—black high-heeled shoes, tight black pants, a shiny black shirt—and lots of jewelry. Rings, bracelets, two necklaces. I hate to admit it, but he's the type of kid you'd be afraid of if you ran into him on the street at night.

"So, Joaquin," Wally began, "we just wanna ask you a few questions about Mr. Banks, OK?"

"You can call me Joe, man," Joaquin said with a heavy hint of his native accent.

"Thanks, Joe, and you can call me Wally."

"I ain't gonna call you nothin', man. I'm gonna answer your questions and get back to class."

Wally smiled and stared at the boy. "Let me tell you somethin', kid," he said. "Just so we both have our cards on the table. I know enough about you to know that you're puttin' me on already. I don't need that. You didn't talk to the local cops like this, so don't pull it on me. I know you can speak English better'n I can; I know you can speak in sentences; and you know you're not under suspicion for anything. So don't give me any hard-guy routine, and we'll get this over with quick, OK?"

Joaquin raised his eyebrows and smiled. "Fair enough," he said. "You can still call me Joe."

"And I think I'd prefer you call me Mr. Festschrift now." Joe Capilla looked surprised until Wally reached over and playfully punched him in the shoulder. They both laughed. "I just want to go over your story once more," Wally added. "Take it from the top."

"All I know is I was coming out of the gymnasium just before lunch, and I see these two guys get out of one of those foreign pickup trucks, the tiny jobs, you know. Big white guy, average-sized black guy, and they look like they're looking for someone or waiting for someone, looking all around the parking lot and moving slowly toward the building."

"Did you talk to them, ask if they needed help or anything?"

"No, they were ignoring me, and I wasn't really close enough to talk to them. Just close enough to see them."

"And they were wearing what?"

"The big white guy had a jacket or sweater on, and multicolored pants. He had long, light-colored hair. Maybe not too light-colored. The only thing I remember about the black guy is he looked athletic and was wearing black, horn-rimmed glasses."

"That's unusual these days."

"That's what I thought. I don't remember what he was wearing, though. Sorry."

"So then what happened?"

"They were heading toward the gym, and Mr.

Banks came out. They immediately stopped and looked around, not really looking at him. And he only looked at them for a second. Then the three of them were walking and talking together but it was almost as if they weren't really together. It was as if they were pretending not to be with each other, you know what I mean?"

"Tell me."

"Well, like Mr. Banks walked right up to them and between them as they turned and headed back to their little truck."

"And they were talking but not looking at each other?"

"Yeah. If I hadn't been close enough, I guess I wouldn't have thought they knew each other or had any business together."

"But it looked like they did?"

"Well, yeah. At first. But when they got near the truck, they all stopped and chatted for a moment. Then Mr. Banks went back into the building."

"Through the gym?"

"Yes, but not the same door he'd come out of. It was one farther south, down by where the phys. ed. office is."

"What did you make of it, Joe?"

"I didn't make anything of it. I went to lunch after that, and then to metal shop."

"Which you hate."

"How did you know that?"

"Which you hate because it reminds you of the manual labor that your father had to do in Mexico to earn enough money to get you to the states, maybe ten years ago."

"Seven years. How did you know?"

"And you had decided from the time you were a child and learned to read so quickly that you were going to study hard and become something other than a manual laborer. And so even though you could do it, you could never enjoy it because of the association that it has in your life. Is your father still alive, Joaquin?"

"No, he died about three years ago. Who told you all this?"

"Anything else about Mr. Banks, Joe?"

"No. That was all I saw, and I didn't think it was important until the cops came around and asked if anyone had seen Mr. Banks late in the morning on the day he disappeared."

"Did the men in the pickup drive away?"

"Yes, but very slowly, around the side of the building. I didn't see them any more after that."

"You know Lewis Milton?"

"Sure."

"Spend a lot of time with him?"

"Not much."

"When do you?"

"Just when the *Academic Bowl* quiz team gets together for a cramming session. He and I have to stick together a little because we're the youngest."

"The older guys get on your cases a little?"

"The older girls, you mean."

"Really? Well, I was led to believe you two were the best on the team."

"We are, but they tease us a lot. We enjoy it."

"But you and Lewis aren't friends?"

"No."

"Are you aware that Lewis's story corroborates yours?"

"He wasn't out there. I would have seen him."

"He saw the same threesome a little later."

"Huh! No kidding?"

"But you two never talked about it?"

"I haven't seen Lewis for weeks, except to pass him in the hall."

"Thank you, Mr. Capilla."

"Thank you . . . Wally."

Mrs. Kolesar was waiting just outside the conference room door, and as soon as Joaquin Capilla was out of earshot, she said, "I think you'll want to get over to the police station. That's where Lewis Milton is."

"You're kidding!" Wally said. "What for?"

"Apparently he thought of something more he wanted to tell the police, so he got permission from his homeroom teacher and called them. They sent a car over to get him and took him to the station."

"That's all you know?"

She nodded. We ran to the car.

"Don't make me get the governor in on this again!" Wally bellowed at the dispatcher in the station house.

"The governor? What're you talking about?" the young man said. "Inspector Rogers is unavailable right now, and that's it. Excuse me."

He turned back to the console to take a phone call and radio a message to a car. As soon as he was free, Wally started in on him again. "You tell Mae Rogers that I want access to this, ah, Milton Lewis or Lewis Milton kid, whatever his name is. And I want it now."

"I told you she was unavailable just now, sir—" and his phone rang again.

Wally tried the door next to the dispatcher's cubicle, but it was locked and had to be buzzed open by the dispatcher himself. And he wasn't about to buzz it. Wally waited until another policeman came through the lobby, and when the dispatcher buzzed the door, Wally hurried through with me in tow.

"Hey, wait a minute!" the dispatcher hollered. The policeman he'd let through tried to grab Wally, but he pulled away and headed toward Inspector Rogers's office. The cop grabbed me instead. "I'm with him!" I said, pulling away as he reached for his gun.

The sight of that weapon so startled me that I almost reached for my own, and I had visions of a gunfight in the police station. Instead, I lurched forward and dove past Wally around the corner, then tripped and slid into the doorway of the room where Inspector Rogers and two detectives were interviewing Lewis Milton.

Mae Rogers looked up and saw Wally standing behind me. She shook her head in disgust. And just as our trailing cop caught up, gun drawn, she said wearily, "Come on in, gentlemen. The fun is just beginning."

Our pursuer holstered his gun before Rogers could see it and moved on down the hall. I stood, red-faced, to enter the room. The phone rang. "Yes," Rogers said. "They're here. It's all right." She hung up. "Did you have to sneak in past my dispatcher?"

"No choice," Wally said. "He wouldn't tell you we were here." She shook her head again. "You're really

Keystone Cops, aren't you?" Wally didn't respond. "Pull up a chair," she added.

We were introduced to Lewis Milton. He sat, long and lanky, with his legs crossed and his bare calves peeking out from under navy blue pants. He wore black oxford shoes, grey socks, a belt about one-fourth the width of his belt loops, a white shirt buttoned to the top, and wire-rim glasses. His hair was greasy but mercifully short.

Mae Rogers whispered something to one plain-clothes detective, who leaned and whispered to the other. They left without a word. "Tell these gentlemen what you told us," Rogers said.

"Well, it's just that I think I saw one of the men this morning that I saw with Mr. Banks the last day he was at school."

"Where?"

"At a car wash, of all places."

"What were you doing at a car wash this morning?"

"My father always has the BMW washed on Wednesday mornings. We go to the car wash on the way to school. Mother has the Volvo washed on Fridays."

"So, which one did you see, the black guy? And how did you know for sure it was the same guy? Workin' in the steam with a raincoat on, probably no glasses—lots of black guys doin' that kinda work."

"Excuse me, sir," Lewis said. "But it was the white gentleman. We were just coming out of the wash, and Father had turned the wipers on. As the window cleared, I saw the tall, white man with the dark wavy hair, only it wasn't as long today as it was the first time I saw him."

"What was he doin' at the car wash?"

"I don't know. I just stared at him because he was wearing the same pants and boots he'd worn before. He was standing outside the window where the guy sits who runs the equipment. I thought maybe he was the manager or owner or something."

"Was his foreign pickup truck there?"

"I don't know. I didn't see it, but then I wasn't looking for it, either."

"Why not?"

"Didn't think of it."

"That surprises me, Lewis. You're pretty observant."

"Thank you."

"Was this tall man wearing a jacket or sweater?"

"No. He was wearing a short-sleeved, Hawaiian-type shirt."

"But you're sure it was him."

"Pretty sure, because of his height, his pants, his shoes, and his hair."

"And the black guy?"

"Didn't see him."

"Would you mind if I asked you about your original version of seeing the two men with Mr. Banks?"

"Again?"

"I've never heard it. Only read it."

"I'm pretty consistent, sir. It won't change much."

"That's all right. Let me hear it."

"Well, I was having my lunch outside alone, as I usually do."

"Why?"

"I just prefer it, that's all. I eat quickly, and then I read. Anyway, a small pickup pulls up not far from where I'm sitting and waits. After a few minutes, both men get out. A small black man and a taller white man, the one I saw this morning. That's when I saw what they were wearing. When Mr. Banks came out of the front of the building, they walked up to him and talked for about thirty seconds, and then all three of them got into the truck, with Mr. Banks in the middle, and they drove off."

"Fast?"

"Not particularly."

"Did you think anything was strange about it at the time?"

"Not in the least. I thought they were friends of his who had an appointment for lunch."

Lewis looked up suddenly, and his eyes widened as if he had seen a ghost. "That's him!" he said. "That's them! That's both of them! You got them!"

The two plainclothes detectives who had left the room soon after we got there had two men in custody and were taking them down the hall to another room. The identification of them as the same men who had allegedly abducted Willie Banks would have to be made a little more calmly, professionally, and officially, but for all practical purposes, the prime witness had just fingered the two prime suspects.

We followed Inspector Rogers and Lewis Milton to the end of the hall, where the suspects were sitting uncomfortably and apparently unwillingly on either side of a long conference table. The taller man was insisting that he be allowed to phone his lawyer before answering any questions. The black man looked scared to death and said nothing.

Inspector Rogers motioned her men out of the room and told one, "You know they are allowed to call lawyers. Just before these gentlemen and I question them, give them that right. They're not under arrest yet. We just want to talk to them. But they don't have to answer anything they don't want to, and they do have the right to have a lawyer present. After you've done that, get scarce. I only want Mr. Festschrift and his friend and myself in the room with them."

When the door was shut on just the suspects alone, Rogers pulled Lewis to the little window in the door and asked him for a positive identification. "Are you telling me that to the best of your recollection these are the men you saw with Willie Banks at your school on the day he disappeared?"

"No doubt about it," he said. "No doubt whatever about either one. Where'd they find them?"

"At the car wash, just like you said," she whispered. "When our guys got there to check out the taller man, the black man was just getting to work. The tall one owns the franchise, and the black man is the manager."

"Hm," Lewis said. "And all this time they were just a couple of miles from the school. Can I go back now?"

"Sure," she said. "We'll have someone take you. We'll be in touch."

One of the detectives carried a phone into the room and reminded the men they got just one call each. "That's if I'm under arrest," the black man said, defiant for the first time. "I can make all the calls I want otherwise."

"Make more than one and I'll see that you're under arrest," the cop said. He came out with the phone a few minutes later. As Wally and Inspector Rogers and I prepared to enter, Inspector Rogers whispered to Wally, "Feel free to lead. They're all yours."

"Why the change of heart?" he asked.

"June Kolesar tells me you're a pro," she said. "That carries more weight than two governors. Let's get to the bottom of this thing."

Chapter Twenty-Six

"You gentlemen wanna introduce yourselves to us?" Wally began.

"No," the big white man said. "We want to know what we're doing here."

"You weren't informed? You weren't told that you were being brought in for questioning in connection with a young junior high school teacher, a black man named Willie Banks? And that you're being questioned because there are people who think they saw you with the missing man on the last day he was seen at the school?"

There was no response.

Wally raised his voice and spoke slowly and deliberately. "Will you gentlemen tell me whether you were informed of that so that I may apologize if you were not?"

"We were," the black man muttered.

"Then let's stop with the baloney about wanting to know why you're here. What's your name, sir?" he asked the white man.

"You have it."

"If I had it, I wouldn't be asking for it, would I?"

Inspector Rogers slid the man's identification documents over to Wally. "Sandy Ashford," he read aloud. "That you?"

The big man said, "Read the description and play detective."

"You're not funny," Wally said. "And you could be in big trouble."

"So could you," Ashford said. "False arrest, among other things."

"I think I know the law better than you do," Wally said. "And we have every right to bring in for questioning anyone who fits your description."

"I'm not that unique."

"Something tells me you are. And Mr. Daniel, is that you?"

"Yes, sir," the smaller black man said. "Lee Daniel."

"You sound a little more cooperative than Mr. Ashford, am I right?"

"Don't count on it."

"Wonderful."

"Inspector Rogers, would you be so kind as to take Mr. Daniel to another room for questioning?"

"We stay together," Ashford said.

"Yeah," Daniel added. "Together."

"You think you're runnin' this show?" Wally said. "Get Daniel out of here. You guys get your lawyers, or what?"

"I don't have one," Lee Daniel said. "Don't need one or want one."

"Mine says it's all right to answer your questions," Ashford said.

"Good," Wally said, as Mae Rogers and Lee Daniel left. "Let's get started."

"Save your breath. I got nothing to say."

"Meaning?"

"Meaning I've never even been over to that junior high school. My former wife and kids live in Georgia, and I have never had a reason to be there."

"Not even for benefits, trying to sell one of the classes on renting out your car wash to raise money, nothing like that?"

"Nothing."

"You know we have someone who saw you at the junior high?"

"I read the papers. Everybody knows the teacher disappeared and that the students thought they saw him with two men, one black, one white."

"And that couldn't have been you and Lee Daniel, because you've never been over there."

"Right."

"Never?"

"Never ever."

"We have a witness who says he saw the two of you with Banks the day he disappeared and that he has no doubt about either of you. He's an honor student, a genius, very perceptive, good memory, rather serious-minded."

"And wrong."

"Where's your tan vinyl jacket?"

"Who says I got one?"

"Just guessing. Could be leather, but I don't take you for a leather man. You're more my kinda dresser, aren't you? Go for something that maybe looks like leather but that doesn't cost an arm and a leg."

"Matter of fact I do have a leather jacket, Mr. Know-it-all. Matches these boots."

"That's what our witness remembers about you."

"I'm sure."

"What kind of automobile do you drive, Mr. Ashford?"

"Three kinds. I do pretty well at the car wash."

"In Florida? C'mon! I was surprised to see one here. Cars don't get dirty here. I haven't seen a dirty car yet."

"But the rich people want the salt rinsed off. I do OK, really."

"So what kinds of cars do you drive?"

"I have a T-bird convertible, a '69."

"Really? Must be worth some bucks."

"I should say it is. At least ten grand. Perfect condition."

"What else?"

"I have a two-year-old Buick four-door with all the goodies, a real gas hog."

"And?"

"A pickup truck."

"Foreign?"

"Yeah."

"Beige?"

"Cream."

"Like the difference between leather and vinyl."

"What?"

"It's just that you care about appearances, Mr. Ashford. Why would you want to be seen with Willie Banks the day he disappeared?"

"Never knew the man."

"Never met him?"

"Never."

"What if I told you he said he knew you?"

"I'd say you were a liar."

Wally stood and smiled at Ashford and at me. "Did you catch that, Philip? The man would call me a liar. He takes his car wash manager with him in his cream, not beige, pickup and drives over to a junior high he swears he's never been at, picks up a man who has not been seen since, and he calls *me* a liar."

"You *are* a liar!"

"And why don't you say that Willie Banks is a liar?"

"Because I don't believe you even talked to him. If you'd talked to him, he wouldn't be missing."

"And you have personal knowledge that he's still at large?"

"How would I know?"

"That's what I'd like to know. Philip, go tell Inspector Rogers that we have all we need from Mr. Ashford."

"What do you mean you got all you need from me? You got nothin' from me. All you're tryin' to do is make Lee think I've broken down."

"Broken down?" Wally said. "You mean you're withholding something, Mr. Ashford?"

"I didn't say that!"

"Then what breaking down is there to do? And what harm is there in telling your accomplice that we have all we need from you?"

Ashford glared first at Wally and then at me as I left. As soon as I stepped into the hallway I could hear Mae Rogers berating Lee Daniel. She was almost screaming at him. "How can I believe you?" she said. "You change your story all the time. You say neither of you have ever been to the junior high, then you tell me that maybe Sandy has been over there a time or two. You're not a credible man, Lee! I can't trust you!"

As I opened the door it looked as if Daniel was relieved for the break. He breathed a big sigh but was on the verge of tears. "We got what we needed from Mr. Ashford," I said.

"Oh, good," Inspector Rogers said, rising slowly. "Stay put here, Lee. I may be back."

"What'd he say?" Daniel pleaded. "What'd he say?"

"Apparently he said enough," Mae told him. "Probably sold *you* down the river."

"He better not have said I got any money. I didn't get any, at least not much."

"What an amateur you are," Inspector Rogers said. "What a weak-kneed amateur."

"What'd he say?"

The inspector leaned over the table and rested both hands in front of the suspect. She spoke softly. "Who says he said anything, Mr. Daniel? All I heard was that we had all we needed from your partner."

"He's not my partner! He's my boss! I do what he says; I don't ask questions. I know he got money from this deal, and all I got was a few dollars. I don't even have it anymore. And we didn't *do* anything! You know that?"

She sat down. "Tell me about it."

"If he tries to say I was as involved in this as he was, he's lying! I don't care if I lose my job. All I did was ride along."

"What did you do, Lee?" she asked, almost soothingly.

262

He looked up at me self-consciously. "I just rode along."

"Where?"

"Not far."

"What happened to Banks?"

"What do you mean, what happened to him? Nothing happened to him."

"You didn't do anything to him? Take him somewhere? Rough him up? Lock him up? Hide him? Hurt him? Kill him?"

"Is that what Sandy said? Because if that's what he said that's something I know absolutely nothing about. All I did was ride along with them for a few miles, and then I drove Sandy's pickup back to the car wash and parked it inside, where it stayed for more than a week. For that I got fifty bucks."

"You got involved in this mess for a measly fifty bucks?" Inspector Rogers said, almost mocking him. "If you had any idea how much Ashford got, you'd be sick."

"Yeah, but what'd he do to Banks? I swear I don't know." Daniel was nearly in tears. "He says he'll give me fifty bucks to ride along with him on a little errand; that's all I know. He says just do what he says. So I rode with him to the junior high, and we parked in the back until this Banks guy comes walkin' out. Sandy says follow me, so I follow him and we talk with Banks, and Sandy tells him to go out the front way and we'll meet him there, or maybe Banks told Sandy, I don't remember because I'm just there for the ride, see?"

"So you drove around front?"

"Sandy did. I was just along. And we get up there

and there are kids all over the place. It was lunch time or something. And Banks isn't there. Now I don't know if that bothers Sandy, because I don't know what he's up to, but he says follow me again, but when we get out of the truck, he doesn't go anywhere. He just stands around, like he's lookin' for Banks or something. Then when Banks does come out, we go up to him again, and then we all get in the pickup, me on the outside, Banks in the middle, and Sandy drivin'."

"You didn't get fifty bucks for just that, Lee," Mae said, almost as if she were his lawyer now.

"I was almost gonna ask Sandy what else he wanted me to do. I didn't know if he was up to no good or was kidnappin' somebody or something. That didn't seem like a very logical way to do it. I mean, we coulda followed the guy home and pulled him over before he got to his street. But I'm no kidnapper, and I don't think Sandy is, either. At least I didn't."

"You do now?"

"I don't know what to think now. I read in the paper about Banks disappearing, and I asked Sandy what happened to him, and he said that was what my fifty bucks was for, to shut me up. He said not to worry about Banks, but I sure did."

"You ought to."

"I do. What did Sandy do to him?"

"You tell me."

"I told you! I was just along for the ride. I dropped them off at a bus stop. About three hours later Sandy comes back to the car wash, walking from the bus stop near our place. He's got a hair cut and he's wearing different clothes, and I figure maybe he's robbed

Banks because he asks me if I'll get rid of Banks's wallet for him. I asked him how much did he get, but he told me it wasn't anything like that and to quit askin' so many questions. I asked him why didn't he get rid of it himself, and he said didn't I want another little piece of the action. I said what's in it for me and he hands me another ten spot. Not much, but pretty easy money for ditchin' a guy's wallet that's empty anyway, except for his cards and stuff."

"So what did you do with it?"

"I popped it into an oil can in the back where we were burning some old oily rags and junk. Not really supposed to do that inside the city limits—well, you know that—but we do it anyway, sometimes. Not too often. A little while later Sandy asks me what am I gonna do with the wallet, and I tell him I burned it up already and he starts in swearin' me up and down like he's gonna kill me. Makes me give him back the saw-buck, and I don't know why."

"What'd he say?"

"He said I was a fool not to keep it and use the credit cards or something. But I never break the law. I knew something was fishy when he's payin' me fifty and then ten to do pretty much nothin', but I figured I was clean 'cause I didn't know the man he was fleecin', and in fact, I didn't really know he was even doin' a number on him."

"Even when he brought that wallet back?"

"Well, yeah, I didn't figure that was *Banks's* idea, if you know what I mean."

"I sure do. You expect me to believe all this?"

"I'm tellin' you, lady, this here has been the honest truth, I mean right down the line. Sandy already

265

probably tried to blame it on me, but that's everything I know, whether you believe me or not."

"I believe you, Lee. Maybe I should have my head examined, but then, whether I believe you or not won't get you out of trouble. It's who else believes you or what we can get Sandy to say now that'll make the difference for you."

"You tellin' me you've just been putting me on? That Sandy hasn't already told you a story? C'mon, what'd he say already?"

"Not much, but he will sing now."

Chapter Twenty-Seven

Mae Rogers waved at Wally in the room where he was staring down Sandy Ashford. He rose to meet us in the hall, leaving Ashford a little worse for wear.

By the time Inspector Rogers finished filling in Wally about Lee Daniel's account, Wally was ready to tell me to call for reservations to Chicago. "Why?" Mae Rogers said. "You think we're that close to wrapping this up?"

"Oh, yeah," Wally said. "In a way it's shaping up like I feared."

"You don't think Willie Banks is down here somewhere?"

"I don't think so. We'll see if we can get a lead on him from Ashford."

"I want to see this," Miss Rogers said.

"So do I," I said.

"Then let me have one of my people make your reservations for you," she said.

"OK, but I still have to call my wife."

Wally looked at his watch. "Hurry up. I'll wait till the three of us can talk to Ashford. Then we'd better hit the road."

I didn't want to admit in front of Inspector Rogers

that I had no idea what Wally was onto, but then I didn't think she was sure, either. The other thing I was going to ask him on the way home was how he came up with all that stuff about Joaquin Capilla without ever having met the kid before.

I reached Margo at the Schaumburg office and learned that she and Larry were indeed in the middle of their operation. "I didn't feel well this morning," she said, "but Bubba and Earl and Larry helped some hired men move the stuff in, and we're up and running. I'll be over there this afternoon and evening."

"Earl's back already? I thought he wasn't coming until tonight."

"That's what we thought. But he didn't come back alone, Philip. He's back with Gail Durning. She's a special lady, and they've announced their engagement."

"You're kidding!"

"Remember the cooling-off period she wanted? She got tired of it and wanted to see him again. He flew down there, reestablished the relationship, asked her to marry him, told her he couldn't stay away from this case long, and she drove him back up here. She's staying in a hotel for a few days before heading back to make wedding plans. As soon as this case is over, they're driving back to Springfield to be married."

"Where will they live?"

"Depends on what Hanlon wants Earl to do with IDLE."

"He might just as soon stay up here."

"Hope so."

"Me too."

I told Margo what was going on and when to

268

expect us, then hurried back to Wally and Mae Rogers. Wally led us into the conference room and to the uncomfortable Sandy Ashford.

"No matter what you got outa Lee, you'll get nothin' more from me," Ashford began. "I wasn't at that school, I never saw that teacher, and you can't prove otherwise."

" 'Course we can't," Wally admitted. "Nobody can ever really prove anything, can they? Truth is though, we don't need to prove it. We have two eyewitnesses who'll swear in court they saw you at that school with Willie Banks, talking to him and driving next to him in your pickup. And what's better, we've got your accomplice's testimony that you paid him fifty dollars to go there with you. Why'd you do that, Sandy?"

There was no response.

"Why'd you take Banks's wallet, Sandy? You get much? Is that where Lee's fifty and his ten bucks came from? He thinks you got a lot more than he did. That true?"

Still no reaction.

"Lee thinks you robbed Banks and hurt him, maybe killed him. What I wanna know is, why did you try to plant Banks's wallet on Lee?"

Ashford's eyes narrowed, but Wally didn't slow down.

"That's the part I can't figure yet, Sandy. For some reason, you wanted Lee to have Banks's wallet on him. What were you going to do to him? Have him knocked off? Knock him off yourself? You're a low-life, Sandy. You've got a record in this town for petty crimes a mile long, am I right?"

Mae Rogers nodded. Ashford nervously eyed them both.

"Anybody can look up someone's record," he said.

"Mr. Festschrift didn't look anything up," Inspector Rogers said. "He can just smell creeps like you a mile away. He knows you better than you know yourself. He knows everything you did and said to Willie Banks, whether you admit it or not."

Ashford was clearly spooked. "So tell me," he said. "Tell me more. Tell me all about it."

"No, I want you to tell me," Wally said. "Tell me how a jury will react to hearing that you came back with the wallet of a man who was never seen again. How you paid your friend a total of sixty dollars to ride along with you, and then you sent him on his way while you did the dirty work."

"Wouldn't they have to produce a body before I'd be in trouble?"

"You're already in trouble. If Banks never turns up, or if he turns up hurt or dead, you're going to spend several semesters in the Florida State Penitentiary."

"No way I'm goin' to jail," Ashford said. "Not for this little job."

"What was the job, Sandy? You gotta have some explanation, or you won't leave this station house except on bond."

"I did nothing wrong."

"What *did* you do?"

"Nothing."

"You did something. You just called it a small job."

270

Ashford stood and thrust his hands in his pockets. "It sure wasn't worth *this* hassle," he said. "No way."

"I'm listening," Wally said.

"Banks told me if I squealed, he'd get more than his money back."

"I'm still listening."

"OK, I don't care if I have to give him the money back. But I want to be protected if he comes lookin' for me, all right?"

"Why would he come looking for you?"

"Because I didn't knock off Lee for him."

We all sat staring at Sandy Ashford. Apparently only Wally was not stunned by this bit of news.

"And Banks didn't really know Lee, did he?"

"Not really. See, Banks found out Lee and I used to deal a little dope. We don't anymore. Honest. There's no future in it. So he shows up at the car wash one night, just before closing, and he starts talkin' dope. I can tell he knows what he's talkin' about, but I tell him how do I know you're not a cop, and he says you don't, and then he says that's not what he really wants, anyway.

"What am I supposed to make of that? I don't know. I ask him what he's after, and he asks me if I know anyone who wants to make big money in a short time without doing anything illegal. I say sure. Me. He tells me he thought maybe I would because I look like the kind of guy who knows a good deal when he sees one, about which he was right as rain."

I resisted the temptation to agree sarcastically.

"So what was the deal?" Wally asked.

"He said he wanted to disappear, and he wanted help. All I had to do was get him someone else's papers, you know, license, draft card, stuff like that, then pick him up at his school and be kinda obvious about it. He was going to drop some heavy hint that some old enemies of his from his hometown were after him, and he was sure people would think that's who we were. He had it all planned out, a meeting place, everything. And he suggested that I get duplicates of Lee's papers for him. That wasn't hard. I know where Lee puts his stuff when he fills in on one of the short shifts. I lifted his wallet one night and had the thing done. Out of the six hundred I got from Banks, I gave fifty to Lee and never told him what was going on."

"How did the part about knocking off Lee come into it?"

"Not till the very end. I didn't ask any questions. I mean, I make a good piece of change owning the car wash, but six hundred bucks, minus a nickel to Lee for about an hour's work, was too good to pass up. The only thing illegal was copying those papers, but that wasn't much. The plan was that we ride from the school to a bus stop, then Banks and I get out and let Lee drive my pickup back and hide it awhile.

"Then I was to take a bus back into town, and Banks was to take a bus to the terminal where he'd catch a bus to wherever it was he wanted to go. Said southwest, but why should I believe him? When we get out and are standin' there at the bus stop, I give him his phony i.d.'s, and he gives me his wallet with a ten in it. I say what's this for, and he says plant it on Lee and have him turn up dead, the more mutilated the better, and he'll send me the other halves of the bills inside the inner pocket."

272

"Which you hadn't noticed?"

"Not until he told me. There were ten halves of five-hundred-dollar bills. He told me if Lee was dead with his identification, and if Lee's head and hands were destroyed to the point where it couldn't be proven that he wasn't Willie Banks, Banks would send me the other halves to those bills."

"Were you going to do it?"

"I thought about it."

"For five grand, you'd have wasted your friend."

"For five grand, I'd do a lot of things."

"But he thought you were serious about getting rid of it for you, and he burned it before you got a chance to kill him."

"That's the funny thing. I was thinking of tossing him into one of those burning barrels, and wouldn't you know he picks one of 'em to burn the wallet. Once the wallet was gone though, I figured I wouldn't be doin' Banks any favor by snuffing Lee, and then I was kinda glad I hadn't done it. I didn't need the money that bad. Or the grief."

"You would have grieved?"

"Nah. I mean I didn't need the hassle. Which I got anyway."

"Aren't you worried that if Banks would pay to have a stranger killed for his own purposes, he'd pay to have you killed for failing in the mission he assigned you?"

"Yeah, I am. But I figured if I kept quiet and didn't get him in trouble, he'd know I upheld one end of the bargain and might listen to my excuse about Lee. You gonna protect me from him now?"

"Why should I?"

273

"Because I told you the truth."

"Truth that distasteful isn't worthy of reward."

"I gave you what you wanted and needed."

"You squealed to save your own skin, which is what you always do. I gotta give you that, Sandy. You're consistent. I'll tell you what, Inspector Rogers here can decide whether she wants to bust you on the phony documents rap or for burning oily rags within the city limits. And we're going to turn you and Lee loose. You're such good buddies. I can just about guarantee that Willie Banks will never set foot in Florida again, but I wouldn't put it past him to send one of his drug scene friends around with a message or a blade or a bullet for you. I am going to ask you for the halves of the five-hundreds, just in case we find the other halves on him."

"You're not really going to leave me unprotected."

"You think you're worth a full-time bodyguard. Why don't you pay your best friend, Lee, to watch over you? And then hope he never finds out how much you mean to him. Five grand."

I was full of questions as we headed back to the hotel to check out. I asked Wally when he first suspected that Banks/Robinson engineered his own disappearance.

"When I heard his wife talk about him," he said. "I wasn't sure, but that got me thinking. And then the two most credible witnesses we had made it look like there was no force whatever. When I found out that the two suspects were two-bit local hustlers, it started coming together. I gotta admit the whole messy scheme was more than I expected."

Wally got a kick out of how impressed I was with his guessing about Joaquin Capilla's past. "Just lucky," he said. "But not that hard to come up with."

At the airport he was finally able to reach his wife at home. He was glum on the plane. "Bad news," he said finally, after we had eaten. "She's sellin' the house and wants to split the money with me. I don't want any of her money. I just want her. I want someone to do for."

Earl met us at O'Hare and brought us up to date. "Margo's home with a nervous stomach, Philip, which doesn't sound like her, though this is probably the most dangerous case either of you have ever worked on. I made her promise she'd see a doctor tomorrow morning if she wasn't feeling better."

Earl was deep in thought after Wally told him about our day. "If Robinson isn't clean," he said, "that means IAD probably *is*. Ol' Buchanan will be thrilled to hear that little bit of news."

"He'll say he knew it all along," Wally said.

"And he did."

We talked strategy at the Glencoe office until the wee hours. Earl wanted Larry and me to make some sort of a foray, even if only a preliminary one, into the territory of the cops' operation. "Wait till you see the front we've got set up," he said. "It looks more real than the real thing. You'll love it."

"All I want is a good night's sleep," I said.

"Yeah. You'll be meeting Gail tomorrow. You'll love *her,* too."

"Looking forward to it," I said, yawning.

"Dress grubby," was his parting advice.

"For Gail?"

275

"For the sting."

Chapter Twenty-Eight

Gail Durning was a beautiful woman, but not so much in a conventionally physical way. Although she was pretty, she was a woman whose real beauty glowed from within. Quiet, at peace, deeply happy. You could just tell.

When she asked about people or told them how pleased she was to meet them, it was clear she was sincere. Her perfect, creamy complexion was her outstanding feature, and it was easy to see how Earl could have been attracted to her from afar and even more impressed up close.

And all those great first impressions were made on me at the crack of dawn Thursday in the Schaumburg office. When I say crack of dawn, I mean it. We were up earlier than we would have been for a fishing trip.

Margo had slept fitfully, but she felt good in the early morning hours. She was nervous, sure, but this would be a big day. Bubba Buchanan showed up with a huge box of fast-food breakfasts, and by six o'clock Wally and I had been brought up to date on all the details and shared a few of our own.

Everybody was ready to get rolling, but Bubba and Earl were emotionally flat at the news of Johnny Ray

Robinson and the likelihood that he had engineered his own disappearance. "Maybe you jumped at believing those guys because their story clears your friends in IAD," Margo suggested.

Buchanan shook his head slowly. "No, if there was another person on earth who had the classified information necessary to get to the hidden informants, it was Robinson. We just assumed he was clean because his own life would be endangered too. But now it's obvious he's been a double-dealer since the beginning."

"Which is hard for me to believe," Earl said. "Or at least to accept. I believed in the guy. I liked him, never suspected him. In fact, I even admired the way he would never give names, just other details that would allow us to make significant busts. Now I see why. He was being selective. He was being groomed as a hit man for dirty cops. He was to get selected as an important informant, get in deep enough that he had to be sent away and have his identity protected, and then carry with him the knowledge of where the other informants were."

"So he would have had them hit?"

"He may have hit them himself," Wally said, almost spitting out the words. "You all know how I feel about crooked cops. You can imagine how I feel about this slime."

"Let's keep our heads," Earl said. "This is a very dangerous man with nothing left to lose."

"Where do you think you'll find him?" Margo asked.

"No idea," Earl said. "Could be in the next room.

Could be in South America. Depends on how much unfinished business he has."

"I've got some unfinished business with him," Buchanan said. "Those were brave, selfless men with families who have now made the ultimate sacrifice for the sake of a clean police department."

"For once I agree with you wholeheartedly, Bubba," Wally said, rising and clapping the old cop on the shoulder. "Hits pretty close to home, doesn't it?"

Larry was fidgety. "Let's move, huh, Earl?" he said.

Earl went over the plan for the day one more time. He and Bubba and Wally would stake out the second-hand shop front that Margo and Larry and I would run as a legitimate business. By midmorning, Larry and I would check out the cops' phony operation less than a half mile away.

"This could take weeks," Earl said. "Let's just take it one day at a time."

I was amazed. I had been told by everyone how realistic the used clothing and appliance store would look, but I couldn't have imagined it. The reason it looked so real was that it *was* real. Everything in the place was stolen property in good condition and priced to sell.

The building was dingy and worn, but the shop occupied the many-windowed ground floor and was easily accessible to the street. I was dumbfounded by how quickly the people in the neighborhood discovered the place and began to come in droves to peruse the merchandise. It was like the most successful garage sale anyone could ever want, with toasters and rain coats and video games and everything else for sale.

"Where'd you get all this stuff?" was the most commonly asked question.

Larry was always ready with an answer. He knew the point was to get the word out that this was a shop dealing in hot items. He figured that if it was worth it to the city to actually let all this stuff be sold, rather than kept as evidence in home burglaries, it was his job to clarify the picture for everyone as soon as possible.

"Ask me no questions, I'll tell you no lies," he'd respond. Or, "You don't ask me where I got it, and I won't ask you where you're taking it. Fair enough?" And the people would giggle. He was a master. To the question "How can you sell this stuff so cheap?" he'd reply with a snicker, "Low cost to me, low price to you."

By mid-day of the second day in business, the shop was doing famously. We were actually thinking of ordering more merchandise and wondering where the money would go. Should Margo and I get into such a business if it were legitimate? And if it was legitimate, where would we get the merchandise? Closeouts? Fire sales?

But for all the dreams and questions, the clientele turned to a seedier sort. We had begun with a steady stream of housewives and retirees, and now the street people were showing up, trying to shoplift stolen property and to talk us down to even lower prices, offering vague threats about turning us in if we weren't willing to bargain.

Then we were paid a visit by the local protection

agency, and I don't mean environmental. Three young members of a gang that called itself the Park Princes of Death wanted to talk to the people in charge. Larry played a little tough himself, telling them that if they didn't want to buy something, they'd have to wait, because he and I were busy.

For several minutes, the Princes hung around the entrance, hurting business, and finally Larry called them in. We went to a stuffy little room in the back where we wound up talking with only one of the boys. We were glad to have Bubba and Wally in another back room, from which they were able to keep an eye on Margo. With the hoodlums away from the door, business had begun to pick up again.

"It works like this," the spokesman, who introduced himself as Ace, said. "We protect your place from vandalism, and we're always on call to throw out anybody you don't want in here. And we watch the place at night so there aren't any fires or broken windows or nothing like that."

"And who do you protect us from?" Larry said, staring him in the face. "You?"

"There's no telling who might want to do something bad to a place like this," Ace said. "But if you pay us regularly to protect you, we won't be tempted to do anything bad to it, either."

"So we pay you, one way or the other."

"You got it."

Larry looked at me and back at Ace. "Why don't you grow up, Ace? Get into the big time. Deliver us stuff we can sell, and we'll split the profits with you. You'll be like partners with us. That's better than robbing us or getting insurance money, either one."

Ace's eyes lit up. I suppose mine did, too. Where had Larry come up with that on the spur of the moment? As it turned out, he hadn't. It had taken some time to think through—time he had bought when he sent the Princes out the front door.

They would be partners for only a little while, and then they would be caught in the same sting that was intended for much bigger bait. Larry saw them as a nuisance we couldn't afford and didn't have time for, and thus, his idea.

Ace jumped on it. "How much will you take a day?" he asked.

"From you I'd take a hundred dollars worth of stuff."

"A hundred? Man, I can deliver that in an hour if I put everybody on it. Make it two and we got a deal."

"But we set the prices," Larry insisted.

"You put the price on it in front of us and pay us half, up front. That's it."

"Except you have to protect our store as part of the deal."

Ace nodded and slapped a high five on Larry. As soon as Ace was on his way out the door, Larry stuck out his tongue at me in a gagging pantomime, and I knew he'd have just as soon beat the rascal to a pulp as made a deal with him.

"Hey!" Larry called after him as Ace hurried out to tell his underlings. "Can you get me some auto parts?"

"Why, man? You wanna branch out? There's enough auto parts places around."

"Lot of money in auto parts. And it'll bring the husbands of all these housewives in."

"We'll see what we can come up with."

Another stroke of genius by an old pro. "Anything to get out of that dangerous assignment this afternoon," Larry said. "Something about that hasn't made sense from the beginning."

"Going over there, you mean?"

"Yeah. They'd see right through us immediately."

Our three older law enforcement mentors were thrilled with the new tack, and by late afternoon, the ruse had worked. We would never know why or where they found out about it, but a man from the phony auto repair shop visited our store. Bubba recognized him and almost gave us all away by trying to let us know without making a scene.

No questions were asked, and nothing suspicious arose. But the fact was that we had flushed our quarry out of hiding, and they wanted to know what we were up to. We hoped their interest would speed up the process.

But it didn't. We waited a full week to see if anyone from the other operation would return. When no one did, Larry and I were briefed again on just how to approach their shop.

Meanwhile, Gail had returned to Springfield. Margo's bout with whatever stomach flu she'd entertained was almost over, with only residual discomfort occasionally. Shannon Shipman had moved Larry's and her stuff from Fort Wayne, had found an apartment in Winnetka, and was looking for work. And business was better than ever at our second-hand shop.

With the city pound running dry on us, we had to resort to more and more of our wares coming from the Princes of Death. Bubba Buchanan and Wally were engaged in an all-out search for Johnny Ray Robinson and had—on the side— tipped off the Burglary Division about the activities of the Princes. They were under constant surveillance, and Burglary was under strict orders to make no arrests until our victims had been stung.

All of Johnny Ray Robinson's relatives were assured that they were out of danger unless they were afraid of him. They weren't, and so his mother returned to Biloxi, and his wife moved back to Tallahassee to pack up and move in with her own people.

The Chicago IAD had been brought back into the picture as Earl and Bubba became convinced that Lee Daniel's and Sandy Ashford's stories checked out. In the ensuing days, feelers had gone out all over the country. The boys in IAD knew that only Robinson could have set up the other informants, and regardless whether he had put them to death by his own hand or had only played a part in their slayings, to the IAD he was a murderer and had to be caught. The morning of Larry's and my scheduled advance into the enemy territory, we received the biggest news to date.

"Johnny Ray Robinson may be in Chicago," Bubba reported. "In fact, our information says he may be personally involved in the action on Cornell Street North."

"Why would he be so stupid?" Margo asked. "He showed Earl the place himself. And he'll be easily recognized. He has to know that one day soon, IAD's going to crack down on that operation."

"That's what we're afraid of. My people think

they're arming for one last stand in the hope that they'll damage the morale, the reputation, and the manpower of IAD. They want to make it an unattractive place to work."

"By damaging the manpower," Larry said, "you mean—"

"Just what it sounds like," Bubba said. "They're hoping to be personally investigated, and when they are, they'll shoot down as many IAD officers—and anyone else—they can before surrendering or escaping."

"I still don't understand why Robinson was stupid enough to allow himself to be seen in Chicago," Margo said.

"Well, he doesn't know we've seen him," Bubba said. "We have reports that he purposely injured himself so he'd have a realistic limp, and that he shaved his head, had some teeth pulled, and wears glasses."

"What'd he do to himself to cause the limp?"

"No one is quite sure, but the limp is real. Since we can't get close, and he only comes and goes in the middle of the night, we can't make a positive I.D. We do know that a slight, wiry, athletic-looking black man leaves the auto repair shop every night after midnight and goes out for booze and food that he brings back about an hour later.

"He's bald, has teeth missing, limps painfully—almost as if he's chopped off a toe or two—and wears wire-rim glasses."

"You're saying he's staying—living—at the auto repair shop?"

"Exactly."

"Flaunting it."

"He doesn't think so. He thinks we don't know. But he knows we'll find out. And he plans to be ready. Some of the shipments they've taken over the last few days have been from some of the biggest munitions and gunrunners in the midwest. They'd better know what they're doing, or the whole place will go up in smoke."

"And that's where you think you're sending my husband today?" Margo said. "Why keep playing the game? You know what's going on in there; why not just raid the place and bust them on weapons charges and for dealing in stolen property?"

"No probable cause."

"Probable cause?"

"Of course. We have to have it for them the same as for anyone else. We can't just go busting in on someone's home or business because we think we know what's going on inside."

"But you *know* what's going on!"

"We need more. That's why Larry and Philip are going in today."

Chapter Twenty-Nine

"You got all your lines down?" Wally asked at the Schaumburg office the next morning.

"I studied the script for hours last night," Larry joked. I nodded.

Margo was not happy, but she wasn't saying much. I thought she looked a little peaked, but Earl confided that he thought piqued was more like it.

"She'll be happier when you guys come back in one piece," he said. "We don't want her on the stakeout, nor do we want her to be the only person running the second-hand shop this morning. I've asked her to stay here until she hears from us. Then she can join you two in the shop this afternoon if nothing comes from the effort this morning."

Margo was frustrated by having to be so far from the action, but she admitted she would be too emotionally involved to be able to handle it otherwise. All she could think of, she said, was the stockpile of munitions purported to be in the phony auto repair shop where Johnny Ray Robinson was holing up.

Bubba had assigned one IAD man each to himself, Wally, and Earl, and they would stake out the Cornell Street property, arriving at least twenty minutes before Larry and I did. "Remember, Larry," Bubba said, "no heroics. All you want to do is make them aware of your own shop and get them jealous and territorial. If they see through you and think it's the beginning of the end of their business, they may start shooting."

"But if we can get in—"

"Don't. There's no way. They've probably got code words and everything. Anyway, if you got in, what would you do?"

"Look around. Get an idea of what's going on. Give you ammunition to raid 'em."

"Problem is, there's real ammunition in there. Just handle the assignment the way it's written."

Just before we left, Wally did something a little out of character. He asked if he could pray for us. "If that makes anybody uncomfortable, you don't have to listen," he said.

Bubba Buchanan immediately rose and moved toward the other side of the room near the window. "Becoming lily-livered in your old age isn't going to help you today," he said. "Not on a case like this."

Larry, a bit wide-eyed, stayed right where he was, and I sensed he was watching us as we closed our eyes. Wally prayed an awkward, halting, heartfelt prayer for safety and clear thinking, and he added a request for love for our enemies, "that can only come from God."

Most impressive, though, was his prayer for the courage of selflessness, that we would be willing to give of ourselves the way Christ gave Himself for us. We were silent and still when he finished, but Bubba was ready to roll—in much the same way Larry had been the week before when he thought that was D-Day. Now he was calm and professional. Bubba, the old veteran, was jumpy.

Wally and Earl and Bubba pulled out at about seven to rendezvous with their partners from IAD just outside Oak Park. We didn't know, nor did we want to know, exactly where they would station themselves. But they'd been carefully surveying the area for days, looking for just the right places. We knew that between the six of them—our three and the three from IAD—they'd have us covered.

Margo was distant before Larry and I left. She didn't even remind me to be careful, which was her usual understatement. I couldn't tell whether she was under the weather again or just worried. And she wasn't saying.

Larry and I loaded the back seat and trunk of an old, beat-up Mercury Marquis with junk from our shop. We took so much junk we couldn't get the trunk lid completely shut, which was just the look we were after.

As we cruised the neighborhood near Cornell Street, I asked Larry if he was nervous. "Scared to death," he said. "See our guys anywhere?"

"No, but you know they're here."

"How do I know that?"

"Because of who they are. If they couldn't make it, they'd have gotten to us by now."

"If they couldn't make it, how would they get to us?"

"Don't get *me* spooked now," I said.

"You're not scared already?"

"To death."

"Even after praying?"

" 'Fraid so."

"You know I'm gonna try to get in that place, don't you, Philip?"

I turned to face him. "Of course not. What are you talking about?"

"That's why I'm here, man. That's why they asked me back. Because I'm a little crazy."

"Don't give me that, Larry. You're back here because you want to be and because they asked you. And they asked you because you're good, one of the best, and you're too smart to do something stupid like changing the game plan at the last minute."

"You don't think they know I've got it in my head to get in there? Why'd they put you and me on this? Why didn't they put you and Margo on it so it would really look innocent, and so there would be no chance of anyone trying to get in there? Why do they have the place staked out with six of the most talented law enforcement people in this state? They may pretend later like I made a mistake, but I'm going in. If you don't want to, tell me now, because I don't want you messing me up."

He turned north onto Cornell South. Three more blocks and we'd be at Cornell North, a block from *9679*. Neither of us had even seen it before, but we were close. "You'd better circle around once more," I said, "if you're determined to do this. I have to decide."

"What am I supposed to do? Drop you off? They'd see that and head me off and not let me try it. Or you'd go running to them."

"You think I'd do that?"

"You might."

"Only if it was the right thing to do."

"That's just it, Philip. I admire you for always wanting to do the right thing, but does it ever occur to you that the right thing doesn't always mean going by the book? Sometimes you have to be unconventional. You think I'm successful, that I'm good, that they like me? What do you think has made me that way?"

"I've never known you to be a grandstander, Larry."

"I'm *not* a grandstander. You call something this dangerous grandstanding? I'd have to be crazy to show off in a situation like this. I'm doing it because my hunch tells me it's right. Because I think it's what, down deep, they really want me to do. You with me or not?"

"I have no choice."

"You do too. In or out?"

"In."

"Reluctantly?"

"Of course."

"Then keep quiet and stay close. If you're not comfortable with the ruse, stay out of it. Don't try to be something you're not."

"What am I supposed to do then?"

"Just stay with me and look like you know exactly what I'm talking about and agree totally. You got a gun?"

I shook my head. "We're not supposed to be carrying weapons—"

Without giving me a chance to say anything more, he wheeled around the block and wound up in front of the auto repair shop. He pulled up next to the old man with the clipboard, turned off the engine, and hopped out. "No need to get up, old timer," he said. "Just wonder when you can schedule me for a brake job. We run the new second-hand shop a half mile away, and I can leave the car anytime."

The old man scowled at him and said nothing, looking down at his clipboard and then up at a half-open second floor window that had a long shade blowing out. It was too chilly a day for that.

"Well, how 'bout it, Pop? Can you schedule me or not?"

"Nope."

"Why not?"

"Closed for the season."

"Whadya mean? What're you doin' out here then, soakin' up some rays?"

"We're closed, kid," the old man said. "Beat it."

Larry squatted next to the old man and spoke more softly. "Seriously, I'm here on business."

The old man squinted in the sunlight, his face folding into wrinkles. "What kinda business?"

"Your kinda business."

"What kind is that?"

"Pickups and deliveries."

"You delivering or picking up?"

"Both."

The old man hesitated. That wasn't the answer he wanted.

"Delivering stuff," Larry said. "Picking up information."

"Like what?"

"Like what else you boys need, other than what I've got."

292

"You better give me a password before I have you run outta here, you hear?"

"Oh, boy, yeah," Larry said. "Well, I been dealin' with this man on a lot of secret stuff, and we've used all kinds of code names. Which was it for this one?" He looked at me, and I appeared deep in thought too. I prayed silently he wouldn't try to guess a code word out of the blue and get us shot up.

Two black arms reached out and shut the upstairs window, catching the bottom of the shade. Larry was still stalling. "Oh, let's see," he said. "We've used IAD and Johnny and Ray and J.R., and oh, yeah, we used Banks once before."

The old man's eyes lit up. "That's close enough," he said. "If you know Johnny, you're OK."

The old man pushed a button, and the garage door opened. I slid over to the wheel and pulled in, wondering what Wally and Earl and Bubba and their associates were thinking now.

Two average-sized white men stood on either side of the door, both of whom I assumed to be cops or former cops. The guns at their hips were barely concealed. As the door closed again and the old man went back to his chair, one of the men said, "What've we got here?"

"The usual," Larry said. "But we're in a hurry. We're supposed to be opening our shop not far from here in a few minutes, so let's get unloaded and you can pay us later."

The man looked carefully at Larry. "We always pay later," he said.

"Yeah, I know," Larry said, lifting items from the trunk. "Where to?"

"Just right there on the floor. Where'd you get all this stuff?"

"Same place you get your stuff. You need anything in particular?"

"Maybe. Like who are you and how did you get in here?"

Larry straightened up. "I'm Larry, this is Philip, our last names are none of your business, and you know how we got in here. No one gets in here without giving Douglas the password."

"So what's the password?"

"Listen, you don't want to anger friends of Johnny Ray, do you?"

"I wanna know what the password is. We're friends of Johnny too, ya know."

"The password is Willie," Larry guessed. "Satisfied?"

We finished unloading and heard steps on the stairs. "That'll be the boss," one of the men said.

Larry motioned for me to start the car in the closed garage. "Where you goin'?" the man said.

"Gotta go," Larry said, jumping in. "Lock your door!" he told me, as I backed up to the overhead door.

The men swore and scrambled to get to the button to lift the door. As I backed out, tires screeching, I noticed one of the men had a huge revolver in his hand. As we fled down the street, the other was standing over the old man, berating him.

"How did you know the password?" I asked Larry. "Let alone the old man's name?"

"His name was on his shirt. And what else could the password have been? I suggested everything else I could think of to the old man, but I only came close. Right now he's probably telling them what I told him that convinced him to let me in. I think our mission was successful."

"It was successful all right," Bubba said back at the second-hand store. "No doubt you sped up the process. But you could have gotten yourselves killed."

"It was my idea going in," Larry admitted. "I think it worked."

"Yeah, it worked," Wally said. "Not too smart, though. Too much like I woulda done."

Earl nodded. "I tried to reach Margo," he said. "She must have left already."

"How would she know we were through?" I asked.

"Maybe she just figured enough time had passed. She'll probably be here soon."

"So will Robinson's boys," Bubba said. "We'd better get into position."

Wally went upstairs to a vacant room, which fortunately had strategic holes in the floor. Earl positioned himself in a back room with a view of the front door. Bubba and his three men from downtown went across the street and next door. We all felt better that the confrontation—if there was to be one—would be on our turf, not theirs.

"Open for business," Earl said, and Larry and I turned on the lights, opened the door, and waited for the customers. It was as if they came out of the woodwork.

They would prove a problem if our rivals showed up in the middle of the day. How would we deal with the competition with customers in the store?

I tried calling Margo several times during the day,

but I couldn't reach her at either of our offices or at home. Finally I got hold of Bonnie, who said she had heard from Margo. "Her message is not to worry. She was glad to hear nothing had really gone down yet, and she'll see you at home tonight."

Fortunately for us, no one from the other operation showed up until we were just about ready to close. Then Bubba radioed Earl that he recognized a car moving slowly toward our place from a few blocks away.

"It's one of their cars," he said. "Followed a block or so behind by another. Both are full."

"Shut the store," Earl said, and we began flashing the lights, ringing up sales, and shooing people out as fast as we could. I had just turned the open and closed sign to closed when a car full of men slowed and parked across the street. A mixture of black and white faces peered at our store front.

Chapter Thirty

"Be sure Shipman and Spence have weapons," Bubba's voice cackled over the two-way radio, which was a bold, dangerous move with our adversaries so close by. Within a few seconds, he wouldn't be able to communicate with Wally and Earl that way. His, and their, cover had to be protected at all cost.

"I'm armed," Larry called out to Earl.

"Mine's under the counter," I said.

"Better get it," Earl stage-whispered from the back. "No, wait!"

From the car across the street came hobbling none other than Johnny Ray Robinson himself. He leaned heavily on a bejeweled cane and limped painfully toward the door. When the others in his car got out and began to fan out down the street and around the other side of our building, Earl radioed, "Bubba, we're going to need a lotta help fast. Call anybody downtown you want. It's all gonna go down tonight, the whole thing. Let's try to take 'em all. Robinson has to be high to come in here alone."

Earl was right about that; I could tell as soon as Johnny Ray edged up to the door and tested the knob. He weaved in surprise to find that it had not been locked, even though I had turned the closed sign around.

"You don't wanna close on me now, do you, bro?" he said through broken teeth and gaps where teeth had been. His head was bare and shiny, and he wore glasses. He was a world away from the square-jawed young man we'd seen in a formal police cadet academy graduation picture. I had to wonder what went wrong. Was he bad to start with? A plant by future-minded crooked cops? Or had he been influenced once he joined? Or fallen into dope and needed sources and income?

"Well," I said shakily, "we're closing, but we have a moment if you'd like something."

He cocked his head and looked up at me with one eye closed, the other half-open. "I'd like to take a look at your fine establishment. I'm a neighboring businessman, you know."

"Is that so?"

He just looked at me. Then he pointed with his cane to merchandise high on some shelves. "Tell me about that," he said, quickly returning the end of his cane to the floor to catch himself. He winced as he limped toward the shelf.

"What you see is what you get," I said. "It's just what it looks like, all in perfect condition."

"No doubt, my man. No doubt. And you, are you what you look like, all in perfect condition?"

"Sir?"

"Don't play dumb with me, boy. And you," he said, pointing to Larry, "big mouth. What's your story?"

"Story?" Larry said, stalling as long as possible so

reinforcements from the Chicago PD had time to arrive.

"Your story," Robinson said, "is that you went one step too far when you checked me out today. Makes sense for the competition to check each other out, and you could have pulled it off. You could have kept the whole thing from me a few days longer. I wouldn't have had to know you were a cop."

"I'm not a cop," Larry said.

"Neither am I," I said, lamely.

"You should have just stuck with your story that you were new in the neighborhood and wanted auto work done, or that you heard we were dealing in second-hand merchandise just like you were. You've got a good front here, a nice place, an innocent-looking place. I never would have suspected it."

I heard the floorboards creaking above us and quickly went into a coughing jag for Wally's benefit, allowing him to get wherever it was he felt he needed to get without drawing attention to himself.

"Oh, that's a crafty code," Robinson said. "You don't think I know you're not alone? You don't think I know that somebody ain't goin' out of here alive tonight? Me, I don't care which of us it is, as long as it's somebody. I'm a dead man, anyway."

"What do you mean?" Larry asked.

"What's it to you, cop?"

"I told you, I'm not—"

"Then why do you come to my place today with my password and knowin' my name, man? The password says I got a double-crosser workin' for me, which is ironic enough, isn't it? And knowin' my name proves that."

"Johnny, you're making a big mistake," Larry said. "You don't remember me. Times have been hard for you—you've had some setbacks, you've been overly tired. We've done some jobs together, man."

Robinson hesitated for just a second, but he wasn't buying. "You can't jive me with that! I'm wasted, but I'm not gone. My old lady wants nothing to do with me because she can't handle the drugs. I didn't do a good enough job for the guys I was workin' with, and they're after my bones. And now somebody workin' for *me*, on *my* payroll, is rattin' back to the cops. Well maybe that double-dealer—or I should say triple-dealer—will get himself shot up tonight. For sure, you're not comin' out in one piece."

I heard Wally on the stairs behind Larry, and I began coughing again. It made Johnny Ray Robinson jumpy. His eyes darted about the room. I was only guessing, but I had the feeling Earl was jockeying for better position too.

By now Bubba must have had his back-up men, but what were Robinson's cohorts up to? I could only hope Bubba, IAD, and his support team had them in their sights.

I carefully watched Robinson for any quick move, but I couldn't imagine where he was carrying a weapon. His clothing looked skintight, and there was no telltale bulge anywhere.

I tried to casually move over to where my gun was—at the counter next to the one Larry was standing behind. But Robinson was suspicious of my every move and maneuvered to keep himself between me and wherever I tried to get to. It was a slow, silent,

300

ritual dance, and I didn't want it to end in death for either of us.

Larry and I jumped when Robinson whirled around and looked out the front door to see Bubba Buchanan heading up the operation in the street. Apparently he and his men had completely surprised Robinson's henchmen, and they were being herded into paddy wagons, all of them, with their hands high and their weapons surrendered.

"Well, well, so it starts right at the top!" Robinson hollered crazily, as if he thought Buchanan could hear him. "How ya doin', chief? How's it feel to have a prize pupil gone bad?"

"Did you go bad, or were you bad from the start?" Larry said.

"Let's just say I had the wool pulled over *his* old, ignorant eyes from day one. Now what do you think Buchanan wants? I suppose he thinks his grand entrance means this big operation is over."

"It is," Larry said evenly. "Buchanan will get your friends for loitering, vagrancy, carrying concealed weapons without licenses, and resisting arrest."

Robinson's eyes grew cold, and his chest couldn't camouflage his racing heart. "I'm not even armed, man. Don't you see I knew this was the end? I knew I wasn't gonna come out of this. I hoped to go out in a blaze with my boys messin' up your little ruse, yeah. But let's just talk a coupla more minutes, huh?"

Larry shook his head slowly. "What's the point, Johnny? It's over. Let's go downtown. You're lucky you're still alive. If you go to jail, at least you'll be protected from some of your enemies."

"Don't give me that! You think I don't know I'll be

up on the murders of those two cop informants? That's the death penalty, man!"

Larry just stared at him, and Robinson started in again, as if on the brink of a breakdown. "I'm strung out, man," he said. "I need a fix, I haven't slept, I'm malnourished, I got two toes chopped off that haven't healed yet, my mouth hurts, I cut my head shaving this morning, and I'm unarmed. What more do you want?"

"You *are* in sad shape," Larry said, probably wondering, as I was, why Earl and Wally and Bubba didn't come in and make the arrest. I figured they were waiting for an all-clear signal from each other; otherwise, they would have emerged from their hiding places. Maybe they didn't want to push Robinson toward the brink with any fast moves.

I was scared. More so when Robinson started ranting again. "All I want to do is jaw with you brothers here a minute," he said. "This one was pretty slick, slippin' by my best guys and almost poisoning 'em to death in my garage."

In the street I could see Bubba Buchanan lined up with the glassed-in front door, his service revolver raised to eye level, aimed at the back of Johnny Ray Robinson's head.

Larry's gun was holstered in his belt at the back, under a shirt with the tails hanging out. I didn't know how he'd reach for it if he needed to. I desperately wanted to get near mine, just in case. I thought I'd have an easier time getting to mine than Larry would to his, but I felt a little better knowing that at least Earl's and Bubba's weapons were pointed at Robinson. Wally, probably behind the door at the bottom of the stairs behind and maybe six feet to the right of Larry, was not in the right position to have a shot at him, but I knew he was close by.

I moved carefully toward my counter as Robinson slowly and obviously painfully leaned heavily on his cane and shuffled in front of us and between us. "You," he said, pointing at me with the cane, "you were good, but you were just followin' orders. The man here says start the car, you start the car. Quick, but a follower. And you," he tried to point at Larry, but he had to catch himself again. "You're something else again. You're the one with the quick word, the quick thought, the quick action, the jive, the number, the action. You two are the ones who finally did me in. I faked out the head of the Illinois Department of Law Enforcement and the Chief of Internal Affairs. Man, I got a reputation that'll outlive me for years. But you guys have the honor of havin' started the end for me."

His eyes were beady but ablaze, and I felt naked without my gun. Vulnerable. I wanted to drop behind the counter and scream for someone to just take him out. Outside I saw a man on either end of the sidewalk, flanking Buchanan about twenty feet from him on either side. They were in combat crouches, both hands on their weapons, which were also pointed at Johnny Ray.

He limped forward and lay his cane on the counter in front of Larry. Then he stepped back a few feet and almost fell. I couldn't resist the urge to take a step to my left and reach for my gun, but when I did, Johnny stepped forward again and grabbed the end of his cane, leaving it flat on the counter, but pivoting it so it pointed straight at me.

I hesitated, puzzled, and the end of the cane seemed to explode. I felt a dull thud in my shoulder as I spun in a circle and crashed back into a wall shelf. Merchandise fell around me, and I felt as if someone had slugged my shoulder with a sledgehammer.

My mind was reeling, telling my body to stay up and grab the gun, but I was slowly sliding down the wall to a sitting position, and as if in slow motion, I saw Johnny Ray whip the murderous cane toward Larry, who was reaching behind his back for his own weapon.

Simultaneous to the shattering of the glass at the front of the store with shots from three angles and the blast of Earl's snub-nosed .38 from my left, the door behind Larry burst open and Wally Festschrift leaped out, closing the distance between him and Larry and Robinson in an instant.

He tumbled headfirst and prostrate past Larry to smother the end of the cane, just as Robinson fired it again. It knocked the huge man up off the floor about three feet as a .44 magnum bullet ripped through his solar plexus and down through his stomach and lower intestines, destroying his pelvic bone and exiting through his hip.

The bullet lodged several inches deep in the wood flooring as several more shots rang out, including one from Larry that was probably unnecessary, but which assured from point-blank range that Johnny Ray Robinson would not survive the nine slugs that had entered his head and back in less than a second.

And Wally Festschrift, who had finally found someone to do for, someone to give to, somewhere to invest himself, lay staring up at me glassy-eyed, his jaw set in determination as if there had never been a choice, never a millisecond's hesitation.

Larry and Earl carefully rolled the big man onto his back and cradled his head in their arms.

Epilogue

My wound was superficial compared to Wally's. The slug had torn ligaments and muscle and dislocated my shoulder during its brief journey through my body. Then it had gone through the metal chassis of a heavy-duty blender, an inch of walnut shelving, a half-inch of plaster, an inch of wood frame, two inches of stud board, and finally lodged in the outer wall of brick.

Minor surgery and a lot of pain pills made me presentable in a black sling. It was nearly midnight before they let Margo and Earl and Bubba and me see Wally, and then we were to go in only two at a time. Bubba and Earl insisted we go first.

Wally didn't look good, and the prognosis was pessimistic. But still Margo was able to make him smile. "You'd better be up and around soon," she said, as he fought to keep his eyes open over the tubes and wires. "I'm going to need a godfather for this baby."

I had to sit down. What a way to tell me I was going to be a father! I wanted to hug her, but it would probably be weeks before I could.

"You gonna name him after me?" Wally rasped.

"Walvoord Feinberg Festschrift," she said slowly,

306

turning each name over carefully on her tongue. "Not a chance."

"Pray for a girl," he managed. And he fell asleep.